CAST A LONG SHADOW

CAST A LONG SHADOW

Welsh Women Writing Crime

EDITED BY KATHERINE STANSFIELD
AND CAROLINE OAKLEY

HONNO MODERN FICTION

First published in Great Britain in 2022 by Honno Press
D41, Hugh Owen Building, Aberystwyth University,
Aberystwyth, Ceredigion, SY23 3DY

1 2 3 4 5 6 7 8 9 10

Published with the financial support of the Books Council of Wales.

ISBN: 978-1-912905-58-4 (paperback)
ISBN: 978-1-912905-59-1 (e-book)

Cover design by: Sion Ilar, Books Council of Wales
Cover image: © Arcangel.com/Abigail Miles
Text design: Elaine Sharples
Printed in Great Britain by 4Edge

Introduction

At the time of writing this introduction to *Cast a Long Shadow*, the follow-up to Honno's 2009 crime short-fiction anthology *Written in Blood* (edited by Caroline Oakley and Lindsay Ashford), crime fiction is outselling all other fiction genres in the UK. The great variety of the contemporary crime-fiction market goes some way to explain its popularity. Readers enjoy the warmth and humour of 'cosy' mysteries at one end of the spectrum, while at the other, psychological thrillers probe the darkest reaches of the human mind. The diversity of fiction between these poles means the genre can meet the tastes of a huge range of readers: historical crime spans the ages; noir stories throw light on political corruption; cold cases are reinvigorated by scientific advances; police procedurals reveal the inner workings of the establishment; spy narratives step into the space left by the Cold War. A fascinating current development is the rise of the genre mash-up, which sees crime fiction motifs blended with fantasy, science fiction, westerns... International crime fiction written in English and crime in translation are more widely available than ever. Far from being a genre that rests on its formulaic antecedents, crime fiction today is diverse and in a continual state of reinvention, reflecting life in all its variety.

Within the covers of contemporary crime fiction can be found the worst of human nature: its depravities and cruelties, its selfishness and disregard for the lives of others. The crimes that animate the plots of crime fiction often arise from unfairness and inequality, or at least individuals' perceptions of them. But crime fiction is also about the best of ourselves – as characters seek to right wrongs and go that extra mile to find answers, bringing to light the truth. It's about the murkiness of what is 'good' or 'bad', too, concerned often with moral greyness that resists easy ideas of right and wrong, innocence and guilt. 'Justice' can be a complex and fraught idea to explore, not a neutral outcome. This is especially true for those who lack power in society.

This rich field of contemporary crime writing is one in which women are extremely well-represented – as writers and as readers. But also as victims – a reflection, it must surely be argued, of horrifying levels of real-world male violence against women and girls. For all their trappings of fiction, crime stories often have at their heart a shocking realism, and this is true for this anthology. A number of contributions centre on women and girls as the victims of male violence. Putting together this book in the period in which Sarah Everard was abducted and murdered by a serving police officer in London, resulting in a very public conversation about the safety of women in society, means that the stories women tell of violence, power and justice are more urgent than ever.

Narratives of women as victims do not preclude those that cast women as defenders, seeking justice and to restore order in their world, as they define it. Such characters are plentiful in *Cast a Long Shadow*, in recognisably realist modes as well as in re-imaginings of myths new and old. Women also feature strongly among the culprits, taking the law into their own hands and not always for the good. A similar plurality can be seen in the nature of crime explored within these covers. Murder plots sit alongside those involving fraud, drug production, theft and issues of consent. And the anthology points forward to transgressive acts that should preoccupy us all, now and in the years to come: crimes against the environment.

Exploring the world of criminality and justice in the short story is a challenge: writers must get to grips with its moral complexity as well as readers' expectations of narrative form in crime fiction. If the short story is its own distinct form of fiction, the glimpse it offers inherently different from the complex tableau of the novel, then the crime short story must surely be classed as a separate entity within the world of that glimpse. Such stories are an art form all of their own, offering crime fiction in miniature, akin to the 'Nutshell Studies of Unexplained Deaths': true-crime scenes rendered in dolls' houses by Frances Glessnor Lee. Lee created the Nutshell Studies as a way to train homicide detectives in America in the 1940s and '50s. The small-scale horror of toy bedrooms covered in fake blood, dolls drowned in their mini baths, their homes turned over by burglars, is uniquely unsettling. Crime short stories achieve much the same effect as we peer through a window onto a tiny world, and the tales are all the more satisfying for it.

The women writers of Wales have risen to the challenge of this narrative form and the number of submissions for this anthology confirmed the popularity of the genre here, as well as the wealth of talent: crime writing, in all its myriad styles and preoccupations, is a hugely active field in Welsh writing in English. *Cast a Long Shadow* offers a snapshot of the Welsh women crime writers at work today, with the promise of much more to come.

Contents

Song Fox

Tiffany Murray

The knees of her white thermals were black because the sand was black. Arctic wind cut, terns shrieked, and Lilith dug with the small spade. They had been in the cabin spring through summer, and now winter was calling; there was little autumn here.

Lilith knew the waves on this beach could creep up behind you, scoop you up and throw you back at the rocks like laundry, so she faced the sea. She sang with numb lips in that high thin voice he'd so taken to. She sang with a pretty tune but no particular meaning: the song was a list. Ravens on the cliffs bobbed. She heard the vixen and her cubs chirruping from the outcrop above her.

'Arctic fox. *Vulpes lagopus*,' she sang against the wind, 'Melrakki, little dog on the snow. White, brown,' she jerked the spade, 'and blue.' There were so many words for fox in Icelandic it still excited her. He'd taught her the words, sometimes moving her mouth into the right shape with his fingers.

'Tófa. Refur. Melrakki. Skolli. Holtaflór. No, Lil, *hol-tah-floor*,' he'd said.

Then there was her very own nameless fox. Lilith had spent that first sunny June day following the vixen along the shoreline: she was blue with copper eyes. It was her fox up on the cliffs now, sucking up gull eggs, feeding on carrion, and oblivious to all she'd done. Lilith tore off her gloves; she was burning up.

'I know,' she shouted at the wind, 'a sign of bloody hypothermia!' She laughed, which she knew, of course, was an added tic of madness. Wind-blown sand stabbed her legs through her thermals; she'd remembered boots, a scarf, a hat, and she'd taken his coat, but she'd forgotten her trousers. It's the simple things, she thought. She touched the bite mark on her thumb; it had healed well. Black and white eider ducks watched her from the shore and she glanced up at the cabin. She wanted to get in there and pack. This business on the beach was taking too long and as sure as she had been, now she didn't quite know why she had to do this. Still, Lilith picked up the guitar, a fine 0018 Martin (because he said if it was good enough for early Nanci Griffith then it was good enough for him, and that had made Lilith's skin itch). She placed the brown guitar in the black hole and sang again, this time a lullaby about going to sleep while the waves wash you clean, and your lover waits on the cliffs until darkness catches him. Lilith stood, wobbly in the growing wind. The raven-boys and her foxes had long gone from the cliffs as she shovelled the last of the sand, and buried the guitar in black. It was done.

Dillon Bar in Reykjavík, that's where she first saw him play: Timotei hair and beard, and ice-blue eyes. He was such a cliché it hurt. He called himself 'Thor', though he confessed to a softer 'Einar' after their first night in the van. Lilith knew she was a cliché too when she found herself paying for petrol with her mother's credit card and sitting at the side of the stage at each of his pub gigs with a cheap can of Heineken and a permanent smile. She took to driving the ring road when the weather wasn't too bad, while he strummed the 0018 Martin in the back.

'What's that?' she asked at most things, because even the light was strange on this island.

He mumbled, 'Pink-footed goose, keep your eyes open.' Other times he said, 'The aurora borealis, silly,' and 'No, they are not spaceships landing, Lil. They're lit-up greenhouses for tomatoes.'

He said 'tom-*ay*-toes' not 'tom-*ahh*-toes', and Lilith sang a song she'd made up about terns dive-bombing the parked van.

When spring storms came, he drove, and she would curl up in the front seat and pretend she was safe. When she saw the glacier river for the first time she stood at the shore, dazzled, while he jumped from one block of ice to the next, freezing water running beneath him. A guy yelled from the shoreline that dumb tourists should go home.

'Where were you born on the island?' Lilith asked one night in the van and he dodged the question by pulling down her knickers. (It was April but too cold to sleep in a van without thermals and underwear.) As they made their way back to Reykjavík for another small gig in a small bar, and then up, up to the Westfjords and a place he told her was his, she found signs of other women in the van: a silver bangle, a hair clip (though she reasoned that both could easily be his). One morning when he was peeing next to short-legged, long-haired horses, she found a hefty white bra beneath his seat and a screwed-up note written in red lipstick beneath the foldaway mattress. 'FUCK YOU', it said. Everyone has a history, Lilith thought.

The cabin was one room with a loft, almost on the black beach, on a peninsula with puffins and not much else. He told her this was the place where he wrote his songs. He worked the pump most mornings, and she couldn't believe there was electric, not until she followed the pylons with her eye along the deserted gravel track. There was one loo, but Lilith didn't like to think where that went. The track built into the cliff was two hours to the town in the van.

They took to eating muesli and UHT oat milk at the table by the window, and as Lilith watched the shoreline he told her about the ideas for his songs. She counted fulmar, those pink-footed geese, little black arrows of puffins, and golden plovers (there was a *Bird Guide to Iceland* on the shelf) and when she first saw the pair of blue foxes play on the beach below, she squealed.

'That's the most excited I've heard you in weeks,' he said, and it sounded like a sulk. He poured her a glass of beetroot juice that she left, so he began to give her facts about the foxes.

'Did you know there's an Arctic fox jawbone, 3500 years old?' He chewed hard on the ungiving muesli. 'Did you know they withstand up to minus 70 without shivering? Did you know those ones are Blue Morphs?'

Lilith put her chin in her hands and wondered why he said,

'Did you know?' because of course she didn't. Iceland was a mystery to her. They had foxes on Grampy's farm: bright red, sometimes orange or black, and Grampy would shoot some and keep a cub or two for her to release and rear, and for Grampy to shoot again. Even Lilith admitted this was pretty grim.

'Lil, did you know Arctic foxes are monogamous?' Beetroot juice stained his teeth and the white blond of his moustache; it dripped onto his beard. She stared out at the grey sea.

'And did you know the assholes can live to eleven. They stink, too.'

His accent was becoming less Icelandic, more mid-Atlantic. She watched the pair of foxes playing, scavenging on the cold beach; they were long blue-grey cats, tearing at kelp and a goose carcass. She counted the chord changes in his strumming: just three.

'What songs do you have for me, Lil?'

'Hmm?'

'Sing to me, baby.'

She wanted to watch the foxes but he pressed the Martin into her chest and it felt like a weight and she sat back and strummed until a song formed in her, and she didn't take her eyes away from the kitten-ish foxes as she sang. He recorded every note, every word, on his phone.

'I'll be gone maybe a couple of hours.'

She wasn't worried but felt she should try to worry, so she asked him if she could come after all.

'You're too sick, baby.' He strung his bag across his chest like a schoolgirl with a satchel and although she guessed it must be her fever, it annoyed her more than anything about him now. 'I can't miss this gig, baby. You'll be fine, you have soup, and water, and medication.'

She didn't like the way he said 'medication' like an American advert for a urinary tract infection. She had Paracetamol. She hadn't shown him the fox bite, she'd wrapped it up and tended to it herself. She'd been bitten before. It was nothing, a few teeth marks on the meat of her thumb, but the fever worried her.

'Stay,' she croaked, and he leaned over and kissed her.

'Ew, you're sweaty.' He smiled. 'See you soon, honey. I'm going to sing your songs.'

He was gone for four days. Lilith's fever broke on the third.

'I can't hear myself think!' he yelled. The foxes lived in the crawl-space beneath the cabin now, and the cubs rolled and slammed against the floor joists, yip-yapping with summer.

'I thought you were singing?'

'Don't be cute.'

Lilith watched his scowl change to a smile.

'Come help me, baby, help me with my song,' he whined. He pressed 'record' on his phone.

There were only four cubs in the litter, this was the way it worked up here in the cold. They were as small as kittens, but the stink was enough. Lilith breathed in through her nostrils, the feral tickled her, and she began to sing. She loved the thought that the vixen – her fox – now lived beneath them and breathed in their breath and listened to Lilith's songs until she howled. The howl was the high-pitched chatter of a monkey in a rainforest, whooping out her territory; then the howl became a cackling witch-laugh, then the chirrup of a coasting songbird. He said the constant noise set his bones on edge.

Lilith found his passport in his computer bag. He was Jonathan Brick, born Rendville, Ohio. He wasn't Thor, he wasn't Einar and it wasn't a surprise. He'd learned the language and the land like he'd learned her songs. After she put the passport neatly back, she walked down to the beach to watch the male fox spend his day catching fulmars. She loved the way the fox gripped the pillowy birds so tight in his jaw, it looked as if he was smiling.

The cubs were bigger now, noisier beneath the cabin, and it was getting colder. Lilith stopped making up songs when she started worrying about the cubs.

'What will they eat in the winter?'

'I don't know, Lil. Will you shut up about the fucking foxes? We're here to work.'

'No,' she said, and a cub yowled so hard it made her laugh.

'That's fucking it!' He slammed his fist on the table and beet juice spilled. He marched up the narrow stairs to the loft and when he came down with a gun, she laughed again and thought, 'He doesn't know how to use *that*.'

She'd forgotten about Rendville, Ohio, but when he shot into the floor of the cabin and the cubs were silent, she knew that everyone must know how to shoot a gun in Rendville, Ohio. She screamed and followed him onto the porch, but he was already chasing the dog-fox up along the cliff's edge. Lilith jumped to the ground and the base of the cabin. She pushed her head into the small gap the foxes used, the one Jonathan from Ohio had blocked; the one she unblocked every day. There they were, spots of eyes in the darkness, eyes that had to be alive, eyes with the luminous spark still in them.

'Shh,' she told them.

Lilith heard more shots from the cliff.

She sprinted, and halfway up the incline it was a shock to see the vixen – her fox, the one who bit her all those months ago – keeping pace with her. Lilith cried out because Jonathan was standing ahead, blocking the path, the gun aimed right at them. As she ran at him Lilith waved her hands, her arms, but still he fired.

'Help me, Lil.'

It had taken him a full hour to come to. She had crouched at the cliff edge and watched him, the vixen snaking her ankles, chirruping. Lilith was glad the gun was out of his reach. It had fallen down to the beach below whereas *he* had been caught on a stone outcrop halfway down. She thought his arm was broken, and the bone was certainly sticking out of his leg. There was blood at his head and he wasn't making much noise, though the puffins and kittiwakes that dive-bombed him were loud. She couldn't reach him, but the vixen could. The dog-fox was dead beside him, nestled into his side like a sleeping child.

'Lil.'

It was beginning to snow and she loved the way the black sand turned salt and pepper, and then white.

Lilith was more worried about the cubs now the dog fox was dead. For a few weeks while the weather turned bad, she hunted with the vixen down on the beach: the gun doing good after all.

The morning she saw all four cubs fat as grubs and walking in a line after their mother along the cliff, to the outcrop where their father and Jonathan lay, she knew they would thrive. That morning Lilith buried his 0018 Martin guitar on the black beach. She didn't quite know why, but it seemed the right thing to do. She cleaned the cabin and the van meticulously, packed every item of hers (which wasn't much), erased every recording of her and her songs from his phone, and wiped it down.

Lilith finished the last of the hard muesli but left the beetroot juice. She took the *Bird Guide to Iceland* and the small book she'd found in his bedside table, *What Do You Know About the Artic Fox?* It was a cold but sunny day, the snow light on the ground, and she began the long walk, following the pylons into town.

Cast a Long Shadow

Hazell Ward

Whenever the shadow of the church spire touches the oak tree, Edris Jones walks into the Plumber's Arms and nods at the landlord. Neither man speaks, but the landlord pulls Edris a pint of bitter, Edris pays and carries his drink to the quietest corner, where he sits looking into the fire. He sips slowly and speaks to no one. And no one speaks to him. Once more he will return to the bar, silently buy a pint, and, just as silently, drink it. When the shadow has moved on, Edris Jones will leave the pub and begin the walk home.

And the landlord will collect his glass. And wipe down the table. And breathe easy again.

On cloudy days, Edris Jones goes straight home after he finishes his work. On cloudy days, Edris doesn't think about the past. Not anymore. On cloudy days he can walk by the church and the tree and on to the farm that is his home.

There is just Edris and his mother now, and, like a good son, he hurries home to her.

A shadow is the absence of light. Where the sun's rays are blocked by a solid object, a shadow will form. As long as there is light, the shadow will be constrained. It can be useful. A shadow can mark the passage of time. Hour by hour. Day by day. Year by year. The brighter the light, the deeper the shadow will be. But as that light dies, the shadows lengthen until they cover everything. For the eighteen years of her life, Carrie Edwards *was* the light. And then the darkness came. For thirty-four years now, Edris Jones has walked in darkness, and he knows that, for him, the light will never come again.

Mari Jones is sitting in her armchair, watching the door and absent-mindedly twisting her wedding ring round her finger, when Edris arrives home. She pretends not to have noticed the time. Edris doesn't like it when she worries.

Edris bends and kisses his mother on the cheek.

'Hello, love,' Mari says, 'what's in the bag? Kippers?'

Mari always hopes for kippers, and always forgets she doesn't like the bones.

'Sausages,' says Edris.

'From the butcher's?'

'Yes.'

'All right. With some nice gravy and mash?'

'Of course.'

Mari is happy and settles back in her chair. Edris potters about in the kitchen and talks to his mother while he cooks. The kitchen is the only place where Edris has a voice. Mari listens to him and she relaxes. Edris has dropped the heavy oak latch across the door, as he always does when he comes home. Mother and son sit comfortably eating sausages with gravy and mashed potatoes, and fat peas that have come out of a tin and look too green to have ever grown from the soil.

Darkness comes over the house. But this darkness is benign

and will disappear with the crowing of the cock in the morning. Then, Edris will get up, make a pot of tea for his mother, who is always awake before him, and he will raise the wooden latch and step out into the old farmyard to feed the hens – all that is left of a once busy farm.

Carrie Edwards gets off the bus at 4.45pm every day. Her backpack is heavy with books. As the bus pulls away, she waves to her college friends who are sitting, as always, on the back seat. One of them pulls a face, and Carrie smiles a lopsided kind of smile, and does a silly dance until the bus is out of sight.

Carrie's home is a fifteen-minute walk from the bus stop, past the church, over the stile and across the field that belongs to Jon and Mari Jones. The oak tree marks the halfway point between the bus stop and home, and Carrie always gives the tree a friendly pat as she passes it. It is entirely familiar. A reassuring presence in an easy landscape.

The tree sits near the top of the field, which slopes gently up a short hill. Carrie's home is not visible until she passes the tree, and then it is just a short walk down the other side to home. And safety.

Once Carrie crests the hill, her mother would be able to see her, if her mother were to stand in the garden, watching. And sometimes her mother does. But not today. Today, Mrs Edwards is very busy. Doing what, she will later not remember, try though she might. If, today, Mrs Edwards had stood in the garden watching, Carrie might have come home. But Mrs Edwards is busy. She is not in the garden. She is in the house, looking through her husband's papers for ... something. Nothing.

And five o'clock comes, and Carrie does not walk through the door and drop her heavy backpack on the kitchen table. She does not turn on the tap and let the water run until it is cold, fill a big glass and drink it all down in one long gulp. She does not open the fridge looking for snacks, or lift the lids of the cooking pots to see what is for dinner. Today there are no pots on the stove because Mrs Edwards is busy. But Carrie won't be home to eat anyway.

It is not until 5.30 that Mrs Edwards notices her daughter has not come home. She puts down the papers she has been looking through and steps into the garden. Carrie will be at the garden gate. Or on the path. Or up on the hill, where the very top of the oak tree can be seen over the brow.

Carrie is not there. Mrs Edwards checks her watch and walks back into the kitchen to see whether Carrie scrawled a message on the fridge before she hurried out the door this morning.

Tea at Joanne's. Back by 7.

Or *Athletics. Back by 7.*

Or *Swimming. Back by 7.*

There is no message, but Mrs Edwards waits until seven o'clock, sure that Carrie will get off the 6.45 bus – the last bus from the town. She goes back to sorting the papers, but already she is beginning to forget what she is looking for. She checks her watch. And the kitchen clock. The back door and the gate. She looks up the path, and up the hill. Carrie will walk over the hill at any moment, and her mother will scold her for forgetting to write the note on the fridge. Mrs Edwards looks up the hill and rehearses tart words that she will never speak.

At seven o'clock, Mr Edwards comes home. He looks tired. He checks the stove, where there are no pots. He looks around the living room, with papers scattered over every surface. He turns to his wife with the beginnings of a scowl on his face.

'Carrie's not back.'

Robert Edwards looks at his wife. She is worried, he can tell, though she is trying not to show it. Not to feel it.

'She probably had something after college. Did you check the fridge?' Mrs Edwards doesn't reply, and he knows there's nothing there, but Mr Edwards checks anyway. 'She'll have forgotten. She'll be back.'

'She's missed the last bus.'

Mr Edwards checks his watch. 'Have you called her friends?'

'Not yet.'

'That's where she'll be.' Mr Edwards sounds confident. He has to.

Mrs Edwards calls Joanne. She calls Megan. She calls Rhys. They are all at home. Safe. She speaks to their mothers and they sympathise, in a distant way, glad that their children would never worry them like this. But they don't say so to Mrs Edwards. They say, have you tried Megan, or Rhys or Joanne. Mrs Edwards has tried them, and the mothers sound a little worried now, about a horror that isn't theirs. Mrs Edwards reassures them. She will have forgotten. Or the message on the fridge might have been wiped away. But she'll turn up.

'She'll turn up,' Mr Edwards says, but he stands in the garden and stares at the hill, as if waiting to see his daughter walk over it. At nine o'clock the summer light is beginning to fade. 'I'll have a drive around, see if I can find her.' And Robert Edwards leaves, glad to be out of the house.

Mrs Edwards waits until the sound of his car fades away. Then she picks up the phone and calls Mari Jones.

'Mari? It's Alys Edwards.'

'Oh! Hello.' Mari's voice is surprised. And cautious.

'Is Carrie there?'

'Oh! Carrie? No. I don't think so. What makes you think she's here?'

'She hasn't come home. I was wondering... Well, I was wondering if she might be with Edris.'

'Edris isn't here. I'm expecting him any moment.'

'Oh.'

'Are they... I mean, is she likely to be with him?'

'I don't know.'

'I'm glad you called, Alys, because I wanted to say—'

'Not now, Mari. I've got to find Carrie. If she comes in with Edris, will you ask her to give me a call?'

'I... Yes, of course. But I'm sure she'll turn up.'

Mrs Edwards hangs up the phone and walks into the garden again. She walks to the gate and up the path. The light is fading and the hill is being swallowed by shadows. But Alys Edwards stands on the path until the hill is lost to the night, and she waits, and she waits, and she prays.

Mr Edwards returns. 'I can't see her anywhere. I think we should call the police.'

Alys breathes a sigh of relief. The police will find her. Thank God.

Edris Jones no longer works his own land, which is now little more than the farmhouse and Oak Tree Field, the field left fallow for over thirty years. The rest of the land was sold after his father's death, and sold cheap, too, since no one felt inclined to let Edris and his mother make a profit. Now Edris works for other farmers, on land that he once owned. But he works hard, rarely even taking a break, unless to answer a call of nature or to open his lunch box and swallow a sandwich whole.

Edris does not push his company on his employers. He does not make conversation or crack a joke. One or two of the farmers, discomfited by the silence, have made half-hearted attempts to draw him into a conversation over the years. But Edris always rebuffs these overtures, and the farmers breathe a sigh of relief, and conversation again falls back into instruction and acknowledgement. No one mentions the past. What, after all, could one say? Edris Jones, hard worker that he is, has become one more piece of farm machinery: reliable, stolid, and needing only to be pointed in the right direction.

So what does Edris do, if he does not speak? He remembers. On sunny days, he remembers Carrie Edwards cutting across Oak Tree Field on her way to the bus stop in the morning, and again in the afternoon on her way home. He remembers her patting the tree as she passes it, marking the halfway point of her journey. He remembers her skipping sometimes, or singing as she carries her backpack, full of books, on subjects Edris Jones knows nothing about. He remembers Carrie waving at him, not in the embarrassed way that adults wave, but as children do, using both hands, using wrists and elbows. She smiles, and her smile is a bit lopsided. Sometimes she dances a little too.

In his memory, the sun is always shining when Carrie crosses his field, but she does not cast a shadow. Edris knows that this memory must be faulty, because only at noon would there be no shadow, and by then Carrie would be at college. Safe. Edris knows that this memory is faulty, but he lingers inside it for as long as he can, before it is pushed out of his mind by memories composed entirely of shadow.

'She'll probably turn up,' says a bored policeman. 'Has she ever stayed out overnight before?'

'No.'

'Never? She is eighteen, after all.'

'Not without letting us know. She's very responsible.'

'Hmm,' says the policeman. 'Have you tried calling her friends?'

Alys Edwards presses her hands together, watches as her fingers turn white and then mottled red and blue under the strain.

'Any boyfriends?'

'No,' says Mr Edwards, firmly.

'Edris Jones,' says Alys with a sigh. Her husband looks at her sharply, and she says, 'I think so. Maybe. He likes her anyway.'

Mr Edwards snorts. 'Everybody likes her. But Carrie wouldn't go out with the likes of Edris Jones!'

The policeman looks a trifle less bored. 'Do you know anything against him?'

Robert Edwards looks uncomfortable. He glances at his wife briefly, but she is not looking at him. 'No. Not as such.

But, well, all the Joneses are a little odd. Get strange ideas in their heads.' He glances again at his wife, but she has begun to gather up the teapot and the cups.

'Where does Edris Jones live?'

Robert blusters a little. Alys gives him the address and stands up to put the cups in the sink. She grips the edges of the enamel tightly and stares through the window, although it is pitch black outside now, without even a moon to cast its shadowy light across the garden. 'So, what happens now?' she says.

'Well, I'll speak to this Edris Jones now, just to be on the safe side, and, if she hasn't turned up by morning...'

Alys turns on the taps.

'We can start making enquiries among her friends,' the policeman says.

'We've already done that!'

The policeman pretends he hasn't heard as he scrapes back his chair and turns to go. 'I, or one of my colleagues, will be in touch in the morning. If I were you, I'd try to get some sleep. She's bound to—'

'Thank you,' says Alys, opening the back door.

She closes it firmly behind him and turns to her husband. 'We need to get a search party together to look for her.'

'The police will do that.'

'They'll do nothing! She's my daughter! You can do that, can't you? Goddamn you, if nothing else, you can do that.'

Robert Edwards flinches. 'Yes ... but... It's dark now. We'll have to wait till the morning.'

Alys Edwards calls almost everyone who lives in the surrounding farms, and in the village. She rouses many from their beds. But they all agree to meet at 5.30 at the Edwardses' house to begin the search.

Alys has not called the Joneses, but Mari Jones is standing outside with the others the next morning. Mari looks white, and scared, but Alys cares for nothing now, except finding her daughter. And of course, it is Mari who finds her. It is Mari who tells Alys that her daughter is dead. It is Mari who catches Alys as she falls, holds her while she sobs. And it is Mari who rocks Alys Edwards in her arms while she lets out that low and terrible moan which begins somewhere deep in her gut and goes on forever.

Edris Jones has been held for questioning for twenty-four hours and he must be released. For now. He has not requested a lawyer, despite repeatedly being offered the chance to do so. Three different detectives have questioned him, and his answers are always the same.

Yes, he knew Carrie Edwards.

Yes, he liked her.

No, he wasn't her boyfriend.

Would he like to be? Well, maybe. But he wasn't mooning over her all the time. He just liked her, that's all.

Asked where he had been from 4.45pm onwards, Edris does not have a satisfactory answer. He was working in the fields.

'Alone?'

'Yes.'

'Do you usually work alone?'

'Since my father had an accident and lost the use of one arm.'

'Can anyone corroborate that?'

'About the arm?'

'About working alone.'

'Well, no. That's what alone means. There's the fence that was mended. And the crops that were sprayed.'

'Sprayed crops are not an alibi. Have you seen Carrie's backpack? It wasn't with the body.'

Edris can't help. He is sorry – sorry for Mrs Edwards. And for Carrie, too.

'And for Mr Edwards? Are you sorry for him, as well?'

Edris Jones spits on the floor. There is nothing he wishes to say about Robert Edwards.

Don't go anywhere, Edris is told. We'll be watching you. Further enquiries will be made.

Mari Jones is awake, but she remains in her bed. Edris will be up soon and he will bring her some tea. And it will worry him if he thinks she has not slept well. From her window she has a clear view of the oak tree, though she averts her eyes from it automatically. She has blotted it out of the landscape. She hears her son's foot on the stair. She hears him fill the kettle, and open and close cupboards as he sets things ready on a tray.

There is a pause, and Mari knows that Edris has left the kitchen and lifted the big oak latch of the front door, set it back against its catch. A minute more and she hears Edris outside, knows he has gone to feed the chickens.

She twists her wedding ring absently and listens until she hears her son re-enter the kitchen. Soon he comes up the stairs, and she can tell by his tread that he is carrying a tray. She arranges herself to look as if she has just woken up, though she knows he isn't fooled.

'Egg and soldiers,' he says, laying the tray on her lap.

'Lovely,' she says.

He kisses the top of her head and looks out the window to the oak tree. 'Summer will be over soon.'

'Yes.'

They both sound a little relieved.

Mari is up by the time Edris leaves for work. He opens the front door and sniffs the air. 'Going to rain, I reckon. I won't be late back.'

Mari waits until Edris's footsteps have died away before she quietly eases the catch back down. Better to be safe than sorry.

Carrie Edwards passes the oak tree and reaches the top of the hill. And now she can see her house. Her mother is not in the garden, and Carrie is a little disappointed. Her mother has been upset for days. She hasn't said why. But if dinner is cooking when she gets home, everything will be Okay again. And she really hopes it is, because Carrie loves her mother, and she loves her mother's cooking.

Carrie is looking only at her house as she walks. She does not look around. She does not look behind her. If she had, she would have seen a man that she knew. If she had turned around, she might also have seen the look on his face, and then she would have known, and she would have dropped the backpack full of books and she would have run, and run fast, until she had reached her home and the safety of her mother's arms.

Edris is already in the butcher's when Alys Edwards walks in. She doesn't see him straight away. She is looking through her bag for her single-serving shopping list – one chop, two sausages, half a small chicken – and Edris can't leave without walking past her.

Alys finds her list and looks up. She catches the butcher's eye first. He looks embarrassed, lowers his eyes to the parcel of mince he is wrapping in waxed paper. Alys knows Edris must be there even before she turns her head to look at him. And she does turn. She does look.

'Edris,' she says, with a small nod. Edris turns too. He's not a coward, she'll give him that.

'Hello, Mrs Edwards.' He holds out a note. The butcher snatches at it and slaps the parcel of meat on the counter before rushing to get the change. 'How are you?'

She doesn't answer, but she nods to him as the butcher holds out the change, and she steps back so that Edris can leave the shop. Only her hands betray her. The shopping list is quivering in her hand, and when the butcher takes it from her, sympathetically, she clasps her hands together and watches as the fingers turn white, and then mottled red and blue under the pressure. Alys keeps her eyes on her hands, pressing them together, draining the blood from them, until her breathing has returned to normal and her heart has resumed its natural rhythm. Then she pays quickly, adds her shopping to her bag and leaves, to sighs of relief from the butcher.

Three days after Carrie Edwards is found dead, Edris Jones walks past the village church, and looks up past the stile and up the hill. The spire of the church casts its long shadow in the sunshine, and points, like an accusing finger, straight at the oak tree. Edris's eyes follow the shadow and he knows that there is something wrong. There is another shadow now, this one suspended from the tree. The shadow of the hanged man reaches the crest of the hill and disappears, not over the hill, but into it.

Edris starts to run, but other people are already coming over the hill from the other side. They reach the tree long before he does. They cut the body down. They blow air into lifeless lungs. They try to restart the silent heart. Everyone agrees that Jon Jones did what he did to save his son. What they don't agree on, is why.

There was a note, the coroner says. Jon Jones has admitted killing Carrie Edwards. But he gives no reason. He has asked for forgiveness from God, but not from Alys Edwards. He has said he carried out his crime alone, but he never said how he did it, with only one good arm. He has told his wife and son that he loves them, and he finishes his note with a psalm. Everyone knows the psalm, and no one knows what he means by it.

The police have a confession and a culprit has been punished, albeit by his own hand. Are they satisfied? Well, hardly, but without evidence, what can they do? And there is no evidence. If they had found the backpack, perhaps things would be different. But they have not. They close the case and release the body of poor Carrie Edwards for burial.

And that is all there is to say, except that Robert Edwards left the village the day after his daughter's funeral, and no one has seen him since. No one in the village blamed him. Those who still remember him, and there are few enough of those now, believe that Carrie's death broke him. They said he stood at his daughter's graveside and looked haunted. And maybe that is the literal truth. Who knows?

The whole village attended the funeral, with the exception of Mari and Edris Jones who were warned by the police to stay away. They stayed inside their house, and the oak latch held even when the men came from the wake, angry with drink, and with mourning. The latch held as they pounded on the door and challenged Edris to come out and face them like a man. Mari Jones watched from her bedroom window, begged her son to stay inside. To protect her, she said. And so Edris stayed.

The police came when the men set fire to the door, though they took their time about it. The heavy oak door resisted burning, just as it resisted being broken down. Apart from a little charring, it was no worse for wear. The men wandered away as the police arrived, and the police advised the Joneses, coldly, not to press charges.

Few villagers remember Carrie Edwards now, though they feel the absence of her. And people still talk of the time when they gathered outside the Edwardses' house at first light to look for Carrie. They talk about how scared Mari Jones had looked, even before she found the body. And they all agree that that was bloody queer.

But some people remember.

Edris Jones remembers Carrie. He remembers meeting her in Oak Tree Field one evening, a week before she died. He remembers her smile, and her silly dance, and the way she waved to him using both her hands and wrists and elbows. And how they walked past the old tree, and she patted it, as she always did, and how he almost asked her out, but his courage failed him at the last moment. He remembers how he stood on the brow of the hill and watched her until she reached her garden gate, and home. And safety. And he smiled to himself then, and went to the tree and put his hand where her hand had been, and told himself, next time he would be braver.

And Edris remembers how his mother looked just then as she staggered over the brow of the hill, her face bloody, her clothes torn. He remembers how she collapsed into his arms, and how she let out a terrible groan, one that began deep inside her and went on forever.

Mari Jones remembers the anguish on her husband's face, when Edris carried her home. And she remembers calling Alys Edwards. She remembers the silence on the other end of the line when she told Alys that her husband was a rapist. It was not the silence of disbelief, of shock. It was the silence of a woman who has come to the moment of reckoning, and can no longer hide from the truth: she is married to a monster.

And Alys Edwards remembers, too. She remembers telling her husband she wanted a divorce, that she wanted him out of their lives, forever, or she'd tell about all the things he'd done to *her*. And she remembers how Robert snarled at her. 'I'll destroy you,' he said.

Alys remembers the morning of her daughter's funeral, when she stood in her garden, looking up to the hill, waiting and waiting and praying for an answer. And she remembers looking at her husband's car, parked at the side of the house, and how she walked with sudden certainty to the car and opened the boot. And how she moved aside the boxes of papers that Robert had removed from the house – marriage certificate, bank statements, debt notices – and how, right at the back beneath a scrap of old blanket, she found it: Carrie's backpack, still full of books, some of them splattered with her daughter's blood.

Alys remembers whispering in her husband's ear at the graveside, and how terrified he looked when she told him she knew.

She remembers her husband telling mourners at the wake that he was going to leave for a while, one eye on his wife. Alys said nothing, but watched her husband, a stranger and a monster, as he accepted drinks and condolences for the loss of a daughter who wasn't his. And when the men had drunk enough and had marched on the Joneses house, Alys remembers how she made him stay behind, though he had not wanted to be left alone with her. And how she took the big kitchen knife and stabbed her husband, and stabbed him again. And again.

And Alys Edwards remembers how, at daybreak the next morning, Edris Jones came. She'd known he would. She was standing at the kitchen door, the bloody knife in the sink, the body of her husband on the kitchen floor. She was pressing her hands together, watching the colour drain from them, looking up to the hill, waiting, and waiting, and praying.

Edris looked at Alys, and at the body on the kitchen floor. He looked for a long time.

'I was thinking, I would plough Oak Tree Field this morning.' He looked at Alys, and she nodded. And he took her husband away.

And they had never spoken of it again.

It's all a long time ago now. Memories fade. On cloudy days Edris Jones doesn't think about the past. About the good man found hanging from the oak tree, or the bad man buried beneath it. Edris does his work, goes home to his mother and cooks her dinner, finds his voice in the kitchen of his old farmhouse. On cloudy days he doesn't think about Carrie Edwards at all.

But when the sun comes out and the shadow of the church spire points to the oak tree near the top of the field, Edris Jones walks into the Plumber's Arms and silently buys a pint. He sits in a corner and stares at the fire, and he remembers a beautiful girl with a lopsided smile, waving and doing a silly dance. Edris likes to remember. He will buy two more pints, and then he will walk slowly home, pass the tree and place his hand where her hand once lay, then go home to his mother, lamenting only that he did not seize his moment to kiss Carrie all those years ago.

Edris knows that shadows are the absence of light. For the eighteen years of her life, Carrie Edwards *was* the light, and now Edris Jones is content to walk in her shadow.

Play it for Me

Maggie Himsworth

DCI Elin Owens registered the shudder of the grey BMW as she crossed the first cattle grid on the main road rising up over the Preselis. The landscape here could fall two ways: misty, bleak, with barely enough visibility to follow the white lines, or, like today, a view that took your eye up the west coast of Wales, the immediate moonscape becoming dotted with small dwellings and family homes. Families no doubt sitting around their kitchen table, doing homework, arguing, planning the next day.

The car dropped down into the descent, rattled across the second grid and turned left. Up ahead she could see the flashing blue lights, the blue and white tape.

As she parked a young man approached the car.

'What have you got for me, Mark?'

'Not quite sure yet, guv. Builders doing some work for the new owners and got more than they bargained for.'

'Who found it?'

'Bloke over there, by the JCB. Gwilym Williams, local builder.'

'Is he okay?'

'A bit shocked. Place has been empty for years ... in a terrible state. He thought it was going to be straightforward. Until he found Bert.'

'Bert?'

'Oh, you know, guv. We give them a name until we find out who they are. Do it alphabetically like they name the hurricanes.'

'But you're only at B.'

'Well, this is only my second down here.'

Mark had recently transferred from Thames Valley. He had a young family and wanted a quieter life. Elin wasn't sure if the move was completely living up to expectations.

'Okay. Well, you'd better show me what we've got.'

'Right. Come this way, it's a bit stony but you'll be okay.'

Inside, Dr Raabe, the senior pathologist, was carefully examining something. A large blue-grey flagstone had been moved to one side.

'Doc, this is DCI Elin Owens, the investigating officer.'

'Thank you, Mark. Dr Raabe and I have met before.'

'Lovely to see you Elin. Although I haven't seen you about for a while.'

'Oh, I've been busy, you know how it is. What can you tell me?'

The man looked at her for just a second too long, clearly curious, but then reverted to professional mode.

'Well... Male, age – difficult to tell at the moment.'

'How long has he been here? Are we looking for a forensic archaeologist?'

'I don't think so. Not unless sheet music dates back further than I think.'

'What do you mean?'

'Well, he has something shoved in his mouth. It's not completely intact but I think it's sheet music.'

'So, we're looking at something suspicious?'

'The back of his head was smashed in and he was buried beneath what would have been the hearth, so, yes.'

'Not much to go on so far?'

'Not yet no, but let me work my magic in the lab and I might have something more for you. Late afternoon tomorrow I would think.'

'Thanks, Andy. I'll see you then.'

Elin walked around the outside of the dilapidated building, trying to picture what once had been someone's home. She could just make out the perimeter of what had probably been a garden, the Pembrokeshire banks eroded over time by weather and sheep.

'Guv...?'

'Sorry, Mark, I was just trying to picture what it would have been like with a family living here.'

'Might have been some old boy on his own.'

'Maybe. First step, take a statement from the builder, get the details of the new owners and check them out.'

'Okay. But it's not likely they've got anything to do with this, is it?'

'Probably not, but we still need to check.'

'Yes but...'

Elin sighed.

'Mark, do it please. Ducks in a row and all that.'

'Yes, sorry, guv, you know me.'

'I do. Impatient. While you do that, I'll get someone to start on contacting the Land Registry to find the previous owners. I'm hoping Andy will be able to narrow the time-frame a bit.'

'Andy?'

'Dr Raabe. Andreas.'

Mark raised an eyebrow. Elin felt herself blushing and tried to control the redness threatening to flood her face.

'Friendly are you?'

'Not really. Now, I'm going back to the station. By the time you've finished with Gwilym Williams it will be time to knock off, so I'll see you in the morning.'

'Thanks, guv.'

Making her way back to the road, Elin saw a small red car slow down. The driver was a dark-haired woman, older than Elin. When she saw Elin approaching she moved on, but not before having a good look at what was going on.

'Probably just curiosity,' Elin thought. But she filed it away in her memory, just in case.

Back at the station she instructed one of her team to start the Land Registry checks, then went upstairs to report to her boss.

Home for Elin was a small stone cottage, just over a mile from the crime scene. It had a view down towards Newport Bay, or Tudrath as the locals called it. It was big enough for one and Elin could see no reason why that would need to change. She poured herself a glass of wine and sat enjoying the view from the window. Dr 'Andy' Raabe had been one of her more recent mistakes. She'd had a bad experience with a colleague when she was in her twenties, and since then nothing seemed to have been right between her and men. She had liked Andy well enough, but something always held her back. She thought he'd been keener than her, remembered meeting his father, a charming man, still with a strong German accent. As a prisoner of war, he had opted to stay and make Wales his adopted country.

The team room was already busy when she got in the next morning. Mark was standing at the kettle making coffee. When he saw her, he raised a mug towards her and she nodded.

'There you are, guv. Two sugars included.'

'Oh dear. I should cut down really.'

'Nah. We all need our fix in the morning. Kids were up half the night last night throwing up, off school today. I was glad to come into work to be honest. Amy's going to have a tough day.'

Elin thought briefly about what it might have been like to meet the right man and have a family. She pushed the thought away. No point going down that road... 'How did you get on with the builder?'

'He has no connection with the place other than being employed to do the work. A couple from London bought it, looking for somewhere to escape. Wait till I tell them there was a body under the fireplace.'

'Get hold of them this morning, before the briefing at eleven if you can.'

'Okay. Builder's statement is on your desk.'

'Thanks. See you later.'

Elin was just reading through it when one of the younger members of her team knocked on the door.

'The information you wanted from the Registry, ma'am.'

'Thanks, Hannah. And no "ma'am", thank you. Guv or boss will do fine.'

'Sorry, boss. Can't seem to get out of the habit.'

Elin's predecessor had been a woman of retirement age and Elin had no wish to follow in her footsteps. She looked through the paperwork and prepared herself for the briefing.

'Okay everyone. Unidentified remains, male, found in the ruins of Tŷ Newydd, underneath the hearth. We don't know yet how long he's been there, nothing in the remains of his clothes to identify him. Dr Raabe is working on it now. Discovered by a local builder.'

'Where are the owners?' A voice from the back.

'Mark, can you help us with that please?'

'Plastic surgeon and his wife, Jacob and Lisa Petersen. Live in Fulham, planning the place as a holiday home. Minted by the sounds of it.'

'Have they spent much time in the area?' Elin asked.

'Only in the last few years. No family connections.'

Mark looked down at his notes.

'I didn't pick up anything, guv.'

'Well, it's probably unlikely that someone would bury a body and then go back years later and dig it up. Let's move on. Hannah, can you take us through the Land Registry information, please?'

The young woman shuffled her notes and cleared her throat nervously.

'The current owners, the Petersens, bought it last year from the widow of a chap called Huw Davies. Huw had bought it in late 1969, from someone called Martha Howells. The records show that it had been in the Howells family for decades, handed down through several generations.'

'So, why suddenly sell?'

Elin knew what these families were like. It meant something to have the same piece of land to pass down to their children. It was unusual for them to sell unless there was a very good reason.

'The Petersens told me that they believe Huw Davies died a couple of years ago. His family were strapped for cash and this raised a nice little sum.'

Mark looked around anticipating a reaction.

'How much?'

'250k.'

Someone whistled.

'Bloody hell, more money than sense.'

'Oh, go on Davo, you're only jealous.'

'Too bloody right I am. I wonder if someone would pay that for my bungalow?'

'Does it have a sea view?'

'No, it looks out over next door's oil tank!'

'There you are then, you daft bugger.'

'Okay ... okay.' Elin raised her voice over the din.'I want names and addresses for Huw Davies's family. Mark, you and I will pay them a visit. Hannah, can you try to establish when anyone last lived in the place? Electoral register maybe? Davo, you can start checking missing persons. Start ten years ago and work backwards. It's a long shot but maybe after we've heard from Dr Raabe we might be able to narrow it down a bit. Okay, that's it for now.'

Huw Davies's widow lived in Fishguard, in a house overlooking Lower Town. It seemed a world away from the bleak little house they had left on the mountain.

'Mrs Davies? I'm DCI Elin Owens and this is my sergeant, DS Mark Hargreaves.'

The woman who had answered the door must have been in her late seventies. She led them into a sitting room looking out over the garden.

'We're really sorry to trouble you Mrs Davies, but we wanted to ask you some questions about a property you sold recently, to a Mr and Mrs Petersen.'

Elin had already told Mark that she would take the lead. She didn't want him wading in with his size tens.

'I didn't really want to sell it to them, I don't agree with second homes, but I couldn't afford to keep this house after my husband died. Huw had always said if the time feels right, sell, but it was difficult.'

'How much time did you spend there?'

'None. That's what never made sense. He bought it from his sister Mattie, all of a rush, nothing else to be done, and then he never went near the place, just let it fall down.'

'Was his sister's name Howells?'

'Her married name. Funny lot. Huw never wanted her to marry him, Caleb, but I suppose she'd made her bed...'

Elin glanced at Mark.

'How do you mean, she'd made her bed?'

'Well, her husband wasn't easy. But in the circumstances... Anyway you can't come between husband and wife can you?'

'Did they have a family?'

'Yes, one daughter, Rhiannon. Her father adored her.'

'You said that your husband bought it from his sister. What happened to Mr Howells?'

'Oh, he left them. Went out one night and never came back. It was after that Mattie wanted to sell; she couldn't stand the place. She and Rhiannon moved away and we didn't see or hear from them for years.'

'Didn't you think that was a bit strange?'

Mrs Davies looked at Elin and then at Mark.

'What's all this about? Is there some problem with the new people?'

'No, Mrs Davies, nothing like that. We're just trying to establish what happened to the property prior to the Petersens buying it.'

Elin hoped this would satisfy the woman for now.

'I don't know where Rhiannon is, but Mattie is in a care home. They got in touch with Huw not long before he died and he went to see her. She's got dementia, didn't really know him, he said, but Rhiannon had asked the care home to contact him.'

'Do you remember which care home?'

'I don't know the name but it's a big white house with a long drive up to it, about five miles down the main road.'

'You said the name of Mattie's husband was Caleb Howells?'

'Yes.'

'Did anyone report Mr Howells missing?'

'I don't know. I think Mattie was glad to see the back of him, to be honest.'

'Well, thank you very much, Mrs Davies. That will be all for now. We'll see ourselves out.'

Elin and Mark walked back out through the hallway to the front door. It was one of those houses with nothing on the walls, no photographs, no paintings, no memories.

They got back in the car, Mark driving.

'What do you think, guv? Do you think we've got our man?'

'I think there's a good chance. We need to check if he was reported missing at the time. We have the date of the sale between Martha and her brother so I would say maybe two years before that?'

'Okay. I'll get someone on it. I have a good feeling about this.'

Elin looked at him.

'Don't get carried away with yourself. We're not there yet.'

She smiled though. Optimism was very endearing.

Elin punched in the code on the lab door and pulled it open. She'd left Mark phoning round local care homes to establish if they had a Martha Howells with them.

Andreas Raabe looked up from what he was examining when he heard her come in, and pushed his glasses back up.

'I don't remember you wearing specs, Andy?'

Now why did she say that? Elin wanted to keep this meeting professional. Plus, she didn't want to give him the wrong idea.

'Only for close work.' There was a slight question in his look.

'Well, what does your close work reveal?'

'No surprises. A blow to the back of the head with our old friend the blunt instrument. The remnants of his clothes indicate a rough timescale though – materials which became popular in the 1960s, used in Crimplene, so that's useful.'

'Anything else?'

'Yes, and this is where it gets really interesting. It is a small piece of sheet music in the mouth cavity; I can only really distinguish it under a microscope. It's lasted remarkably well.'

'So can you make it out?'

'Come and have a look for yourself.'

Andy pointed her towards the bench where various microscopes were set up.

'Here, take a look through this.'

Elin was looking at what she thought was a strip of paper torn off the top of a piece of sheet music. She could see a treble and bass clef and notes from the first three bars. The title had disintegrated, but there seemed to be an A and an M.

'Can you send me a slide of this?'

'Already done. Should be in your Inbox.'

'Thanks, Andy. I need to check in with Mark, see what he makes of it.'

'Maybe catch up later for a drink? You can let me know how things are going?'

'I'm going to be busy.'

'All work and no play and all that?'

'That's how it is at the moment, I'm sorry.'

'Have it your own way, you usually do.'

Elin tugged open the door, forgetting that it had to be

released on the inside. She could sense him smiling as she fumbled her way out. Hopefully she wouldn't need to see him again for a while.

Mark called her over as soon as she got back to the team room.

'I've found her, guv. Mrs Davies was right, she wasn't far.'

'Well done. Have you made arrangements to see her?'

'No, I thought I'd better wait to see what you came back with from the lab. You know me, slow and steady.'

'Well, that's a first.'

'Right, listen up everyone.'

The undercurrent of chatter stopped and all eyes turned to Elin.

'Cause of death's what we thought: blunt trauma to the back of the head. We won't get hung up on what was used, it will be long gone. But we do have a time-frame. Fibres in his clothes suggest the 1960s onwards.'

'Oh, Mr Drip-Dry then!'

There was always one clown in a circus, Elin thought.

'One other interesting thing to note, and I think it's probably the most significant. Dr Raabe's hunch was right. Someone pushed a piece of sheet music into his mouth. Mark, could you get that slide up for me, please?'

Everyone was quiet as they studied what was left of the scrap of paper.

'Anyone here read music?'

A hand went up at the back of the room. As everyone turned to look, Hannah blushed. 'I play the piano a bit.'

Elin smiled at her. 'Great. Take a look at this would you? See what you can make of it.'

'What shall we do about Mrs Howells, guv?'

'We'll leave her for now Mark. I'd like to find out a bit more about this music. I wonder if we should go back and see Mrs Davies?'

'She was definitely holding things back, I reckon.'

'Definitely. Give her a ring and ask her to come here tomorrow morning. Give her tonight to worry about it. We'll see her together.'

Elin never slept well during a major investigation. Although there wasn't the same urgency to this case, the optimum time for evidence gathering was long gone, it still needed to be solved and her mind kept going over the possibilities.

Hannah was the first to approach her when she went in the next morning.

'I've had a bit of luck ma'am – sorry – boss. I played the first three bars and my dad recognised it, said my gran used to play it. "Carolina Moon".'

It meant nothing to Elin.

'What are the words?'

'My dad doesn't remember but it's something about the same moon shining on someone far away.'

'A love song then?'

'Yes. About lovers who are parted. I looked it up. It was a big hit in 1958.'

'Good work, Hannah. I wonder what the significance is?'

'I don't know but...'

'Go on.'

'It just seems such an angry thing to do. I mean on top of

bashing someone's head in, this final punishment, a type of degradation somehow.'

'Mm, I see what you mean. Could you get me a recording of the song?'

'I expect so. I'll have a look.'

Hannah was true to her word and an hour later had supplied Elin with the recording. As she was listening to it, Mark knocked on her door.

'Mrs Davies is downstairs.'

Elin had forgotten about her.

'Could you take charge of her Mark? Get Hannah to sit in with you, it will be good experience for her.'

'Sure. But I thought you'd want to see her yourself.'

'No, you're fine. I thought I'd go to see Mrs Howells.'

'Really?'

'Yes. If she's as frail as we think she is, one of us will be less intimidating than two.'

'Okay.'

Mark didn't sound convinced but he didn't argue.

Lunch was just finishing when Elin arrived at the care home.

When she explained the reason for her visit, a large woman in a light-blue uniform escorted Elin down a corridor into one of the two bedrooms at the end of it.

'Mattie, there's someone here to see you.'

Elin looked at the tiny, frail woman, hunched over in the armchair. She looked at the thick support stockings, the Velcro fastenings on the slippers, the cotton nightdress visible through the gap in the dressing gown. There was no response.

'She's not having a very good day today I'm afraid. She refused to come into the dining room and hasn't eaten any of her lunch.'

'Does she have many visitors?'

'None.'

'But she has family?'

'A daughter who pays the bills, but she doesn't visit.'

From what Elin had seen of the place she knew it wouldn't be cheap.

'Do you think she'll understand if I ask her a few questions?'

'You can try, but I doubt it. She doesn't ever say much apart from "no" when she's refusing to do something. Most of the time though, she's quite passive.'

Elin sat down next to Martha Howells and took her hand. She had long fingers, which probably would have been shapely when she was younger.

'Mrs Howells, I'm a police officer. I wanted to ask you a few questions.'

There was no response.

'I wanted to ask you about your husband, Caleb.'

No flicker of recognition.

'I'm going to play you some music Mrs Howells, it might help you to remember.'

As the music began, Mattie pulled her hand away from Elin's, wrapping her arms round herself as she started rocking. Her frail frame seemed to be moving of its own volition, her head hitting against the back of the chair as her mouth opened in a keening wail of pain.

Elin switched the music off. 'I'm sorry, I wasn't expecting that. It's all right, Mrs Howells.'

Elin tried to take the old lady's hand but with surprising strength she lashed out at Elin's face, drawing blood as her nails raked across Elin's cheek. The nurse pressed a buzzer as she tried to stop Mattie from hurting herself or Elin.

Elin pulled a few tissues from a box by the bed and held them against her face.

'That looks nasty. Ask at the desk and someone will put a dressing on it for you, but you'd best go, you're upsetting her.'

Elin wasn't concerned about first aid for herself, although she was a bit shaken. She would deal with it later, but she did need an address for Rhiannon Howells. Despite protestations from the manager about confidentiality, mention of a murder investigation proved to be the trump card.

An hour later, having done a quick detour home, she was back at work, the surprisingly deep scratches cleaned and covered up with a dressing.

'Blimey, guv, what happened to you? Are you all right?' Elin could hear the concern in Mark's voice.

'Mattie Howells happened to me.'

'Why did she do that?'

'She didn't like my choice of music.'

'You played it to her?'

'Yes, just a hunch. But it certainly struck a nerve.'

'Did she say anything?'

'Not a word. But her reaction was extreme.'

'But that could be for all sorts of reasons.'

'I know. It doesn't tell us anything except that it was a song that had special significance for her.'

'Mrs Davies wasn't much help either. I pressed her quite hard but she's not letting on anything more than she did the other day.'

'No further on then.'

'Doesn't look like it, guv.'

'You know what? I think we'll finish a bit early today. Mull things over. Think about where we go from here. I can contact her daughter in the morning.'

Elin was just switching off her computer when someone poked their head round the door.

'Someone downstairs to see you, says it's urgent.'

'Who is it?'

'Rhiannon Howells.'

Elin could see Mark just going out through the door and called him back.

'Sorry, looks as if we're not clocking off early after all.'

They made their way downstairs and introduced themselves to the dark-haired woman sitting in reception. Elin was fairly sure that she drove a red car, a red car she'd seen before. She had a shoebox on her lap which she handed to Elin.

'You should see this.'

Mark found them an interviewing room and they all sat down, the shoebox on the table between them.

'You'd better open it. I'll explain it all to you after.'

Rhiannon Howells seemed calm, as if she'd been expecting this moment for a long time.

Elin opened the box. Inside was a small bundle of letters,

addressed to Martha Davies, in a beautiful copperplate hand. Underneath the letters was a pair of knitted baby's bootees, the white wool yellowing with age but the blue ribbon still in good condition.

'I think you need to do that explaining, Rhiannon.'

'Yes. I've been prepared for it, ever since my uncle sold the farm.' She paused.

'Go on.'

'The remains you found are my father's. Caleb. I was ten years old when he died.'

'Well, he didn't just die, did he? He was killed.'

Elin poked Mark under the table. Sometimes it was better to just let people tell the story in their own time.

'My parents' marriage wasn't a happy one. I didn't realise it so much at the time, but there was always a tension between them. My mother was always distant, not just from my father but from me as well. The only time she seemed happy was when she played the piano. She was a wonderful pianist. Then one night there was a huge argument. I hid upstairs under the bed because I was frightened. I remember the lino was very cold, and it was dusty. All I could hear was my father shouting: "Play it for me, play it for me." My mother wouldn't play whatever it was. Then I heard my father go into the back kitchen, come back in and start smashing up the piano. My mother was crying and begging him to stop. Then it went quiet.

My mother came upstairs a bit later, put me into bed and got in with me. She put her arms round me and told me it would be all right.

When I woke the next morning, my mother was already up and my uncle was there. There were suitcases in the porch and my uncle drove us to the station.'

'Where was your father?'

'I didn't know. My mother took me straight outside. The door to the best room, where the piano was, was closed.'

'Where did you go?'

'To a friend of my mother's in the Valleys. I loved it there. I thought we were going on a holiday, but we never went back.'

'So, when did you find out what had happened?'

'When I was about sixteen years old. She brought the box out and told me the whole story.'

'Which was?'

'My mother and father had grown up together, their families knew each other. Gradually as they got older, it was assumed that they would marry. Then my mother met someone else. He was very different from my father, well educated, although the war had disrupted his education. They fell in love and she got pregnant. He wanted to marry her but her parents wouldn't hear of it. They persuaded my father to stand by her, but it was on condition that she gave up the baby. She was sent away to some place where girls "in trouble" got sent. She had a little boy and he was taken away for adoption. She came back, married my father and a year later I was born.'

'So, the letters are from this other man?'

'Yes, but I've never read them.'

'Why not?'

'Because I loved my father. It felt disloyal to him.'

'What happened the night of the argument?'

'The care home staff told me that you played a piece of music to my mother.'

'Yes, I did. I had no idea it would upset her so much.'

'It was a song that she and this other man used to play and sing together. Even after she married my father, she'd often play it, usually when he was out, but he always knew. It drove him mad because he knew that she still loved someone else. He just wanted her to play it for him, that's what the argument was about. And when she wouldn't, he got an axe and smashed up her piano.'

'Then what happened?'

'He went and sat in his chair in front of the fire and waited for her to make his supper. But she hit him over the head with something.'

Elin waited for more, but Rhiannon was silent.

'I think she did a bit more than that didn't she?'

For the first time since she'd started speaking, Elin saw some emotion in the woman's face.

'I'm sorry, I don't really want to talk about it anymore. I've told you that she hit him over the head.'

'Yes, but I'd like you to tell us the rest of it.'

''She pushed something in his mouth.'

'She told you that, did she? And told you what it was?'

'Yes. I was repulsed by it. I couldn't stand to be near her. I wished she'd just gone away and left me with my father. He was right about her. She was cold as ice.'

'But she didn't. She took you with her and sold the farm to her brother.'

'Yes. She couldn't sell it to anyone else in case they'd find him. She knew that as long as Huw was alive it would be fairly safe. We moved away and that was that.'

'But it isn't, is it?'

'What do you mean?'

'You have a half-brother somewhere. Wouldn't you like to find out about him?'

'No, I have no interest in finding him.'

'And you don't know who the other man was?'

'No, but there's a photo of him in the box.'

Elin took out the tiny bootees and held them for a moment in her hand. At the bottom of the box was a sepia photograph, face down. She looked at it, immediately recognising the likeness of a man now much older, and felt a great sadness for him. Did he feel the loss of his firstborn as keenly as Mattie had? She returned the photograph to the box without showing it to Mark.

She would have to see Andy again after all.

Simon Says

Ellen Davies

It was my idea to break into the school, only, later, I'd say it wasn't. We were sitting on the spray-painted smiley face in the back lane when I came up with the idea. Simon was teasing me, saying I never had any good ideas of fun things to do. Saying I was just a stupid girl.

We're not friends. Not really. We live in the same street, but my best friend is Katie. Katie was on holidays that weekend in her caravan. Simon knocked for me on Saturday morning. My mother doesn't like me playing with Simon. She says he's grubby and smells like stale washing. I don't like the way he always sniffs up his boogers, trying to make them go back inside his nose. That day, I didn't have anything else to do.

'Want to come out?' Simon asked, his scooter slung across the pavement in front of my doorstep.

I shrugged. 'Yeah, okay.'

It was a hot day and we got tired quick from riding up and down the street on the scooters. I had fifty pence tucked in my pocket and I wanted to buy sweets.

'Let's go to the shop,' I said to Simon.

He shook his head, pushing his scooter faster up the street. 'Can't,' he shouted over his shoulder.

'Why not?' I called after him, pushing my trainer hard against the pavement to catch up with him.

'Got no money.'

'I have.' I stopped my scooter, propped it up against a lamp post. The fifty pence was shiny and I spun it round and round in my fingers the way my father had showed me. It felt good to show it off. Simon scooted over to me, leaving it until the last second to press his foot down on the back break.

'Give it here then.' He swiped for it, nearly knocking it out of my hands.

'No. It's mine.' I put my hand behind my back where he couldn't get it.

'Not fair. Friends share.'

'Are we friends, yeah?'

'Of course,' Simon said. 'You're my best friend this weekend.'

Even though I had my own best friend, I smiled at the thought of being Simon's best friend too. It didn't matter that I didn't like him much, because he liked me.

In Mr Prashad's shop, Simon took ages deciding what he wanted. He kept running his sticky hands over the different rows of chocolate bars and sweets, asking loudly how many things he could buy with his 25p. In the end, I let him spend 30p.

We went to the park and ate in the tree den. I crawled in first, getting my favourite seat in the crook of the conifer branch. The tree den is where all the kids from the street go. It smells of car air freshener and I like the way I can smell it on my clothes, on my hands, for hours afterwards. Simon scoffed his pick-and-mix in handfuls, chewing the jelly sweets loudly.

'What should we do next?' I said.

Simon shrugged. 'Dunno.'

'You could push me on the swings, or we could see how fast we can spin around on the roundabout before we're sick.'

'Those are stupid kid ideas. I don't wanna do that.'

I felt silly then for suggesting we play in the park. 'Have you got a better idea?'

'Yeah. Let's go play in the lane and see how many gardens we can climb into.'

I didn't like the idea, but I didn't want to show Simon that I was scared. My mother doesn't like me playing in the lane. She says she'll tan my legs with her slippers if she catches me garden hopping. I swallowed the sticky saliva pooling in my mouth.

'Yeah, okay,' I said, wriggling out of the branch. Simon moved towards me, put his sweaty face close to mine. I could see the film of clear snot running towards his lip.

'Not scared?'

'No.' I swallowed, squaring my shoulders. He leaned over and grabbed my arm.

'Not a scared girl?'

He twisted the skin of my forearm, his dirty nails digging in. I tried to yank my arm free, but he kept holding it, turning his hand in a tight circle around my wrist.

'Get off!'

'Not until you give me a kiss.' He grinned.

'No way.'

I tried again to wriggle my arm. Simon squeezed hard, a slow smile creeping across his lips. He licked them, moving his face closer. I leaned back until my shoulders were touching the tree bark. He smushed his face into mine. His lips were slimy and wet. I tried to tuck my lips away, held my breath. He slipped a slug into my mouth, bashing my teeth with his.

When he pulled away, he gave my arm another squeeze and said, 'You're my girlfriend now. Race you!'

I didn't race him. I let Simon run ahead, pumping his arms and legs, breathing hard to go faster. My legs felt strange, like they weren't mine. I dragged them slowly. My arm throbbed and I could feel the sweat from his palm on my skin. My stomach felt tight like a belt – like when you're watching a scary film or going too fast on the waltzers and you can't make it stop. Even if you close your eyes and scream, you can't make it stop. I thought of going home, letting Simon run ahead and then taking the right at the steps and slipping down the street. Just five minutes and I'd be home. But without looking, I knew my face looked strange. Crumpled, different from the face that went out to play in the morning. I didn't want to tell my mother about what happened. I knew it was a secret. I locked it away in my pocket.

'Slowcoach, slowcoach,' Simon chanted as I rounded the corner into the lane. He was leaning against Mrs Jones's back gate, scuffing his trainers on the tarmac. 'What took you so long?'

I shrugged.

'Mrs Jones has already seen me. Told me she'd have me with her slipper if I even think of hopping the wall.'

I breathed out a breath I didn't know I was holding.

'Don't look so happy,' Simon chided.

'I'm not.'

'Yeah, you are. You never wanted to do it anyway. You're always too scaaaaaaaaared.' He stuck out his bottom lip, mimed wiping his eyes.

'Am not!' I'd had enough then. This wasn't fun. I just wanted to go home. I didn't care that my face was different, and that Simon had made me kiss him. I wanted to go and scrub my skin, get rid of all the grimy places where he had touched me.

'You're not my friend!' I turned, started walking back up the lane. I kept my eyes down, tears pricking in their corners. I watched my trainers on my feet carry me away, the laces bobbing like bunny ears. My blood was loud in my ears.

I didn't hear Simon until he was behind me. I turned too late as his shoulder smashed into my stomach. His weight drove me backwards. My trainers scrambled for grip on the tarmac. I grabbed onto his T-shirt to try to stop myself, but we were both falling. Bits of his greasy blond hair were in my mouth. He smelled like unmade beds, and pine trees. When we hit the floor, he didn't roll away, but kept pressing his weight into me. His elbows were like daggers in my sides.

'Stupid bitch. Stupid, stupid bitch.' Spit flew out of his mouth.

I tried to wiggle from underneath him, to use my legs for leverage, but he had me pinned. Small stones from the ground bit into me. Somewhere down the street, a tinny radio played pop songs, too faint for me to recognise the words.

'Get off.'

Simon pushed his weight on me again. 'Say please,' he said, grinning.

'Get off me. Please.' My voice sounded small, pathetic. He stared at me and I knew then that I was crying. Hot tears tracked down my face. I wanted to screw my eyes shut. I turned my face away from him, tried to disappear into the ground.

Without warning, he released me. I scrambled back pulling my legs close. He crouched down opposite me, smiling.

'Don't look so serious. I was only messing.'

I wiped the back of my hand across my cheeks.

'You're not going home. We haven't finished playing.' Simon reached out his hand to pull me up.

I hesitated. A storm flashed across his face, so I grabbed his hand. He pulled me to my feet.

'Come on. I've got an idea.' He still had hold of my hand and he squeezed, watching for my wince.

Simon took us to the smiley face. 'Sit down,' he ordered.

The smiley face is the place where all the older kids go to play. It's on a patch of scrubland next to the school. I heard that there was a different school there once, but it burned down. Someone has spray-painted a smile on a clear patch of tarmac among the bricks and weeds. Two white dots for eyes, a wide curving mouth, a circle for a head. I pushed sweet wrappers and bits of plastic away with my foot. A plastic bottle rolled into the bracken.

'Right, now for a bit of fun.' Simon rubbed his hands together. 'Truth, or dare?'

I didn't want to choose either, but truth seemed the safest option. At least with truth Simon couldn't make me eat slugs or lick a worm.

'Truth.' I tried to sound more certain than I felt.

'Are you scared of me?' Simon tilted his head, stared at me.

I shifted my legs, pulled them tighter towards me, looked at my fingernails, rimmed with dirt. I started picking the dirt out with my thumbnail. 'No,' I answered.

Simon smirked. 'Remember, you can't lie here or smiley will come and get you in your sleep.'

'What?' My voice sounded strained. 'That's just a silly story.'

'And you're just a stupid girl.'

He wasn't going to accept a no.

'Yeah, I guess I am.'

Simon's smirk expanded into a grin.

'Just a little bit though,' I added.

Satisfied with my answer, Simon said, 'My turn now. I pick dare. But not a stupid girl dare. I want a proper dare.'

I should have dared him to go away, dared him to leave me alone, to go home and tell his mam how he made me cry, and kissed me and hurt me. I wanted to test him, to make him do something that he didn't want to do so he would know how it felt. I looked around, taking a long time to consider each option. I could have dared him to knock on Mrs Jones's gate and run away, or to steal chocolate from Mr Prashad's shop.

'Come oooooooon!' Simon had gotten to his feet and was pacing back and forth, swinging his arms like a windmill.

My eyes settled on the red arrows of the school fence on the other side of the scrubland. He'll never do it, I thought.

'I dare you to break into the school.'

We circled the school fence twice, looking for a way in. I hung back, kept checking the lane in case anyone was coming. Voices floated out from gardens, carried on the barbecue smoke, but no one came. At first, Simon tried to squeeze himself through a gap in the railings. He sucked his breath in until his ribs stuck out like a question mark. He got halfway – one arm and one leg either side of the railings, but he couldn't get his head through. Maybe he'll get stuck, I thought. I could run off then, leave him there. Then I thought about firemen prising the bars open, sirens, people from the street coming to gawp and watch. My mother's disappointed face when I've done something bad. I pulled Simon free when he asked me to.

On the third loop of the perimeter, Simon spotted a grey wheelie bin pushed against the railings on the other side.

'Yes!' He turned to me, satisfied. 'Ready?'

I swallowed the sick rising in my throat. I felt cold all over, even though the sun was still hot and the street lights wouldn't come on for hours yet. I rubbed my arms, tried to banish the goosebumps.

'You go first,' he said.

I walked over to the railings, sized them up. 'How am I going to climb them?'

'Pull yourself up, then drop down onto the bin on the other side.'

I nodded, gripped the bars tight, tried to pull myself up. My trainers slid down the red bars. 'I can't.'

'Of course you can.' Simon grabbed hold of my legs above the ankle and lifted. I screamed. 'Shut up,' he hissed, 'and get your foot on the top.'

I slotted my foot into the narrow gap between the arrows. Simon moved his hand up my thighs, giving my bum a push with the flat of his palm. My skin burned through my shorts. I scrambled forward, threw myself on top of the wheelie bin's black lid. It creaked, hot rubber spongey underneath me. Simon vaulted the fence easily, landing next to me with a thud. He rolled onto his back as though he was sunbathing and started to laugh.

'Shh,' I whispered, putting my fingers to my lip like we do in class. I scanned the yard. Empty.

'There's no one here, stupid.' Simon slid down the bin's side, stood with his arms wide. 'Let's explore.'

Simon led the way, running wildly across the empty stretch of grey yard, spinning in circles. I followed, fingernails wedged between my teeth. I already wanted to leave. This was bad. Not just naughty, but illegal. It was strange too. Too quiet without the other kids running around, the boys calling to each other over the thud of a football. The girls singing as they whipped the skipping rope, jumped in and out and up and down.

'We should go. I feel ill.' I clutched my stomach.

'No way. We just got here.' Simon ran ahead.

'Simon, please,' I called after him as he disappeared down

the stone steps to the lower yard. I looked around at the empty top yard and followed.

I'd just reached the bottom step when Simon barrelled towards me.

'Run,' he shouted, pushing me back up the steps.

'What?'

'Teacher,' he shouted between heaving breaths.

We ran back up into the top yard, ducked for cover by the wall. I put my hand over my mouth to keep my panic in. 'What are we going to do?'

'Let's get out of here.'

Crouching low, we walked like penguins towards the railings where we'd climbed over. My blood drummed in my ears.

An open palm banged against a nearby window, making us jump. I looked up to see the shape of a woman moving purposefully down the corridor inside. My stomach twisted in panic.

I pulled on Simon's arm. 'We need to get out of here before they catch us.'

He nodded, broke into a run towards the fence line, and got to the wheelie bin before me. He jumped, put his arms flat on the surface and swung his legs up. I got there seconds after him.

'Help me,' I said, reaching out my hand for him to pull me up, but he didn't. He stood on the top of the wheelie bin, a triumphant smile on his face.

'Nuh. This was your stupid idea.' He crossed his arms over his chest.

'You made me!'

'So what?' He shrugged. 'I'm getting out of here and the teacher is going to catch you, and not me.' He stuck his tongue out.

I felt as if my stomach was about to drop out and land at my feet. I didn't try to stop the tears. 'Simon, pleeeeease.' I knew I sounded pathetic, like a kicked kitten.

Simon turned his back to me, put one foot in between the spikes of the railings.

I can't tell you now why I did it, but I pulled the bin hard towards me. I only meant for him to stop. I didn't mean to hurt him. I didn't mean it. It's not murder if you didn't mean it. I looked it up.

When the police came knocking doors in the street, I hid in my bedroom, the duvet pulled up to my eyes. My mother called me downstairs. There was a young policewoman perched on the edge of the settee in the front room. She took small sips of tea from the china cup my mother had given her.

'Victoria, we just need to ask you some questions about your friend, Simon.'

I nodded, my tongue like a lump of lead in my mouth. I thought that if I had to open it to speak, I would be sick all over the carpet.

'Your friend Simon,' the policewoman continued, 'it looks like he had an accident at the school. Do you know anything about that?' She opened her little black book and perched it on her knee. My mother put her hand on my shoulder, gave it a squeeze.

'I don't know,' I stammered between sobs. 'I ran home. He wanted to go garden hopping and I was too scared, so I ran home. He's not my friend. Not really.'

'Okay,' the policewoman said, patting my knee. 'Thank you.' She closed her book and looked at my mother. 'I hear he was a troublemaker,' she said. My mother nodded, said she'd never liked me playing with him anyway.

They decided it was an accident. Just a freak accident. A loss of footing while climbing the fence. When we went back to school in September, we had an assembly to remember him. All the teachers said nice things about Simon. They didn't mention the smell of dirty washing, or the trail of snobs he always wore. Everyone pretends that they miss him, that he was a nice boy, except me.

The arrows on the fence were all cut off, replaced by balls of iron. The other kids treat me different now. They go quiet when I walk past, then erupt into whispers. Even Katie has stopped playing with me. She says what happened to Simon has made me weird. I avoid playtime and refuse to go into the top yard. Taking pity on me, the teachers let me spend my break in the library. I've been reading books with characters like me. People who did bad things. I know what I am now. I've been looking up definitions in the big dictionary. I like to re-read the words. I like the certainty they give me.

Red – adjective: 'of a colour at the end of the spectrum next to orange and opposite violet, as of blood, fire, or rubies.' The colour of the railings, the drip of Simon's blood on the pavement.

Impale – verb: 'transfix or pierce with a sharp instrument'. Simon's body stuck through with an arrow, like a fish on a line. I think *manslaughter* sounds worse than *murder*.

Hiraeth

Katie Munnik

It started with the bats and all that noise. Elle had thought bats were silent, their sounds in the wrong register for the human ear, or that they squeaked because they were something like mice, weren't they, only with wings, and didn't they eat insects?

The noise had woken her in the night, a sound like a gathering wind overhead and then screeching in the garden like sharp barking or high, metallic laughter. For a moment, she thought she wasn't awake, that the sounds were clawing their way out from a bad dream, but there was David lying beside her, breathing easily, and all the packed boxes in the corner of the room. She blinked, the darkened shapes came into focus around her, and the sound continued.

It wasn't dogs. Nothing like dogs. Foxes maybe? Were there foxes in Canberra? Dingos? Wild, terrifying, in-the-garden dingos? Something else to ask David about. The sheet over the two of them felt thin, and the curtain at the window breathed as the sound outside grew terrible and louder.

When she woke him up, David told her she shouldn't worry. 'It's only bats. They can't get in.'

She hadn't thought of that. Bats inside. Their voices closer.

'You're fine,' he said. 'Just the way it is here.'

He rolled over and pulled the sheet with him. She got up, put on a T-shirt, and went downstairs, away from the windows.

In the morning, she didn't want to talk about it, but he was lovely. He'd gone straight to the kitchen and found the box with the kettle and the coffee things without asking. She listened from the sofa and then he brought her through a mug on a tray. She put down her book and asked if he knew what the weather was going to be like.

'Hot. Always is this time of year.'

'At least we're not moving any more boxes today,' she said. 'And we don't have to go anywhere.'

They sat together in the living room with boxes everywhere, drinking coffee. She thought he looked tired and wondered if he was thinking the same about her. Around them, the house felt big and unfamiliar.

'Look, I'm sorry, Elle. About last night. I shouldn't have shushed you back to sleep when you were worried.'

He said he'd been tired out with all the stress and the work of the move, and he'd had a heat headache, too, so it had taken him a long time to get to sleep in the first place. He sounded awkward, as if he wished the conversation was already over, which Elle thought made it worse. What worse? She didn't know. She shrugged and tried to smile at him.

'Things are just different here,' she said. 'More different for me than you.'

'I should have warned you about the bats.'

'I didn't know what they were.'

'They do make weird noises. We can watch for them tonight if you like. They're interesting. You'll see. Big as flowerpots and their wings span a metre. I used to love them when I was a kid. I'd wait at the window for them when I was supposed to be in bed and they'd come in a huge crowd. The sky was just dark with them.'

'Cherished childhood memories, I'm sure.'

He laughed and she leaned into him, kissing his neck, his bare skin smelling of Palmolive soap: musky and green.

'Listen, you okay in here?' he asked. 'I want to get some water on the garden before it gets too hot. Give it a chance to soak in.'

The garden had been the big win with this property. The flat in town had been fine for a while – nice enough and close to conveniences – only David had always had his heart set on space to grow things. Put down roots, he said, and she'd liked the expression. It made him sound steady.

Their flat had been small, so they didn't have enough furniture to kit up a house, but David's mother had helped with that. She was almost ready to downsize her own place, or so she said, and would love for some of the old family things to find a new home. David arranged for their movers to stop by her house, which was sensible, making moving a one-day affair, though now the new house was crammed with far too many unmarked boxes. Elle hadn't a clue where to start.

The shelves would need to be installed before the books could be unpacked. She couldn't face deciding about the dresser or the nesting tables, and the curtains were unmanageable on her own. Last night, she and David had started on the kitchen boxes, so maybe that was the place to continue. She could just about face cereal bowls.

There was a large box already open on the counter and when she looked inside, she could see it was full of folded fabric. More things from David's mother. Fancy napkins, doilies, and heavy folded tablecloths, some linen, some lace, many marked with small orange circles of rust. So, not for everyday use then, Elle thought. She remembered the linen cupboard at the top of the stairs, something she'd been excited about when they first viewed the property. A period feature, the agent had said, and the shelves inside were still covered with the original paper: ivory with pale blue forget-me-nots.

The box was heavy to carry up the stairs, and Elle found the unfamiliar staircase tricky. Then at the end of the hallway, she stepped on something that scraped the wooden floor under her foot. She didn't trip; it just caught her off guard. She put the box down and bent to see what it was.

A bit of wood, maybe a stick from the garden. Pale and smooth without any bark. It felt heavy in her hand, and she could see it was broken at one end, and sharp. But running her finger along it, she thought it felt harder than wood should and somehow colder.

Bone.

She dropped it. Picked it up again.

It looked clean and dry, nothing unhygienic about it. She wondered how it had got into the house and what it had been. Too large for a chicken. What else could it be? Once, on a walk, she and David had found a lamb's skeleton picked clean by birds. The grass all around was dusty and dry and the bones white as paint. She'd wondered then how long it took birds to strip bone like that, how long the lamb had been dead. But that had been outside in the wind and the weather. This bone was inside and that made it different.

Then she remembered the bats. Had one got in? Did bats eat meat?

Enough. The box of tablecloths could sit where it was. No rush. No bother. She could just leave it, drop the bone in the bathroom bin on her way back downstairs and go out to the garden to find David.

Elle first met David in London. She'd fallen in love before, but this time it happened so fast, and David was different. Suntanned. Loud. And intelligent, too, which was important. He was always reading and liked to share what he knew. Sometimes, he was too quick to assume she didn't know something, but mostly she liked being able to ask and learn something new. And marriage was new, too. She'd been surprised when he asked and surprised when she said yes. She was carried away – happy, of course – but not quite on her feet. Unbalanced by this rescue plan she hadn't anticipated. She developed a habit of attention, of trying to be aware of things happening around her. The angle of walls, the placement of windows. It was a way of slowing time. And she watched David's face while he read, while he slept, as if she was trying to memorise him. When they stepped off the plane in Australia, she'd kept her eyes on him to see his reaction. He took a good long look around the airport and one deep air-conditioned breath. That's what coming home looked like, she thought. She'd remember that.

Canberra was beautiful and everything she hoped it would be. The garden city, cleverly planned. They explored different neighbourhoods before they decided where they wanted to buy. They liked how walkable everything felt and how easy it was to get around. The houses were beautiful and stylish, what the agent had called *proper family homes*. And when they first stepped through the door of their house, it had felt like home, so spacious and full of light and possibility. Sure, it felt different now, crowded with boxes and unfamiliar furniture, but they'd get it set up just the way they wanted it and it would be beautiful.

That night, the bats came back, and they watched them together through the upstairs window. Knowing what they were helped. Elle didn't find the sound as frightening as before. It sounded more like children, she thought, not singing, not quite laughing, something in between, almost elvish. And David's headache was almost better, he said, and she didn't think of any more questions, and then they went to bed.

She only woke once in the night, and on her way to the toilet her foot caught that bone again, sending it skidding away down the dark hall. She'd been certain she'd put it in the bin – she'd meant to at least – but there was no point in looking for it now with the lights off. It could wait, wherever it was, until morning. Back in bed she fell asleep quickly, but her dreams weren't comfortable. Long hallways and shadows, too many doors opening behind her, opening only a crack and then closing too quickly, too many cracks in the floor and the sound of scuttling, scuttling around her, circling, hemming her in.

At dawn, David got up for a run, and Elle stayed in bed. In the garden, the birds were upset about something or maybe that was the way they always sounded. Crazed and furious. It must be the heat. It would dry anybody out. Even keeping perfectly still, it pushed in on you, hard and desperate, and deep breaths didn't help because there were always insects you might be breathing in and they might be poisonous. Elle needed a cup of tea.

On the kitchen counter, there was a bowl of fruit and David's sweaty headband, so he must have come back already. The garden door was open and, when she looked out, she saw him looking at the back wall of the house. The rest of the garden was in full sun, but there was shade where David stood and a drift of brown leaves as if it was autumn already. Everything was drying out early in this weather.

'They're all dead. They aren't going to hurt you,' he said quietly, and Elle looked again and saw they weren't leaves on the ground but bats. A tangled heap of dead bats, their black-brown wings crumpled, their bodies thin and dried and all their bones showing. They were horrible to look at, heaped like that, their mouths open, their teeth.

'It's the heat,' David said. 'It's not normal. They can't take it. I've never seen this before.'

'What are you going do?'

'I don't know.' He turned and looked around the garden, all that dried grass. 'Might set out some bowls of water in case anything else needs it. Not much I can do for these ones.'

Elle went back inside and ran the shower cold. It made her scalp clench and her teeth hurt, but at least she felt clean. She wrapped her hair in a towel and tried to focus on what she'd wear. The new white skirt she'd bought in Sydney. A cotton blouse. And she'd go to the market, buy something nice for lunch. Maybe a picnic they could take somewhere away from the house. But before that, she'd tackle the tablecloths. She shouldn't leave the box cluttering up the hallway. She'd wash everything, she decided, get them all fresh and ready to put away. She could see them already, pinned to the laundry line, flapping pristine white against the summer sky.

As she closed up the cardboard box, she noticed the bone on the hallway floor. It hadn't skidded as far as she'd thought; it was almost exactly where she'd first seen it, just in front of the linen-cupboard door. But she'd heard it in the night, the long scratching slide of bone against wooden floorboards. Only here it was, not moved even an inch. She picked it up, dropped it in the box and took it downstairs.

David was sitting at the table looking at his phone, and apparently plenty of people were posting photos of similar piles; no one seemed to have any reasonable ideas about how to cope.

'Someone's suggesting bagging them to dump at Parliament House for the bigwigs. Thought being they muck up the planet, they can cope with the mess.'

'What are you going to do?'

'Bonfire, I think. Ground's too hard for burial and I don't want to put them in the trash. They should burn fine. Poor dried things.'

'Here,' Elle said, putting the box on the table, reaching in and pulling out the bone. 'Some kindling for you. I found it on the floor upstairs.'

He took the fragment from her and looked at it, frowning. 'This house is going to need a good sweep top to bottom.'

'All part of making it our own, right?'

He tried a smile and headed back out to the garden, taking the bone with him.

She unpacked the first musty tablecloth, and the fabric felt heavy and substantial in her hands. Looked at carefully, the lace didn't look fussy or pretentious, but considered, like something special. It would look good on the new dining table and maybe the matching napkins would be a nice touch. She shook them out, checking for moth damage, imagining dinner parties, candlelight and conversation.

Halfway through the box, she found something wrapped in tea towels. It reminded her of her mother's silver, which had always been kept hidden in the kitchen drawer, wrapped in a triple layer of tea towels and bound with elastic bands to keep it safe, because no burglar would think to look for silver with the tea towels. But this was lighter than silver and tied with string. David would probably know what it was. She should wait for him. His family things after all. And the smell of the tablecloths was beginning to get to her, or maybe the heat was bringing on a headache. She put the bundle down and poured herself a glass of water. Yes, there was definitely a headache starting. She could hear a hum, and the acrid smell of smoke from the garden came in through the open door. David had started with the bats. That wasn't a pleasant thought, but then he hadn't been terribly fazed. More sad than anything. She looked at the bundle.

The string was regular kitchen twine, and the knots didn't look tight. She pulled and the string came away. The layers of tea towels were old and softened with years of use, and whatever was inside must be fragile, all wrapped up like this. It was probably glass, maybe crystal. She wondered if it was valuable. As she unwrapped the layers, the shape became obvious. Some sort of dish, like the kind you might put on a coffee table filled with mints or boiled sweets.

When the last layer came away, she found she was right. It was a shallow bowl, like the hollow of a palm or a thumbprint in soft dough. The surface looked natural and was marked with fine lines like cracked glaze on an oil painting, the edge filed and smooth. It was beautiful in a way, but not what Elle had expected. Not elegant, but pleasing and somehow familiar. A most satisfying shape.

'You've found him, I see.'

David stood in the kitchen an arm's length away. She hadn't heard him come in and his voice startled her.

'Him?' she said.

David pointed to the dish. 'Dad used to call him our Celtic gentleman. I always found it a bit creepy having a skull about the house.'

The shape was obvious when you knew. Obvious and wrong, because a skull in a kitchen was out of place, out of order. She shuddered and watched David pick it up.

'He's a Welsh saint, actually. Been in the family a long time. Dad said anyone who drank from it was instantly healed. Whooping cough and the plague and who knows what else. The family back in Wales used it to scoop well water into bottles to sell as holy water. Clever, but creepy. I wonder why Mum thought I'd like to have it now?' David said.

'Maybe she wanted it out of the house.'

He put the skull down gently on the table, and Elle felt embarrassed, watching his care.

'Shouldn't it be in a church?' she asked. 'Or buried in the ground?'

'It was always on the shelf at home.'

'It's stealing. It shouldn't even be in Australia. Skulls aren't things other people should own.'

'It's in our keeping.'

'You want to keep it.' She knew she was pushing, hand against glass, and if she pushed too far, she'd crack the pane. How was he going to explain this? She watched herself pull back.

'It's not really stealing,' he said. 'He's long dead, whoever it was. What harm can it do?' Then he laughed and said maybe they should go out somewhere.

'But the fire. You can't just leave it burning.'

'I haven't lit it yet. It can wait. I want to take you out.'

'I smelled the smoke.'

'Not yet, sweetheart. You must have imagined it. Where do

you want to go? Downtown? The lake? We could have lunch somewhere nice. Take a break from all this unpacking and house fuss. You up for that?'

She said she'd go upstairs to get ready and be down again in a minute. She wouldn't be long.

'Take whatever time you need, gorgeous. I'm ready when you are.'

Halfway up the stairs, the bone sat waiting for her. She stooped and picked it up, knowing it was impossible. She'd already taken it downstairs, already handed it to David and even if he hadn't lit the fire, that bone was out of the house. But here it was. The same bone? She looked at the broken end. Was it the same? Or was this a piece that had broken off? She ran her thumb along the sharp edge. How could she be sure?

She put it away in her pocket because she couldn't think about it now. They were going out. Sunshine and laughter. Her white skirt, his open shirt. She could focus. She could breathe.

The market crowds helped, and the lemonade. The striped awnings and tourists and pop music on the speaker when they sat down to lunch. When they finished their sandwiches, David suggested coffee.

'Useless you think it's too hot.' He was being nice, maybe being distracting. The rose-garden café had been his idea, and it was lovely sitting there with the fragrance coming and going on the breeze.

'A coffee would be lovely,' she said.

David went inside to order, and Elle watched the wind push dry leaves across the pavement. Sitting down now, she felt tired and wondered if she was coming down with something. The bone was still in her pocket, and she felt its weight against her thigh. It bothered her. She wished things could just be nice.

She closed her eyes and tried to picture the clean hallway upstairs at the new house with sunlight coming in, and the nice linen cupboard at the end with its glass knob, and the wide wooden floorboards all swept and gleaming. But the bone must have scratched them. She'd heard that scratch. She could still hear it now, if that wasn't a headache brewing, that sound of something hard against the surface, like the sound the skull made when David set it down, bone on wood, wood on bone. There would be more bones when they got back to the house. She could feel them there already, waiting with the heaviness of the bone in her pocket, all edges sharp in the shadows.

And it was all because of the skull. It didn't make sense, but she knew it was true. The house hadn't been like that when they first saw it or when they got the keys. Bringing boxes in changed things, and now all these bones on the floor, this hum in her ears. The skull was calling somehow and the bones gathering. And the bats? She remembered how dry their bones looked through their thin skin. Her own bones ached.

'There,' said David, setting a tray on the table. Elle opened her eyes and saw the two brown mugs, trendy, handmade things, the two small milk pitchers, two spoons, and his tentative smile.

'Thank you,' she said.

He relaxed and handed her the mug, and then he

apologised for being difficult earlier. 'It's just always been on the shelf at home,' he said again. 'But maybe it is a strange thing to have in the house. I don't know.'

'You said it was creepy.'

'Yeah, but Dad thought it was fascinating. He was always reading about stuff like that, Celtic skull cults and druids and things. Bought books online and talked about his research to anyone who'd listen. He was going to write to the newspaper about it, maybe some museum, but he didn't get the time. He went pretty quick in the end.'

David didn't often talk about his father. He'd died while David was away travelling, and his mother hadn't got in touch before the funeral. By the time David heard, she'd had the stone arranged and even flowers planted on the grave: dusty red geraniums that shed their petals in the heat.

The roses in the park were nice enough, though they needed better tending and the beds could do with a serious afternoon of weeding. David was taking his time, snapping photos of the signage to research varieties later. Elle walked on ahead, weaving her way between the curved beds. They struck her as weird, all these English-looking roses gathered together, over-irrigated to keep them lush. They were out of place, she thought, as stolen as the skull. She wondered if it *was* Welsh. It might have been, or it might have come from anywhere. Been anyone.

Which might explain things. What if thought and emotion left echoes behind? What if theft left a sting that lasted, and homesickness lingered long after the mind that felt these things had turned to dust? Then what if that ache of distance strengthened and climbed into hidden places, into locked places? Dream places. The dark of closed eyes. The hollowness of the heart. What then?

Elle stood at the edge of the roses, feeling nervous. Her joints hurt and she took shallow breaths. She tried to stand still and think about other things, like this garden full of old roses and all the work of tending it. David had told her the garden was designed to be viewed from above, the beds themselves shaped to resemble roses. He'd been excited by that idea, that shift in perspective, but it was hard to see from the ground.

Elle reached out and cupped a rose in her hand. The bloom might have been red once, red or orange. Now, it was brown like a crumpled paper bag. She cradled it gently for a soft moment before closing her fist and pulling it away.

A sound behind her, a bird taking flight, and she started, but David didn't see. She put the rose in her pocket, theft on theft, and the smell of smoke lingering around her and the dusty smell of roses.

There were roses at home in the garden, weren't there? The garden where she grew up. Where was that? Which garden? And for a moment, she didn't know. She couldn't picture it. Only hazy green hills, a river, sunlight on church stones, but home? Like sand through her fingers, or water, or smoke.

'Elle!' David's voice cutting through now. 'Are you coming?'

He sounded concerned, and she turned towards him.

'Sorry. I must have been a million miles away.'

'It's the heat. Let's go home out of the sun.'

Back in the car, there was talk of the weather on the radio. Continuing hot and windy conditions were a serious threat to crops and wildlife, and were increasing the risk of new bushfires. This year, like many recent years, looked to be the warmest and driest on record. Again, the authorities were declaring that the weather this year was unprecedented.

She closed her eyes and saw those green hills again, the shape of the river. She folded her hands on the cool field of her skirt, and David drove the air-conditioned car along the wide streets, but all she saw was distant green. Memories pushed in. Mornings when the trees were hung with grey rain. Evenings and the sound of bells echoing, echoing. She pushed back. These weren't her hills. She put her hands on the dashboard, her eyes on the road ahead and tried to see what was there. Longing, remembering. No. Focus. Something must be done. Concentrate on the radio, that might work, but the talking was over and there was music now, ringing, echoing. She changed the station. That was better. Talk. Even talk about the terrible weather helped her focus. She wished David would say something, but he was quiet, only glancing at her from time to time with that concerned look on his face and those lines on his forehead. Another headache coming on. No. Stop. Push back. Don't let the pull of the past pull everything together, pull everything down.

The bones were waiting at the house. She opened the door and saw the first one in the hallway. No, the first two. They were in the middle of the floor, lined up parallel as if they'd been placed. Stepping over them, she noticed more on the stairs and followed their trail. There was dust underfoot and dust in the air. She could feel it on her tongue, gritty as ash. In the hallway upstairs, more bones lined up against the skirting boards, and dust drifted on the floor, pulled by the wind. She must have left the windows open. She hadn't. And she had decided not to open the cupboard door, but her hand was on the knob, the glass cool to the touch, the bones in her wrist turning as she watched; then the door opened a crack, then wide and wider to the clatter of bones, more bones than she could count, every shelf full of bones, full and falling.

David ran up the stairs at the sound, David with his shirt open and his collarbones clear. He hugged her close and pulled her away from the open door. He'd clean it all up, he said. She didn't need to worry. He would take care of it. Everything would be all right.

Only it wouldn't. Not if the skull stayed in the house and its old thoughts persisted, strengthened. Sitting in the kitchen, Elle made her decision. She'd wrap it in clean bubble-wrap, put it in a box, and seal the flaps tightly with packing tape. There'd need to be a letter, too, a formal typed thing, explaining the situation. She'd get David to write it; she'd tell him this was what his father would want. And she'd find the address for a museum in Wales. That would be the right place because the people there would know what to do. She could send it away. Fix the crime. Send the evidence back, wrapped up carefully, with no return address, no way to get lost, and then everything would be all right again, completely fine after all. Then everything would be peaceful and calm and green.

Quirky Robbers

Alison Layland

Despite the tabloid headlines and the accusations in court, I did not kill my grandmother to get my hands on my inheritance. I didn't even know that I was the main beneficiary. And in any case, what would I want with the house when the woods were gone? What I did was no crime compared to the ecocide being committed here and the world over.

My grandparents' house was more home to me than the succession of fancy apartments and houses I lived in with Mum and Dad. Gran had brought me up during the long periods when my parents were away on business. She stayed at our house when needed, but I far preferred the school holidays when I insisted on staying with her and Grampy. Then, eventually, just her. They lived in a row of houses that backed onto a wood. I was entranced by their long, narrow garden, which ended in the lovely orchard Grampy had coaxed back to productive life. Beyond it, we'd explore the woods that seemed to stretch away into fairy-tale land and they'd teach me the names of the trees, flowers and birds, collecting all manner of natural treasures to bring home and make things with. I'd string shiny triangular beech nuts into prickly yet attractive necklaces, until Gran taught me how to shell and toast them, or we'd collect cones, twigs and acorns to add to the family of little woodland figures we'd made and arranged on a mossy blanket. The kind of thing my parents always intended to do with me but somehow never had the time for.

So, when the road came, it stole my childhood.

It was the summer after my first year at university. I hadn't seen Gran for many months, caught up in my studies and the exciting life with my new friends that I told her about when I wrote – real letters, in ink on paper, another old tradition she'd instilled in me, like knowing the ways of the woods.

Any guilt I felt at being away for so long was soon dispelled by the warmth of her welcome. The sad shadow waiting for me at the bus stop immediately blossomed into the special Gran of my childhood years.

Back home, we sat down at the table for her traditional welcome supper of cheese, ham, salad and buttered bread. The latest in a long line of suppers where I'd shed childhood tribulations, talked through teenage traumas, and we'd shared anxieties. I'd never thought about how Dad's long absences might have affected her until he cropped up in the conversation and she said wistfully that if you really loved someone you could prove it by letting them go. With the taste of her special ploughman's platter and orchard-apple chutney making me feel I'd never left, I realised that she'd allowed me that – to grow up. In the first flush of young-adult freedom I'd abandoned her, but now I'd come back – something my dad rarely did.

She asked me about university life, the course, friends, field trips, and I shared her reminiscences of her recently departed friend, Martha. I felt sorry for Gran, but I had mixed feelings about Martha. Whenever we went round to see her and her sister Jenny, two doors away, they'd eye me with suspicion. Martha was pleasant with me, though I suspected only for Gran's sake, until the road scheme was announced. Without asking my opinion, an assumption that annoyed me even though she was right, she'd accused me and 'my kind' – whoever they were – of throwing away all the advances and the progress she and her generation had fought for.

'You like to gad about the country, don't you? How did you get here?'

It made no difference when I said I'd walked to Gran's house from the bus stop. So we needed this bypass, she continued, which would be more efficient and less polluting than queues of standing traffic in town. Anything I said about solving it with a decent public transport system that would mean fewer cars fell on deaf ears. On our following visit she'd fallen ill and, though Gran and I visited her with comforting fruitcakes and flowers from the garden, we never mentioned the road again. Whatever our differences, she was part of my life with Gran, and her death saddened me.

Gran spoke angrily of the way her dear friend had suffered at the end. I knew she was also thinking of Grampy, who'd quietly begged her for release when he still could. I remembered long days by the hospice bedside three years ago. That was one gift neither doctors, nurses nor Gran herself could give him.

Gran cleared the plates and went through to the kitchen. When she returned with two cups of tea, I asked about the road. She went quiet for a moment.

'Let's just enjoy the evening.'

She'd show me the construction site in the morning. We shut out the destruction of our beloved woods, ignoring it just as we'd pushed aside my absence of almost a year. It had been dark when I arrived, so all I'd seen was the unnatural glow of the security lights behind the houses, which I now noticed bleeding out from around the thick, flowered curtains to infect the homely dining room. It insinuated its way into my consciousness and I was surprised I hadn't noticed it from the start.

My room at the front of the house was just as it had always been. I drifted off to sleep with the occasional lights of passing cars tracing the same beams on the ceiling as they always had. The oak-apple faces of the little woodland folk we'd made, preserved since childhood on the shelf, watched over me as I slept from beneath their pointy beech-mast-husk hats. I woke to the sleepy anticipation of pottering in the garden, walking in the woods, hearing the birds she loved to talk back to as we named their distinctive calls...

Then I remembered what was actually going on out there.

When I went down to the kitchen and looked out onto the back garden, the reality of the destruction struck me. Beyond the orchard I could still see our favourite old oak, but it stood alone, its magnificence incongruous without its companions. Everything else was gone. There was no army of garish yellow machinery – they'd done their dirty work and the site was ominously quiet, anticipating horrors to come. Apart from the starkness of absence, the only present threat came from the metal panels of a security fence beyond Gran's hedge.

It was the tents that really caught my attention. A circle of six or seven among the trees of Grampy's orchard. A group of people were sitting around at various heights on camping chairs, crates or groundsheets, with bowls of what looked like porridge. Gran was walking up the path through the vegetable garden towards the house, coffee pot in one hand, teapot in the other. She saw me and raised the familiar teapot in a cheery greeting.

'Who are they?' I asked as she entered the kitchen. 'What are they doing here?'

'Protectors,' she said with a smile.

'...protecting,' we said together.

Something shifted between us. Ever since the spat with Martha, I'd shied away from the topic of the road protests in my letters to Gran. Despite my growing concern for environmental issues – I'd been on a couple of climate strikes during my first year at uni – I'd been reluctant to broach the subject of campaigning with her, and even more wary of joining the protests in her neighbourhood, fearing that, deep down, she shared her friends' view of it all. I gazed on the little encampment and asked myself who'd been making unfair assumptions this time?

Over breakfast, Gran sought to reassure me by saying she probably wouldn't have got involved either if Martha, or even Grampy, had still been here. He would have hated the idea of destroying the precious woods for a bypass, of course, but he'd never been one to challenge the establishment. She couched it carefully in terms of giving herself something to do in his absence, rather than going against her beloved's world view, but I sensed a hint of liberation. She was also more scornful than she would once have been of her neighbours' disapproval. Martha's sister, whom she hadn't seen since her friend's funeral, had even gone to the press to say the great unwashed had invaded Gran's private property and she was acting under coercion. Gran's insistent 'no comment' had only fuelled the suspicions.

'But between you and me, Tilly, it's not bravado. Refusing to speak to them is easier than saying what I really think.' She poured me a fresh coffee. 'I'm glad you're here.'

I felt a surge of warmth and was about to hug her when we heard a loud whistle outside. She jumped up and hurried down the garden. Coffee mug in hand, I followed. I saw the high-viz bulk of a security guard lurking by the fence panel at the bottom of the garden and fully expected her to shoo him away. I stopped and watched in amazement as he lifted the panel and shoved a large canvas sack underneath. Glancing over her shoulder, she took another from under the hedge and passed it back to him.

As he bent to retrieve it, I heard them talking in hushed tones.

'I'm going off duty now. Back on eight till midnight. Have them ready near the Halbury Lane gate.'

He straightened the panel, making it look as secure as all the rest, then paused. I could sense a more threatening demeanour settling over him, like an actor getting into his role.

'That's Lee,' she told me as if it explained everything.

He picked up the sack and strode across the wasteland, dumping it at the foot of the oak.

'What's going on?'

'Wait and see.'

I watched Lee make his way across the desolation towards the Portakabins by the works entrance. Gran nudged me and drew my attention back to the oak. I saw a hook on the end of a rope making a jerky descent like a spider coming for its prey. After a few attempts, someone from above managed to catch it onto a loop on the bag, which began an elegant ascent into the tree.

From this angle I saw what I'd missed from the house: a colourful platform nestled among the foliage. I could also see that the woods weren't completely gone. The line of the road was a wide swathe of mud and debris, like a mortal gash that cut the ends of the gardens off from the remaining trees a distance away.

We made our way back to the camp in the orchard.

'That's the Quirky Robbers fed and watered,' Gran said.

We exchanged a look. There was no need to explain. I smiled as I remembered our secret names from when I was little. *Quercus robur*, the oak. The Quirky Robbers were its guardians, keeping the old soul alive when all around it had been killed.

We stopped at the camp and they called an impromptu meeting. Gran introduced me, then told them Lee was on duty from eight that evening. They nodded as if there were nothing more to be said.

'I'll leave you to explain to Tilly,' she said, rising stiffly. 'I'm off to town.'

'I'll come with you,' I said.

'No, no, I can manage. Any one of my friends here would be happy to help, but if I go on my own it shows *them*,' she waved a disparaging hand towards the neighbouring houses, 'that I'm not being guarded or forced to do anything I don't want to. Anyway, you need to get up to speed.'

'Isn't she amazing?' a tall guy they called Leafcutter said, as she vanished into the house.

I thought to myself that I had a lot to live up to.

They told me they were here to witness the ecocide, posting live streams of the felling and other destruction online, but also making sure the Quirkies were safe from over-eager contractors. Now things had fallen quiet – in more ways than one; I'd noticed the birdsong was nothing like the joyous sound of my childhood visits – the protectors spent most of the days making their presence felt at the site entrances, and sending supplies and people to protests further along the route of the road. Some of them also took turns as tree-dwellers, relieving those up in the oak's branches for days at a time.

I asked them about Lee, the rogue security guard. The stories had grown since the trees no longer could: that he'd been to one of their talks and come over to our way of thinking, or that he was a protector who'd sacrificed years infiltrating the security company – whatever the cause, he'd helped them foil the ongoing attempt to starve the tree-dwellers down, distracting the guard who patrolled with him and bringing them inside information. The contractors' patience was wearing thin but they were reluctant to risk adverse publicity by using force. Once they snapped, the protectors were sure Lee would see to it that the Quirkies' inevitable removal was done as safely as possible.

'How do you fancy a turn up in the tree?' Gran said over lunch.

'What?' I wondered if I'd heard her right. 'The oak? I'd love to; I've always admired people who have the courage to put themselves on the line. One day I will. But I'm here to be with you, Gran.'

'Not a problem. There are always two up there, for safety and support.'

She gave me her secret smile.

'You don't mean...?' She nodded. 'Gran! You can't—'

'Why can't I?' Her eyes sparkled, challenging me to say what I never would, that she was too old.

We spent the afternoon in the orchard with Leafcutter, who'd stayed behind to teach us climbing techniques in the sturdiest of the fruit trees. It was strenuous but doable, though I couldn't help wondering about scaling a tree twice, three times the size, with the threat of Lee's co-worker snapping at our heels. And then staying up there on a flimsy platform.

'I want to do this,' Gran insisted breathlessly, looking down at us through the leaves. 'I don't have much longer, you understand. Call it making up for lost time.'

'And making headlines,' Leafcutter said.

We certainly made headlines, though not the ones we'd intended.

'I'm under no illusion that this will save the tree,' Gran said to me that evening as we walked down her respectable street towards the construction site gate beyond the row of semis. 'It didn't save the rest of them. But it's still important that we do it. They need to know that people care.'

I loved the way she thought of the trees as sentient beings. Or she could have meant the wider world. I didn't ask; both mattered, after all.

We reached the small group of protesters at the gate, and hid with our packs behind one of the trucks, poised to move when Lee gave the signal.

Dusk had deepened when I heard it. Normally, I'd hardly have distinguished his low whistle from the bedtime chatter of the woodland birds but, in their absence, it reached us clearly. We arrived at the foot of the oak without incident and I saw a shadowy figure descending the spider-fine rope.

'You're doing it then,' a woman about my own age said to Gran, as she unhooked her harness.

'Of course, Carys. This is Tilly, my lovely granddaughter.'

The woman smiled. 'I've heard a lot about you. So glad you made it. Are you sure about this, Agnes?'

'We've been through it a thousand times,' Gran said, in her best no-nonsense voice, as I donned my harness ready to climb. 'In any case, being up there will give me and the prodigal granddaughter time for a good catch-up.'

I peered up and saw a face beaming down at me. Joe, I was told. All I could see in the twilight was a thumbs-up, but that was enough and I ascended as quickly as I could. Joe grinned as I unhooked the climbing gear and sent it down. He stayed to help me brace the ropes for Gran.

She wearied a couple of times on the way up, and I could

sense a growing edginess as we thought about Lee's colleague returning. At last, she climbed almost level with us, breathless and shaking. All that was left was for her to reach out and scale the edge of the platform. She paused, gathering herself, then made an awkward attempt. She fell back and I gasped.

'I've got this.' Joe was straining to keep the safety rope tight. The branches rustled around us. With my nerves on edge, it sounded as if the old tree was sending out a warning. Gran shook her head, sadly.

'I'm sorry, I'm not sure I can do this after all.'

'Of course you can,' he said.

She rallied and tried again; this time he reached over and took hold of her arms, pulling her up physically. I reached down for her ankles and she ended up on her back on the rickety platform.

'Not the most elegant entrance I've ever made,' she said, a smile crinkling the corners of her eyes in the dim light. She managed to breathe a heartfelt thanks before dissolving into a fit of laughter. Even the whispering of the leaves all around us seemed lighter, relieved.

'Have fun,' Joe said as he vanished, leaving us to our hysterics.

We hadn't laughed together like this for a long time. Relief, achievement, togetherness, the absurdity of the situation... Holding onto one another, checking the safety harnesses were clipped in place, we looked around our temporary home. They'd got it set up well, with bags of provisions hanging from an adjacent branch, a large container of water, a bucket we were forbidden from emptying when contractors were underneath – however great the temptation – and, slung from the branches slightly above us, two rickety looking hammocks. A sealed box held a couple of tattered paperbacks and a pack of cards. A large tarp was stretched out above, to keep off the rain and sun.

Gran reached down to a larder bag and emerged with two tin cups of juice and a piece of her fruitcake each. Voices drifted up to us from the group between the tents, and the rippling sound of a guitar, but I didn't envy them. Gran and I caught each other's eye and smiled. We both wanted to be here.

We noticed the other security guy had joined Lee; Gran christened him Hedgehog because of his hairstyle; I said that was rather unfair to hedgehogs. After another fit of laughter, we watched the pair patrol the perimeter of the site. Hedgehog threw a couple of disparaging glances in our direction as if to make sure the nutters were still tree-hugging, making his job worthwhile, but showed no sign he suspected any change had taken place, or noticed Lee's single surreptitious grin.

We retired to the hammocks, which felt more secure than they looked.

'I guess we'll get used to the swaying,' Gran said. 'Like being at sea.'

'Sailing off into the sunset,' I said and we smiled.

The night had seemed still, but up here an evening breeze was playing with the branches. I wished I'd checked the weather forecast, but it was probably best not to know if the wind would be getting up in the next couple of days. Others had survived safely in all weathers, so why shouldn't we? We watched the last traces of light fade from the sky and the stars battling for attention with the glare from the security lights surrounding the site.

'We should have done this ages ago, when it was part of the woods,' I said.

'Oh, Tilly, there's no way we'd have done anything as daft as this if we didn't feel we had to.' She was probably right. 'Mind you, your Grampy would have loved it.'

'But you said—'

'Oh, not the protest. Though he was a kind-hearted soul – I'm sure he'd have let them camp in the orchard, even if he disagreed with them. I meant spending the night in our oak. Never get old, Tilly. Up here,' she tapped her head, then her heart, 'and in here.'

'Fat chance,' I said. 'Not with you as a role model.'

I gazed across at the edge of the woodland a distance away, the trees looking on as if in mourning for their brothers and sisters.

'I let Grampy down at the end,' she said eventually. 'Really let him down.'

'You did everything you could.'

She turned, her silhouette against the night sky radiating intensity. 'Inaction can be just as wrong as anything we choose to do. You get that, don't you, Tilly?'

I shivered, and not with the night breeze. Suddenly the idea of not getting old – or sick – took on a whole new meaning.

'But you were there for him. There was nothing more you *could* do.'

'Wasn't there? Giving someone a dignified death may be

illegal – for God's sake, we put our pets out of their misery if it comes to it – but so's sitting up a tree when they want to build a road. I've left it a bit late in life to learn it, but sometimes, just sometimes, what's legal and what's right aren't the same thing at all. You do understand?' she asked again.

I murmured agreement and reassurance and we lay back, swaying in our hammocks as we gazed into the night sky. Orion soared above us, protecting, sword at the ready.

'You know where I went this morning?' she said.

'Shopping?'

'Shopping! You know I got the essentials in when I met you off the bus. Maybe you think I'm going daft after all.'

'Of course not. It never occurred to me.'

'No, I had a doctor's appointment.' Something in her voice made me turn to her, causing the branches to sway alarmingly. 'Results of some tests I've been having. He confirmed what I'd suspected. The breast cancer I had years ago? It's back. Much worse than it feels at the moment, if I'm honest, but it's taking me over. I imagine the little dark spots on the scans like the currants in my fruitcake.'

I reached over and hugged her, swallowing the lump in my throat.

'What's the treatment?' I managed to ask.

She sighed. 'Not a lot they can do. Chemo if I want it, which realistically won't do more than give me a few extra miserable weeks. I'd rather just get it over with, to be honest.'

'But surely—'

'My own fault. I've been in denial. Putting off the inevitable. It's too late to do much at all, really.' She laughed.

'Which is probably what made me reckless enough for this. I'm glad we're here.'

'So am I.'

Gran squeezed my hand in the dark. I felt the branches sway as she leaned over and looked down from the hammock towards the ground. 'It's so good to know I've got you here to help me.'

For the first time since we'd ventured off the ground, I wondered if we should be here.

A beautiful dawn, seen from this unaccustomed perspective, dispelled the nebulous fears that laced a night's interrupted sleep. I helped Gran move stiffly from the hammock to the platform, all the while ensuring our safety lines were clipped in place, and after a frugal breakfast we settled in for the day. I had my phone, but only used it to receive messages from the protectors – this time away from the world was ours alone. Inactivism, Gran called it with a smile, though it was never boring. We had each other and the never-still leaves of the old oak.

It's hard to remember details now, but those two days were filled with dappled sunlight and the warmth of togetherness. As well as some beautiful, nostalgia-tinged conversations and some deadly serious discussions about the future, we enjoyed hours of comfortable silence, feeling at one with the tree and watching a cheeky robin who visited us regularly. We were the Quirky Robbers now, sharing a glow of achievement and purpose.

On the second day, we noticed an increased number of car

horns tooting support as they passed the site gate and, peering down through the leaves, thought we glimpsed a growing crowd over there. Lee brought a bag of provisions and told us in a stage whisper that the authorities would be moving in to get us down, by persuasion or force, the following day.

There was a newspaper clipping in the bag.

GENERATIONS OF PROTEST
Seventy-six-year-old Agnes Powell is with her granddaughter in the branches of the last remaining oak of Bluebell Woods, protesting against the town's new bypass.

There was a blurry photo of us through the leaves, taken with a telephoto lens. Gran feigned indignation that they hadn't asked permission, but I could tell she was enjoying the attention. Her delight faded as we read on. After a brief consideration of the controversy surrounding the road, the article went on to suggest she'd been brainwashed by the protestors, who were using me to get to her and gain extra publicity for their cause by endangering an old lady. There was a quote from Jenny Robinson, Martha's sister, calling on the police to come and rescue her. 'I don't know what they're playing at. Her granddaughter's up to no good.' The woman's sentiments were echoed by a chorus of disapproval from other neighbours the journalist had stirred up.

'As if I can't make my own mind up,' Gran said, indignantly.

By the end of the afternoon, the messages of support on my phone had increased, and links to less sensationalist reports highlighting what we were actually there for: to spread the word about the destruction of ancient woodland and vital habitats for the sake of a road that would only add to the climate crisis. They also told us the contractors were gathering ready for action, as were the TV film crews. Real information was scarce as our friends were corralled away from the site entrance and Lee was nowhere to be seen. Gran and I worried he'd been found out.

'If we were here purely for the publicity, we've certainly succeeded,' Gran said as we settled into the hammocks that evening, buffeted by the wind that seemed to have grown with the day's media storm. The noise from the far side of the gates had died down for the night, and all we could hear was the sighing in the branches. 'I really feel we've done something worthwhile. Made something of my last days.'

I murmured agreement. Then she broke the spell.

'It's time, Tilly. You'll keep the promise you made me, won't you?'

An owl hooted across the void from the distant woods. I thought I saw it ghosting across the open space. The oak's leaves rustled more intently, knowingly, silhouetted against the sky.

I passed Gran the sleeping tablets she'd brought to ensure peaceful oblivion, then I unhooked her safety harness like she'd asked me to. Worried that she might not take enough pills, she dreaded unwanted resuscitation.

I reached over and held her hand as she drifted into sleep. Gazing at her serene face, I wished I hadn't made that promise. But it was Gran's choice and I couldn't betray her trust. The owl screeched; a moment later it was met with an answering tu-whoo. I squeezed her hand one last time and a gust in the branches felt like the oak's approval. All it took was a gentle push – the hardest thing I ever did.

The wind in the branches smothered the sound of her fall in a merciful blanket. I spent a restless night thinking I shouldn't have passed her the tablets, should have ignored what she asked, should have called for help as soon as her pulse weakened. Then I imagined pain-filled days in a hospice bed compared with the dignity and joy of the magical time we'd spent in the oak. I told myself it was the malicious gossip putting doubts in my mind. Fulfilling someone's wishes wasn't meant to be easy.

As the sky began to blush with dawn, I'd calmed enough to say farewell to Gran and the oak as she would have wanted. I became aware of panicked shouts from below. I didn't look down, dreading what I'd see and preferring to remember her as the cheerful champion of the woods.

They found a handwritten note, the closest thing to a will Gran had made. There was nothing about her end-of-life wishes. It simply bequeathed the house to her beloved granddaughter, Tilly, and asked that she be buried beneath the oak or, if that wasn't possible, in the orchard.

Jack and the Juniper Tree

Julie Ann Rees

Eyes stare sharp with authority, fingers tap, impatient. Accusing glances flick with muttering, spitting accusations. Whispers rustle, heads nod. Murderer ... guilty ... cold bitch ... evil witch. I am condemned before I've even told my tale, but tell it I will.

Once upon a time...

In a land of blood and bone, my belly swollen with child, I staggered through the forest. He would be home today and I had to get rid of this thing. The dates did not match. He had been gone for over a year and this morning a letter arrived, saying he had docked at the port, and I was to expect him for dinner. I had no meat and no way of buying any. This cumbersome beast in my womb had destroyed my figure and any man that passed my cottage refused my charms, leaving me penniless.

It had been my own fault. I had been careless; damn that old goat who had left his spawn inside me. I had bled as normal so not noticed the life quickening until it had begun to wriggle. The herbs I'd mixed had not helped get rid, but this brisk walk and the tea I'd overdosed on should hurry the birth along. It should be out before tonight.

The contractions began slow and irregular, and then more frequent. I had done this before but never birthed a living soul.

They had all been cold and grey in death. I collapsed and landed heavily. It was about to begin, so I lay back against the rough bark of a juniper tree. I could smell the sharp pungent berries warmed by the late autumn sun. The moss was soft and I began to drift in and out of consciousness, as the pains rose and fell like the sea, and I waited.

Agony tore through my womb and I screamed and scrambled, heedless to being heard. I was deep enough in the forest for my cries not to be noticed by any but old spirits and the dead. On hands and knees I felt the creature free itself from the confines of my body and fall to the leafy floor. Then a sound, soft to begin with, then crying with such force and strength enough to fill the silence, and I realised I had birthed a living child.

I picked up the tiny scrap and placed it to my breast. Eyes blinked with life, lips nuzzled and much to my astonishment it suckled greedily. I had never felt the breath of a child that lived before. Tears flowed down my cheeks to dampen the soft fuzzy head, and for a time I forgot my troubles and did nothing but lie in the late afternoon sunlight breathing the scent of juniper, whilst suckling my new baby boy.

I felt the afterbirth pass and suddenly I was afraid. I would have to go home and make food for my husband. He would wonder where I was and would beat me if I had no dinner for him. I looked longingly at my baby. I could never take him home; my husband would think nothing of sticking him with his sword and roasting him on a spit. 'I will leave you to the mercy of this kind juniper tree and return in the night to feed you again,' I assured him, cooing until he settled.

I had no plan, as I had believed the baby would be born dead like all the others, and then I could have cooked him up and fed him to my husband, but he was alive and well. I gathered soft moss and crackling dead leaves. Under the tree was a hollow nestled in the roots. I made a little bed and lay my baby down, marvelling at his blood-red puckered lips and snow-white skin. He gurgled as I kissed him.

The afterbirth lay dark and slimy amongst the roots, its smell acrid and pungent. I gathered it in my shawl and carried it home for my husband's dinner. I rinsed it in the stream and placed it in a pan over the fire and added some beets. It was thick and rich with blood; surely he would be pleased. I had just enough time to wash myself and put on my best dress before I heard him arrive.

The ground shook and the crockery rattled as his huge form came up the path. I had forgotten just how large my husband was and fear burned within my belly. The door swung inwards and his great head appeared.

'Wife!' he bellowed. 'Where are you?'

'I am here,' I replied meekly, keeping my eyes downcast.

He gathered me in his arms and kissed me. I tried not to show my revulsion as I gagged at his sour breath and struggled in his grasp. I was lucky he was hungry and quickly dished out the stew made of afterbirth. I consumed only the broth to replenish my strength. Noticing he had a large flagon of wine, I slyly added some poppy to ensure he slept after his food. I could have done with the pain-easing properties myself, but knew I had to get back to the juniper tree to feed my baby.

As my husband slumbered, sated and fat, I thought about killing him. Bashing his skull or slitting his throat would be easy would it not? But how would I explain this to his friends and the villagers, who would, no doubt, ask questions. I would never be able to dispose of his body without help, and murder was punishable by death. I'd have to be far away before his body was discovered and maybe they'd come after me, hunt me down for the spectacle of an execution. With these thoughts in mind I grabbed my shawl to return to my babe in the woods.

The juniper tree gleamed silver with starlight as I approached but I couldn't hear my baby. I hoped he was still asleep. Worrying, and praying no predators had come, drawn by the birthing smells, cautiously I pulled the branches and leaves aside, cooing softly, to reveal an empty nest. With a cry I pressed my face into the hollow of the tree, shoving the moss aside, and saw a dark tunnel reaching down at a great distance, but daylight glimmered. Pushing my head and shoulders into the passage I dragged my body inside and struggled towards the light.

Falling from the darkness I found myself clinging to the stalk of a huge plant that branched and joined with the roots of the juniper tree. Of my own land I could see nothing, only mist and fog swirling otherworldly in the silence. Hurriedly, and now terrified for my baby, I began to climb down, passing large pods of dangling green beans and realising it was a beanstalk to which I clung. Soon the fog began to lift, dispersing into marbled swirls, and the soft tones of a woman singing fluttered on the breeze.

The ground was close, only a few spirals of fog remaining, as I jumped the rest of the way and landed with a gasp. The woman immediately stopped singing and I heard a baby cry. Running towards it I reached out my arms through the clearing mist, and saw a tiny, red-caped old woman rocking my baby. She clutched him tight with sinewy arms, her white hair wisped over his face. Eyes widened in shock as she took in my presence. Stepping slowly backwards, squaring crooked shoulders, she demanded my name, told me nobody but her son Jack had ever climbed the beanstalk before, only he had the right.

I began to weep and explained where I had come from and what had happened, assuring her she had nothing to fear. She handed me my baby and he quietened once I placed him to my breast. I noticed she lived on what looked like a prosperous farm surrounded by forest on all sides. There was a track winding through the trees and it was from there I heard the beat of hooves. A horse and cart emerged with a young man at the reins; the back was laden with goods.

The old woman's son was handsome but small like his mother, his eyes flashed when he saw me – making me blush. Coyly, I looked away.

'What brings such a pretty young woman, nursing a babe, out here to our farm?' he enquired of his mother whilst holding my eye.

'She came down the beanstalk after her baby.'

'The beanstalk, eh?' he said, eyeing it and me curiously. 'Only I am allowed to ascend the beanstalk, so tell me how you descended. Do you come from above?'

'Yes, I do,' I said and told my story for the second time that day.

'Then please stay with us for dinner, we have plenty of meat. Surely you do not need to go home yet?' I was frightened, but even more frightened of returning home to my husband and my hunger had the better of me.

During dinner, Jack and his mother assured me that my baby could stay with them and I could visit whenever I wanted. Even stay for good, if that was my wish. Of course I wished to get away from my husband but there was something odd about this mother and son living alone in this strange land. Whatever I decided, I had to get back to my house – where my husband would no doubt have gold and silver from his recent return – I needed to steal enough so I could start a new life with my child.

Jack and his mother promised to look after my baby whilst I returned to my husband. I assured them I would not be long and would pay them for their trouble. They laughed and nodded as they waved me off. Jack had wanted to come with me to help, he was confident he did not fear my husband, but I knew my husband's temper. His sheer size dwarfed both Jack and his mother. Even I was large in comparison to them. So I told him to leave it to me, plus I had an uncanny feeling that Jack may want to steal some of my husband's money for himself and might possibly scupper my chance of escape.

I returned to the beanstalk, to the juniper tree and to my house tucked deep in the woods. Luckily my husband was still asleep; the poppy had worked well. I gathered a few of my clothes, wrapped up in a shawl, and approached my husband's purse. He had been successful during his trip. It bulged with gold and silver. Slowly I edged it open and took some of the shining coins.

'What are you doing, thief!' came his booming voice.

'I am only counting how much money your glorious self has made, my love.' I realised then that I would have to kill him if I was ever to leave with anything that night, and I could not bear to be separated from my baby any longer. I wasn't sure if leaving him with Jack and his mother had been a wise decision and I was eager to return.

'Here, have some more wine and we can celebrate your hard work and fortune,' I said, filling his glass with the poppy-laced wine. He raised it in my direction and downed it in one. I stoked up the fire knowing that the heat would help him sleep and waited. Soon he was snoring once again and I crept to the kitchen, returning with the knife I used for cutting and gathering my roots and plants. I kept it very sharp.

I watched my husband slumber. I had been his since my monthly bleeding began. The night he came to fetch me from my father's cabin lay etched upon my mind. My father cowering as he handed me and my small dowry over to the beast. I had no mother to cling to, as I had killed her tearing myself forth from the womb. I hoped my husband would be loving and tender but he knew nothing of these ways. Killing him was something I'd dreamed of, but until now had never had the courage. Women were burned on pyres for the simple kindness of healing the sick... In truth, men feared us and, as my husband stirred, I wondered if they had just cause.

My thoughts were often evil and more than once I had been tempted to use witchcraft to raise a storm and sink his ship. There had been talk in the village of the small people again, the thieves that crept and stole in the night; I hoped he would be accosted in the forest and murdered for his precious items, but fortune was not my ally as he continued to darken my door, but at least he brought coin. Should I not be thankful, I wondered? I suppose I had been, but not anymore. Now I had a reason to fight, a reason to kill and be free, and a reason to live for the sake of my child – a reason to commit murder.

Holding the little knife tightly, in palms salty with sweat, I wondered how I should do it, how I could end his life fast without the risk of him waking and killing me instead. My hands trembled and I thought of how the pigs were slaughtered: a slice to the neck and his life blood would flow – except that took time and my husband's neck was heavy with jowls. What if I missed the vital artery? Or failed to sever it all the way, meaning he would survive, fight back? I knew I had one attempt to kill or be killed.

My knife was too small to reach down to his heart, so it would have to be the jugular. His heavy boots were propped upon a stool; he had loosened the leather thongs that bound them. I tied the strips together tightly; if he tried to chase after me he would fall, allowing me to complete my crime. I toyed with tying his huge hands, too, but feared he would wake. I had to act now if I was going to act at all. Breathing deeply, I raised the knife, watching closely for the small thrum in his fat neck, and stabbed him deep in his throat.

He woke and roared, clutching the wound, but I acted fast

and quickly ripped the knife to the side pulling it out. The knife slipped from my grip as the blood sprayed forth, drenching me. His eyes registered what I had done, shock flickering as his pupils faded. Lunging towards me, he staggered – the tied leather boots tripping him – and he toppled over: a mighty oak felled. I sprang away and just managed to avoid him before he landed, hitting his head on the hearthstone. A dark stain spread outwards to mingle with the spilled wine.

Trembling with fear and adrenalin I ran to the river, where I washed the blood from my body and hair. The water swirled berry red in the moonlight and I shivered; my breasts were heavy with milk and painful to touch. I must have looked a terrifying sight, a wicked witch who had murdered her husband in cold blood. I returned to the house, strangely nervous at the dead thing that had caused me so much pain. I crept forward and with shaking hands checked for a pulse of life. There was none, his hulk was nothing but flesh, bone and blood. I dressed hurriedly in warm clothes, I needed to be gone. I didn't want any of his friends calling round to welcome his return and accuse me of murder.

Quickly, I ran to the purse of coins and took the lot. Now, if I was ever discovered I could claim I had been kidnapped by the robbers who had killed my husband. I knew his friends would search for me and I'd have to get to the strange land fast. I couldn't leave anything to chance, I had a babe to think of now. As I reached the juniper tree I noticed a striking bird with red and white plumage alight on the lowest branch. It looked at me knowingly then began to sing a beautiful song, but the words that formed in the tuneful trills chilled me:

My mother she birthed me
My Father would eat me
The others they ate me
And my bones lie under the beanstalk

'What is this horror...?' I cried, and shooing the bird away I descended the beanstalk. It was still dark in the land below but I noticed freshly dug earth at the bottom. I scraped back the soil with my hands and there, wrapped neatly in a silk cloth, were what appeared to be the bones of my baby, freshly picked clean of sweet pink flesh. I ran my fingers over the glistening remains and wept, cradling them to my heart. I hadn't even named him.

Seeking revenge I entered Jack's cottage. Loud, even, sleeping breaths slumbered through the hall and a rich, sickly scent of meat lingered in the air. The first door I opened held a comfortable cot bed pushed up against the wall. I approached to see the old lady sleeping deeply. I picked up a soft white pillow. Her eyes snapped open and I relished the fear that flickered behind her rheumy gaze before I smothered her. The small body bucked and kicked as I pressed until her foul life fled. She was an easy kill, but Jack would be harder.

In the kitchen I found a cleaver. I touched the soft silk cloth that held my baby's bones, which I had placed in my pocket, and fuelled by anger I sneaked into Jack's room. A golden egg sat at the side of an empty bed. I remembered a villager complaining of his golden goose being stolen, and it seemed I had found the culprit. It seemed these two must be the same as those stealthy small people I had heard of, who came thieving and killing in the night. Jack was awake and he slammed the bedroom door, trapping me. Smirking, he raised a sharp pointed blade.

I raised the cleaver and lunged towards him, hoping to cut him in two, but although I was the larger, he was a skilled fighter and I was weak. He side-stepped me. My cleaver caught in the door and I felt a sharp stab in my side; kicking out I knocked Jack to the floor, where he twisted to his feet once more and grinned. I knew when I was out of my depth, and tugged to release the cleaver, swinging the door inwards, and ran, toppling cupboards and shelves in my wake in a bid to slow his pursuit. I reached the beanstalk and threw myself into its boughs still holding the cleaver, and climbed as fast as I could. My side pained where I had been stabbed but it was nothing to the hurt I had already endured.

Jack followed swiftly and I could feel him gaining on me. On reaching the juniper tree, I pushed myself through the opening and breathless turned back to hang from the roots. They curled and held me firm, recognising my need, and with all my might I hacked at the top of the beanstalk where it branched into several tendrils that clung to the roots. Thankfully, the cleaver was still sharp and as Jack's head emerged his eyes locked onto mine and I heard the last tendrils of the beanstalk break away from the branch he had ascended. The stalk swayed but Jack hung on and reached for another branch, his eyes full of rage.

I hacked at the next, breaking the sinews, but Jack had reached the juniper's roots. I had the advantage and, caring little for my own safety, in my grief hurled myself forwards swinging the cleaver, slicing Jack's head clean from his body. I watched his head and corpse plummet down through the swirling mist and fog into the silence below. The beanstalk quivered before all the remaining tendrils unfurled to twist and disentangle from the roots of the tree and slowly it, too, began to fall, joining Jack on his descent.

Heaving my body upwards, I collapsed in the hollow where I had birthed my only living child and wept. My tears soaked into the silk that held my baby's bones and I buried them under the tree, marking the spot with a stone. As I wept and mourned for my son, the pretty little bird returned and sat upon my shoulder and sang. The mournful tweets swirled into words as they touched and prodded my mind.

> *My mother she loved me*
> *The wicked Jack ate me*
> *My mother she avenged me*

'Oh shush, shush!' I yelled at the bird, pressing my palms to my ears, not wanting to be reminded of what had befallen my child, but it ignored me and pecked at the stone under which I had buried my babe.

The ground began to move, the fallen leaves swirled and I heard a muffled cry. I pushed the stone aside and a small white finger reached through the disturbed earth. I scraped at the soil and there in the cloth, instead of bones, lay my boy, snuggled in a leafy bower. He gurgled and hiccupped before continuing to cry. I delighted at the sound and held him before me, checking he was complete before holding him at my breast. He latched on and greedily began to feed before snuggling to sleep. 'Thank you!' I cried to the little bird, which bobbed upon the branches of the juniper before disappearing into the air. A soft red and white feather fell to my lap and I tucked it into my shawl.

Exhausted, I lay against the juniper tree and breathed deep the sweet milky scent of my baby mingling with the woody spice of the berries warmed by the sun. I knew I couldn't go home, and the beanstalk was gone, so I would have to hide in the forest like a cut-throat, after all, that is what I'd become. I had killed three people and one of them my own husband.

Murderer said the voices; *murderer murderer murderer* echoed the muttering; *guilty guilty guilty* rustled the condemning whispers in my mind.

'Yes, I am,' I announced, 'and someday I'll pay for my crimes. If those pompous old men in the courts don't burn me, then the lifeless God will dish out his penance no doubt ... but not yet. For now, I am a mother.' I tasted the word on my lips, breathed the word on my breath, watched it form and felt its power. '*Mother...*' I whispered, and laughed. 'I am a *mother* above all else and I would kill again to save my son ... so judge me if you dare.' My babe stirred within my shawl, the red and white feather brushed his delicate skin and he began to suckle.

Street Theatre

Sheila Kitrick

It's 4 a.m. on Saturday, 12 November, 1988 when Manny Saltzman turns his truck into Duval Street and then brakes hard to avoid a pile of curtains dumped in his parking space. He's been driving for two hours already and, with a hard day's work ahead, is in no mood to clear up after some lazy sod of a porter. Another vehicle pulls in behind him and, ignoring the angry shouts, Manny jumps down from his cab and aims a few kicks at the heap which fails to move as expected. Cursing and gesturing, he fetches a flashlight and its powerful beam reveals blood soaking through the fabric and dripping off the toe of his boot.

By 5.30 a.m. the main access roads around Spitalfields and the London Fruit Exchange are blocked by vehicles. A murder victim on market property suggests that business as usual is unlikely. Initial confusion arising over the location of the body leads the police to Brushfield Street and Spitalfields Market, resulting in the actual crime scene becoming compromised by tyre marks and foot traffic. The potential impact of congestion on commercial interests alarms the civil authorities, and political pressure is applied to the police to expedite matters.

DCI John Burns and his team are told to get it done and they do but to no one's satisfaction. Come nightfall they're up the road in the Ten Bells pub.

'Absolute shambles,' declares the DCI. 'Running round like clowns in a bloody circus ring.'

'Bugger all on the body,' comments DI Tom Bailey. 'Knife wounds but no weapon.'

'There's the clothing,' suggests DS Willie Dunn.

'Okay,' concedes the DI. 'Soaked in blood, ripped to shreds and reeking of piss.'

'That will be the curtains,' observes Willie. 'But the gear's identifiable. I'd say it's from the last quarter of the nineteenth century.'

'He's the station's local historian,' explains Tom, addressing the DCI. 'Too keen on Victorian melodrama in my view. More like some coked-up yuppie in drag, straying too far and running out of luck.'

'I'm not convinced,' persists Willie. 'There's something about it that's staged.'

Tom groans and pats his pockets.

'Why staged?' asks John Burns, opening a pack of cigarettes and offering them around the table.

'Look, guv,' says Willie. 'Don't go taking this the wrong way but you've only been down from Manchester for a month and may not be up to speed on the public interest in our manor and its past. The fascination with the Ripper, the murders and every other referenced character and incident from that period never wanes. This could be some period psycho-drama gone wrong.'

'Why?' asks the DCI.

'Here's why,' Willie replies. 'It was the hundredth anniversary of the Ripper's last murder on the ninth of November, and though our man was killed on the eleventh it was a Friday, just like the ninth was in 1888. And another thing – our murder was committed as close as dammit to where Mary Kelly lived and died.'

'When we finally rolled up,' grumbled Tom Bailey. 'Funny how that first caller got the location wrong and that we haven't been able to ID him yet despite his foreign accent.'

The DCI puts a stop to the inevitable sighs with a question. 'Who's drinking?'

Two hands go up joined by a third, that of new arrival DC Connor.

'We've got something, guv,' Connor says. 'When they rolled Manny Saltzman's truck back, a scrap of business card was wedged in the tyre tread and the surname was just about legible. We ran it through records and found a match. This geezer, if he's ours, was one of the suspects in the rape of a fifteen-year-old girl in 1986. She landed herself in lock-up – well secure unit. She'll be easy to track down.'

January, 1987

If you don't know London, you'll be none the wiser when I say I'm just off the Eastern Avenue, somewhere near Chadwell Heath, but no worries, one kid's lock-up is much like any other. The Golf convertible turning into the car park belongs to Dr Khan, our temporary child psychiatrist. She's covering for Dr Jacobs, who's off with his nerves. She's out to impress the councillors by using inner-child therapy to root out trauma and there're privileges on offer for volunteers and my hand goes up.

Dr Khan takes a deep breath, leans forward and fixes me with an 'I am interested in you' look.

'The idea is this,' she says. 'You coax your wounded inner child into speaking out.'

'Who to?' I ask.

'To you, Vicky.' She consults her notebook. 'You are Victoria McCann, aren't you?' I nod and she says, 'Then you write it down.'

'I'm crap at English,' I say.

'Oh, so am I,' she says. 'But as you relax and open your mind to what your five-year-old self needs to say, recording her words will come easily to you.'

'Would the "you" be my fifteen-year-old self that got raped?' I ask.

'Only if she's ready to mother the frightened child within...' replies Dr Khan.

We look at one another and I realise she's serious, so I nod and say, 'By the way, the name's Vix, as in six.'

The day after my consultation with Dr Khan, a care worker gives me two new biros and an exercise book. I get to use a staff sleep-over room and it's a neat set up with coffee on demand. I can give them shitloads on childhood trauma but as for the rape, it's none of their business. I'll deal with it my way. I'm a big girl and chose to believe an arsehole who thinks he's clever.

29 November, 1986

The day before my fifteenth birthday, a couple of things kick off. My mother, or Doll as we call her, swans off for a long weekend with that prick she calls her soul mate.

She wakes me up in the middle of the night and tells me I'm grounded. Don't even think about going out, she says. If them slappers you call mates turn up with booze, it's their funeral. She's left 30 quid stuck in a 'lovely daughter' card and a note to feed the cat and pay the milkman – what a bitch.

I think, right – I'll do it, so I did it. Well, my second cousin Angie, who's seventeen, did it, with some scissors and a ton of peroxide and now I look like that picture of Madonna on our calendar. If I was eighteen or even sixteen I could do a runner, but fifteen? It's a bloody cage.

The girls turn up around five and do a double take at my cool platinum look. Becky's brother's running the bar at this new club up the City where the punters are loaded. We slap on the slap, swallow some speed and boogie on out.

'Right,' says Becky, checking her make-up in a hand mirror. 'I'm the only face at the bar being as I'm legal and you lot ain't. This place Oliver's is a big boys' watering hole, and as for you, Vicky, keep your head down.'

'Who's gonna take her for fifteen?' asks Noreen.

'She's not even that 'til midnight,' says Becky. 'So, Angie – you watch her.'

As if. I'm keeping one eye on Angie, who is otherwise engaged, and one on the clock. When it strikes midnight, I say to this geezer who's been chatting me up – 'You can buy me a drink now. It's my eighteenth birthday.'

'Allow me,' says this super-chilled, Yankee voice.

The geezer turns and clocks a six-foot-plus dude bearing down on him and fades away.

'What's your name, birthday girl?' asks the Yank.

Quick as a whippet I say, 'Vixi. What's yours?'

'Lloyd,' he replies. 'You sure do look like Madonna, has anyone told you that before?'

'Yeah, all the time,' I say, well impressed by his film-star looks.

'You know how I got here?' he drawls.

I shake my head.

'I pierced your crappy London clouds like a javelin thrown from Mount Olympus, just to be with you.'

Oh my God, I'm gazing at him like some nerdy schoolgirl and he laughs.

'I was aboard Concorde at the time.'

I feel well mortified until he tells me I'm the most gorgeous girl he's ever seen and I believe him – my hair looks sensational.

27 October, 1986 – Big Bang!

Lloyd Bradley flies into London from New York aboard Concorde. The day of his arrival marks the deregulation of the City of London and, some say, an invitation for Wall Street to plunder London's gold.

Lloyd is an expert in company acquisition and asset stripping, and he sets the pace for the coming year at Weaver's of Leadenhall Street. By the end of day one spent with Lloyd, the management team are despondent.

'Within two years,' thunders Rufus Weaver, senior partner, 'our square mile will be indistinguishable from Las Vegas and I for one have no intention of serving under the leadership of a thirty-year-old American thug, Princeton education notwithstanding. I can only conclude that he intends to humiliate us into a block resignation and then plunder what's left of the body.'

30 October

A black cab pulls up outside Oliver's just after 2 a.m. and Lloyd hands the driver a note whilst the four girls tumble in. The cabbie, Ed, drives under thirty all the way to the East End, not wishing to draw attention to his cab or its shrieking passengers.

Arriving at the Mile End destination, he turns to the girls and waves Lloyd's note at them. 'The man's paid me to pick you lot up at 9 p.m. sharp on Friday. Right?'

'Halloween party,' they yell.

'Right,' says Ed.

By 10 a.m. most of Weaver's board members have resigned and the remainder find themselves talking to two new senior executives, Lyndon Crane and Edward Blair, Princeton alumni and old friends of Lloyd's. At the close of business, the three friends meet at the Savoy Hotel's American Bar to plan a party. Lyndon is elected to provide the venue for what Lloyd terms a Victorian-themed Halloween night with a Ripper twist.

'What's your contribution?' asks Lyndon.

'I'll bankroll the gig and provide four nubile young ladies.'

'Legal?' enquires Lyndon.

'Legal,' Lloyd replies. 'And if I may speak for Eddie Blair, who has developed a taste for London's rough trade, he'll be picking up a mixed bag of artful dodgers, to my specification.'

31 October

Shrieks of amazement greet the lunchtime delivery of a wicker costume basket. A letter from Lloyd headed 'Jack's Halloween' is handed to Becky, putting her in charge and specifying which costume is meant for whom.

Angie and Noreen, whilst loving the way they look in their scarlet cancan outfits, look on enviously whilst Becky preens herself in an almost sheer red and black wasp-waisted corset with a flimsy green train hanging from its straps.

'You can see everything you've got in that,' Angie accuses.

'I've got the figure for it,' replies Becky, rolling on black stockings and red satin garters. 'Besides, I'm eighteen.'

Vixi is raking unenthusiastically through her bag of white stuff.

At 9.30 p.m. Ed drops the four cloaked figures outside a pillared entrance on Russell Square in Holborn.

'Press the entry phone,' he says. 'Apartment six.'

Angie and Noreen, high on speed, can't stop giggling and push Becky forward.

'Who's calling?' a voice asks.

'Madonna,' they shout.

'No kidding,' comments the voice. 'Come on up.'

Lyndon greets them at the door and raises his hat. 'Well, hey there,' he drawls. 'You little babes look good enough to eat – let me relieve you of those cloaks. I think you'll find it warm enough in here. What can I get you?'

'What have you got?' asks Becky.

'A pantry full of goodies,' he replies. 'Your pleasure is my pleasure.'

'Is it?' says Becky. 'Where's Lloyd?'

'Oh my,' he exclaims as Becky removes her cloak. 'I guess a humble policeman will not do for such a beauty.'

'Where's Lloyd?' demands Vixi.

'All the girls want only him,' laments Lyndon, evaluating Vixi in her white laced bodice, frothy skirt and petticoats. 'You must be his little Madonna for this evening of evil spirits – you'll find him down the hall, the door beneath the lantern. As for you my burlesque beauty,' he says, turning to Becky. 'In my official capacity as Inspector Aberline, I reckon I'll be taking you into protective custody.'

'In your dreams,' she retorts, linking arms with Angie and Noreen. 'We're going with Vix.'

'Whatever you say, sugar,' Lyndon purrs, 'but have a care: Jack's about.'

They find Lloyd dressed in understated Victorian clothing, seated at a desk, going through a pile of paperwork.

'Well good evening, girls,' he says. 'You look just as cute as I'd imagined. Give me a minute and I'll be done with this tedious stuff and then I'll show you around.'

'Who are you supposed to be?' Angie asks.

Lloyd smiles and taps the wide-brimmed hat he's wearing. 'You know the theme's "Jack's Halloween", so if Lyndon is Inspector Aberline, who do you think I am?'

'His assistant,' Angie retorts.

'Wrong, my Victorian beauty. You are looking at Jack the Ripper.'

'He wore a top hat and carried a bag of knives, didn't he?' asks Vixi.

'Okay, that's the stereotype but if I were planning a series of murders, I'd want to look like everyone else so no one would remember me, right, girls?'

'I'd remember you,' says Vixi.

'I sure hope so, baby,' he purrs, holding out his arms.

'Hang about,' Angie protests, 'we're not standing here like lemons.'

'God forbid,' says Lloyd, 'I'll only be a minute or so. Go find Lyndon, or Edward, you'll love him and his friends. Lyndon's got the grooviest jukebox in his bedroom and food and booze in the kitchen – not to mention other goodies that he'll be anxious to share with you. Go on, scoot. If Vixi promises not to distract me she can stay here while I finish up – close the door behind you.'

Vixi skips towards him and he catches her.

'My, my, little miss,' he murmurs, holding her at arm's length. 'Bo Peep all in white to whet Jack's appetite.'

'What's that supposed to mean,' she complains, pushing herself forward. 'You told me I'm your Madonna and she ain't no bloody Bo Peep.'

Lloyd laughs but continues to keep her at arm's length. 'You are my unspoiled Madonna in virginal white.'

'No, I'm not,' she cries, throwing the bonnet on the floor and stamping on it. 'I don't even like this gear. I thought you fancied me.'

'I do sweetheart,' he pleads, 'but to savour not to eat.'

'I don't know what you're on about,' she says. 'You can at least kiss me. I've told the girls I'll do it for you.' She raises her petticoats to reveal blood-red garters and Lloyd's smile fades.

'Where the fuck are my white garters?' he asks.

'I swapped them for Becky's,' she replies.

'Jesus Christ!' he exclaims.

'I can take them off can't I?' she pleads.

'You know what?' he says. 'I hate a lack of care and now I'm weary of your common whining voice. You've got nothing of value to lose and never will have.'

Vixi's eyes narrow. 'Are you playing a part, Lloyd?'

'Yes, of course,' he says, regaining his composure and producing a leather sheath from which he draws a long knife.

'You know what this is?' he asks.

'A dagger – so what?'

'It has history. Carried by gentlemen and scum alike for hundreds of years up 'til the nineteenth century. It's called a "Bollock Dagger" – the balls stop the hand sliding onto the bloody blade. Beautiful, isn't it?'

'Not especially,' Vixi replies. 'Now, if nothing's happening, I'm off.'

'Oh, something is happening,' says Lloyd. 'Not what I ordered from the menu, but I'll make do with a hamburger.' He moves quickly, seizing her by the throat with unusually long fingers whilst pushing a pungent-smelling, lint-covered wodge into her mouth. 'Enough happening now?' he whispers, spinning her around, taping her wrists and pulling her across his lap.

Barely conscious, Vixi watches the tip of the dagger circle her knee and then with an upwards thrust, slice off the first of the garters.

Edward and his selected friends make a rowdy entrance and the men in the group whistle their appreciation of the three young queens of burlesque talking to Lyndon.

'Lyndon,' shouts Edward. 'I've thirsty guests here, ready to party.'

The only two women in Edward's group, also dressed as Victorian showgirls, view Becky, Angie and Noreen with a critical eye.

'Jesus,' whispers Angie, 'look at them old brasses eyeballing us, they've gotta be at least 50.'

'No whispering,' admonishes Lyndon, pinging her garter. 'Stick close to me and prepare to have fun.'

They follow him into a large open-plan space with more alcohol on display than a local off-licence.

'Champagne for my "Hoorah Henries" and their lovelies,' demands Edward, opening a double-doored American fridge and taking out a couple of bottles.

'Ain't there no bloody music at this party?' Noreen complains, swishing her voluminous petticoats.

'Sure is,' says a guy dressed like a Wild West gambler. A few minutes later, ZZ Top's 'Sharp Dressed Man' booms from ceiling-mounted speakers.

'Now, girls,' says Lyndon. 'Have you met "Molly" before?'

They laugh and shake their heads.

'Okay. It's a cooler form of speed. Real dancing gear.'

He hands each of them a brightly coloured capsule and a glass of champagne and exchanges smiles with Edward. They know how long the drug will take to get the girls on their feet and hanging loose. No one notices when Edward and a couple of friends leave the room or at what time someone screams and someone else calls the police.

Sometime later, DI Jean Lyons accepts the girls' protestations that they never took Lloyd for a nutter, but questions the wisdom of leaving a fifteen-year-old girl alone in a bedroom with a thirty-year-old man.

'It was an office, with a desk and we never left her,' asserts Becky. 'She wanted to stay with him.'

'When did you next see her?' asks the DI.

'We didn't, not 'til one of them old scrubbers starts yelling.'

'Old scrubbers?' queries the DI.

'Yeah, there were these two old birds and a load of blokes, stood out like sore thumbs, didn't they, Angie?'

Angie nods.

'Were any of them known to you?'

'No. We heard one of the birds call someone "Mick" and someone else "Johnny". They were dead common. They sort of talked like us, but they were definitely rough trade and we reckon they'd been paid to be here by the Yanks.'

'Did you see any of them go to Lloyd Bradley's room?'

'We're not sure, are we?' says Angie. 'We were pretty wired and the time whizzed by.'

'So, no one thought to check on your friend?'

'Cousin,' interjects Angie.

'Cousin,' repeats the DI. 'Who'd been missing for four hours.'

'Don't say it like that,' protests Angie. 'We lost track of time, didn't we?'

'Four hours is a big chunk of time to lose track of,' she observes. 'Have you or your friends taken drugs tonight?'

'That's so out of order,' protests Angie. 'All them Yanks have been off their faces on coke and stuff all night – what if they slipped us something?'

'We'll bear that in mind,' says DI Lyons. 'Meanwhile we're taking you to the station for further questioning. Your parents will be notified.'

'What about Vixi's mum?' wails Angie. 'What do we tell Doll when she gets back?'

When Doll and her soul mate got back, she had to be restrained from attacking DI Lyons and two other officers. She accused them of doing fuck all while foreign paedophiles preyed on innocent schoolgirls. She continued to cause chaos on a ward at the local hospital where she screamed abuse at everyone, including her seriously injured daughter who said nothing.

So that's what happened, and further down the line one of the low-life scum, name of Mick Watts, was done for cutting and raping me whilst under the influence. He may have had his turn but I wonder how much Lloyd paid him to take the rap. Anyway, I get moved on to a better-resourced centre where I get seriously fit and start passing exams. The Council use me as a bit of an asset at fund-raising jollies designed to attract would-be investors in rehabilitation schemes. As the star toe-rag, some seriously loaded people take an interest and one, this Russian guy, name of Stepanov, offers to mentor me when I walk free.

September, 1988
I land a job at the Savoy Hotel and even get to serve drinks in the American Bar – there's a thing.

My hair's waist-length now and baby blonde, and I'm taller, about five ten. I get hit on a lot but I'm not interested – too busy and well catered for elsewhere.

Lloyd's married now, some Long Island heiress he's parked in a Grade II-listed manor house near Windsor which, apart from the castle, is the place to be seen.

My mentor, being well connected, has organised the launch of a new company called Golden Sugar Developments, to be held in a conference suite at the Savoy. By chance, it happens to be Lloyd's new venture. He's pitching a scheme to twenty potential investors to build some space-age city on the Isle of Dogs. His banking buddies have been talking tax breaks and other incentives with the British Government for months and now it's got the green light. I'll get a recording of the proceedings, for educational purposes, courtesy of Stepanov.

Remember Edward? Well, he still has a taste for the low life down Whitechapel way and don't that lot love to talk. A bit of flattery from a beautiful girl or two in the pubs, clubs and dives will get them bragging about the little jobs they carry out and favours they do for their rich Yankee pals. The word is that Lloyd's wife knows nothing of her husband's appetite for Class A drugs and rough sex and maybe she never will, if we get it right. It's weird to hear myself say 'we' because I'd always reckoned on working alone but I've struck lucky.

7 November, 1988

Landis and Bradley Associates have a permanent contract with a local secretarial agency and when Lloyd's secretary fails to turn up for work on the Monday, they send in a temp. The beautiful young redhead from Moscow is a sensation of speed and efficiency and clears a backlog of work by teatime, leaving time for a tête-à-tête with Lloyd about shared interests. At her suggestion, he invites her to dinner and Katya proves to be engaging company. It is over dessert that his interest is piqued, when she reveals her secret obsession – a predilection for meeting strange men on dark streets.

'Does this turn you on?' she asks in her glacier-cool voice.

'No,' he replies, reaching for his glass.

She pushes the glass aside.

'You are a beautiful looking man,' she says. 'But I'm sensing a blackened soul much like my own and if this is so, you have my trust.'

'Do I?' he drawls.

'Yes,' she replies, 'so here's the question. Will you play for me London's deadliest stranger on that darkest of blood-stained streets to reconstruct a murder and maybe raise the devil?'

He glimpses a badness glittering beneath the surface of celestial-blue eyes and permits himself a smile.

'Specify,' he demands.

She returns the smile. 'Only Jack will do for me in the worst street in London.

Beneath the tarmac of Duval Street lie the cobbles of Dorset Street and...'

'The passageway to 13 Millers Court and Mary Kelly's bed of death,' he continues.

'Just so,' she says. 'Wednesday the ninth is the centenary of his last murder, but our piece of street theatre shall be performed on Friday the eleventh, the actual day. I'll get you close enough to smell blood.'

Katya is class, isn't she? I wish I'd met her properly but she had to go home, as did the driver of our mobile theatre. An old BT box van had been sourced and re-sprayed as 'Kent Gardeners' Produce'. Inside, it's been dressed to resemble the interior of 13 Millers Court with a single wooden bed, thin mattress, worn bed clothes and a small wooden table. Piles of old curtains are strewn over the floor, permeating the space with a sour smell. We had a couple of feral cats living in there for a day or so before the gig. An exit has been knocked through at the front of the van along with a modified access door at its rear, beneath a lamp. Certain market employees are enlisted to ensure that our parking space in Duval Street stays vacant and that a blind eye is turned to the 11.30 p.m. arrival of our van.

Lloyd receives a written invitation the day before the rendezvous and, come the evening of the eleventh, he walks the short distance from the office to his apartment for a quick shower and a line of coke before changing into his finest gentleman's evening suit, cape and top hat, circa 1888.

Just before midnight, he rings for a cab to take him to the Ten Bells pub, from where he can see Katya standing on the corner of Brushfield Street. She's cheaply dressed in an iron-grey full-skirted frock, frayed red shawl, soiled white apron and black straw bonnet and buttoned boots. He likes the detail. Crossing Commercial Street, he pauses and asks, 'Will you?'

'I will,' she replies.

She leads him down Brushfield Street, turning left into Crispin Street and left again into Duval Street.

'Indulge me,' he says, aware of his quickening heartbeat and rising blood pressure. 'A moment, if you please, to breathe in the foul air of this street he knew so well?'

'And Millers Court that he knew best of all,' whispers Katya. 'Close your eyes and let me lead you to where your senses shall be engaged.'

A grey mist distorts the shape of the box van parked against a barely visible loading bay. They walk towards the light of a lantern swinging in the bone-numbing November wind and stop at a small ramp leading up to a wooden door numbered thirteen.

'Open your eyes,' she instructs. 'Listen out for approaching footsteps whilst I step inside. After five minutes, knock and enter.'

The pounding behind Lloyd's temples accentuates the sound of footsteps on cobbles and he reaches down to touch a hilt protruding from his boot.

Crawling in, he's initially overwhelmed by the stench but as his eyes become accustomed to the dim light the tableau is revealed and its effect on his system is like that of crack cocaine. He is Jack and he springs on the reclining body, preparing to use maximum force, but is met with compliance. She lifts her skirt and petticoats, draws her knees up and drops them open to fully expose herself.

'Whore,' he snarls, preparing to tear into her with his teeth, only to have his head jerked away from contact with the soft target.

Finding himself immobilised by a pair of powerful arms, he watches helplessly as the figure before him closes her legs and rises to her knees.

'How's the javelin?' she asks. 'You know, the one thrown from Mount Olympus.'

'Who the fuck are you?' he rasps. 'Where's Katya?'

'Don't say you've forgotten your little Madonna in the white dress and bonnet?' she asks. 'Remember you showed me a cool old bollock dagger that sliced off my garter and then sliced me? No? Well, I just happen to have one here.'

'Why would I remember you,' he sneers. 'A common little tramp on a stinking bed – a loser.'

The arms holding Lloyd tighten and a melodic male voice asks, 'Vy budete?'

'I will,' answers Vixi, lifting Lloyd's chin and neatly severing his carotid artery.

Epilogue: January, 2020
Fucking unbelievable! I've seen my second psychiatrist in

47 years and he turns out to be as useless as the first one. I've made a follow-up appointment that I'll not be keeping, so need to be well gone before they realise that I don't exist. Should I have broken cover? Maybe not but I've been restless of late. Anyway, I didn't reveal much about the early years – not necessary. I needed an opinion on degree of dangerousness in later years and the look I got said it all.

I'll step it out to the car park powered by some rare January sunlight and try to outrun the West End traffic back to the East End which still feels like home despite the razing to the ground of its markets and alleyways. 'Shame on you,' they roared in 2012 when the Mayor of London sided with developers to bury old Spitalfields and its allure of darkness, but I'll remember.

A scheduled flight from New York to London disgorges its batch of young and super-smart Yankee interns, one of whom heads for Stepanov Towers, Canary Wharf, for the interview of his life. Barely minutes before Victoria Stepanov's red Lamborghini glides into view, Randolph Bradley hands a letter of introduction to a security officer.

'Not related to Lloyd Bradley are you?' he enquires, returning the letter.

'My uncle,' replies Randolph. 'Did you know him?'

Before the security officer can reply, Victoria Stepanov walks into reception and comments, 'Many of us knew him. Didn't you used to work for him, John?'

'I surely did,' the security officer replies.

'There you are, Randolph. You are truly amongst friends.

Look, do we need to interview? With your résumé, references and family name, let's do lunch instead. What do you say?'

'Mrs Stepanov,' he exclaims. 'I am totally honoured.'

'Wonderful,' she says. 'Call me Vix, as in six.'

Stone

Louise Mumford

The baby is transfixed by my headscarf.

It was once said that I ate babies but, well, many things have been said about me over the centuries. The baby dribbles, long gloopy trails of spit that coat its chin. I give my headscarf a warning pat.

I like the train. I've tried to find them in many places over the years, but the train is by far the best. Warm. With seating. I don't have a home, or a job, or any of the things that normal people have.

I am not a normal person. Once, a very long time ago, when myths and legends were merely gossip about people I knew, I was a girl. People told me I was beautiful, and I liked that, what young girl wouldn't? But my mother, I remember, told me to be careful and gripped my hand so hard I could feel her fingers digging into the spaces between bone.

I guess I wasn't.

No. That puts the blame on me. I wasn't to blame. Not then. I was just a girl in Athena's temple. In those days gods and goddesses overran the place, like rats – except rats show their teeth, don't they? Gods hide theirs until it's too late.

The train is full of people on their way to work. I doubt I will find someone amongst these, but I stay anyway, rocked gently from side to side with the rest of them, their eyes gritted with sleep, and the smell of toothpaste barely covering morning breath. The carriage is a fug of powdery deodorant undercut by the bitter scent of coffee.

Nowadays people don't have to work in temples unless they want to, and even then, they can be pretty sure their gods won't saunter down the temple steps like Poseidon did, smiling a fish-smile before going for the throat. I thought I'd been clever, that being a priestess of Athena was a pretty safe bet, her being Goddess of Wisdom and all that. I thought she would be fair.

I was wrong.

Wrong place, wrong time. People think they know my story but it's only ever the part about hissing and stone. They remember the monster on a deserted island, but they forget who created the monster. The sharp edge of the steps scraping my legs, the stink of him: wet mud, fish guts and brine, the pain a hot thing, filling me up, pushing the rest of me into the corners of myself, where I hid until it was over. He stayed in human form to do it, and I'm not sure, but I don't think that was a kindness.

He used me to desecrate Athena's temple.

Desecration. This kind of thing still matters, even today. I thought that as humanity built its own artificial constellations to rival the stars, boxed knowledge into shiny screens and plotted ways to the edge of the universe, they would eventually forget about gods. After all, the gods have forgotten about them. They've all buggered off back to their unearthly palaces to play chess and place bets. But words like 'desecration' still have the power to slice, maim and destroy. For Poseidon, I was a means to an end.

The train hurtles me on. It is lunchtime. A woman with skin the texture of dried-out porridge is eating a sausage roll and trying not to get crumbs on her top. No one sits next to me, not even at rush hour. They know. I wear sunglasses, my coat collar is pulled up to my nose, headscarf and hood all firmly in place, but still they sense it, at some animal level.

Monster.

Gorgon.

Medusa.

It wasn't Poseidon who created me though, it was Athena. I remember the disgust on her face as she yanked me up from the steps, the anger thrumming from her so hard I thought she would kill me then and there. Desecration. Disrespect. He was nowhere to be seen, so I took the brunt, like I'd wanted it to happen, like I hadn't been screaming so hard he'd had to snap his fingers and close my throat while he finished.

At the time I thought her stupid and vengeful, not the Goddess of Wisdom I had pledged my life to as a priestess. But now I think on it (and I've had time, oh how I've had time!) I realise maybe she wasn't so stupid after all.

She turned me into a *weapon*.

It was done in the blink of an eye.

I can't say I *didn't* enjoy it, the killing. I didn't go out and find my victims, they came to me, remember that: those men *purposefully* travelled to the island where I'd been dumped with snakes for hair. I'd have been happy enough left alone. They barged their way in, expecting their over-polished swords and bulging muscles to win because that is what their life had taught them up until that point.

The point where I turned their blood to stone and then watched them shatter.

The snakes I don't mind so much. They whisper to me, help me in my search, curl up on my head at night and breathe with me when I sleep. I don't sleep often. Sometimes they nip and hiss at each other, at other times they flick kisses at me when I feel sad and tired.

It is evening when I spot him standing by the train doors. I know it by the tingle in my jaw. Handsome, in a way that in my day would have been written about in songs, the gods flitting to him like flies on dung. He's dressed well, watch glinting in the flickering train light, neat hair, expensive-looking coat. My snakes move. The woman standing with him sways against his shoulder, out of time with the train's rhythm, her bare knees purple in the cold and her gold mini skirt hitched up by the arm clamped too tightly around her waist. He murmurs something in her ear.

It is never about lust.

She blinks dazedly. With her lipstick smeared and her hair hanging over her face, she looks very young, though when you've been around for aeons like I have, it's hard to tell.

The story is well-known, isn't it? My defeat. Perseus cut off my head. He had tricks, the gods shining on him, blah, blah, blah. The simple truth was I'd got lazy, there, on my island, with the stone dust piling up around me.

But in my story, death was not a full stop.

It was Athena. Always her. She is the beginning and end of

my tale. She took back my head, fixed it to her shield for a while, and then, I suppose, had to stare at it every day. Maybe that was what gave her the idea, I don't know. I believe that, nowadays, in retirement, people get gift cards or gold carriage clocks. When I retired, I got a very different leaving present. Athena offered me my little human shell again, the pretty priestess girl, but I'd outgrown that. I didn't want delicate blush skin and a simpering voice; I wanted my snakes and my stone gaze. I was used to them.

Monster.

Not human, not God. Something altogether more terrifying.

It is much later than I thought. The train is nearly empty and there is a pressing darkness outside the windows, the kind that wants to be let in. The train doors open with a whoosh of cold air and the man steps out, gripping the woman, keeping her upright when her ankles wobble in her stiletto shoes.

I sigh. I will have to leave my warm little carriage bubble. My snakes hiss to get me moving and I am out, onto a frigid platform first, and then the wet street, slick like eel skin. She must be cold, I think to myself: bare toes, bare legs, bare neck. In the old days they would have sacrificed girls like her to the gods.

The girl staggers to a halt, almost bending forward to stop the man from simply dragging her on. Her voice is slurred but I can hear it clear enough, 'I don'... I don' think I want to ... to go to yours, I...'

Nearly lifting her off her feet, he pulls her along and now

she starts to flap one arm, looking around for someone to help her, heels grating on the pavement. The street is quiet. Every word gets sloppier and more twisted, 'I ... want ... to go ... home.'

Didn't we all, dearie, didn't we all? But it's time. They've gone into an apartment block and I follow, shrugging my hood back, loosening my headscarf, feeling my snakes untwist. Sunglasses off. I take the stairs rather than the lift because it feels good to finally move.

The door opens at my touch because even locks know when they are in the presence of legends. He didn't bother with the bed and she's thrown on the sofa, now out cold with whatever he's plied her with, skirt up around her waist. I take a breath. This is the thing that irks me about all of this: I don't get much of a moment. No time to shine. I unwind my headscarf and feel my snakes uncoil and stretch.

It is over in the blink of an eye.

He turns and sees me, his mouth already forming words, eyes wide and – in that instant – I am every inch the story, snakes hissing, my whole body incandescent with power but also something more deadly than that: a total, all-consuming, destructive rage...

...and then he's stone.

Disappointing, really. Most men are.

With his trousers around his ankles, he does not make a dignified statue. I poke him and he crumbles, like a cheap garden ornament.

But he is not what I am here for.

The girl is sprawled, unharmed – she is all the girls there

have ever been, and, as well as that, all the girls yet to come. I pull down her skirt and brush the hair away from her face, her breath softly warming my hand. She will wake up, confused and in a strange place, but she will be unharmed and free to continue the rest of her story however she may choose.

With a little help.

I bend down to her and feel my snakes move, just a flicker of their tongues against her cheek, the nip of teeth sharpened by time. For the briefest of moments, her hair writhes.

Monster I may be – but I am *their* monster.

From now on there will be just the tiniest drop of venom in her gaze.

I turn to the open door and the waiting night. Before I leave, I carefully retie my headscarf and give it a gentle pat.

Galata

Caroline Stockford

1.

A woman was paying the waiter, at a table outside Samsun Café beneath Galata Tower. She was in her 30s and although she looked European, she was speaking Turkish as though she had been born here. She thanked the waiter and stood up, pausing for a second before stepping over the invisible threshold that divided the café and its outdoor tables from the stream of people passing into the small square. The steady confluence of tourists broke into eddies, here and there, as some stopped for selfies and group photographs with the landmark tower.

I followed her as she turned left, up the steep, cobbled street heading towards Tünel. The street was full of boys on mopeds and laughing girls in groups of two or three. Head-scarved women held children's hands. The woman I was following approached a very short man, on the left of the street. His head was down and he leaned forwards as he walked. He had a small wooden ledge on his back and two thick cloth straps over his shoulders. She caught him up outside a shop selling alarm clocks and wristwatches. Its narrow shop front was always dirty; the interior cushioned with dust.

I overheard her ask, 'Excuse me, but are you a street porter?'
He turned his head and straightened his back.

'Yes. I'm a porter.'

'Well...' she stopped for an instant, out of breath, 'I've been wanting to make a film about street porters ... for a while. About you. How the profession has survived, and all that. Could I interview you? Some time when you're free?'

'Here.' He passed her a white card from his front pocket.

'How long have you been doing this?' she asked. She was smiling at him, with her head held slightly to one side. I looked at the window display of the watch shop. Each Casio and Seiko in its plastic bubble box was familiar to me. I knew all their numbers and even the position of the dead flies along the white cotton wool that the cases sat on.

They were still talking.

'Thirty-five years I've been doing the job, sister,' he replied. 'Our shop is just a few doors up. There are four of us. Can we offer you a tea?'

She nodded.

They walked together for a few yards until he stopped outside an ornate iron door.

'We're here.'

They passed into a tiled hallway. It was cool, and decorated with dark-green wallpaper, which was ripped in places exposing plaster. To the left was a room where a husband and wife were selling mobile phone cards from behind a counter. A large clock with a picture of Galata Tower on its face was above them on the wall.

'I hate those clocks,' the woman said, quietly.

'What did you say?' asked the porter, looking over his shoulder.

'Oh, I just don't like those clocks that don't stop in between the tick and tock. It's like one smooth rush towards death, with no pause.'

'I see. You are a philosopher like me!' The porter smiled. 'You mean that eternity is hidden between the tick and tock?'

'Haha,' she laughed. 'That's just it.'

I slipped through the door and overtook them in the dark corridor, ducking into the porters' rooms, where I turned left into the kitchen.

They followed me down the corridor. Breeze and the evening light poured through an open door and they entered. An airy, square balcony was located beyond the cramped room. On the balcony, plastic chairs softened with bright cushions were set around the sides and huge geraniums flushed dark and bright reds in pots. I stood on the other side of the kitchen window and listened.

'Sit, sit! Tell me about your film,' said the porter. He called inside to the kitchen. I came out with a tray, my head bowed. 'Bring us tea. Some for the sister, here. And biscuits if there are any.'

The old man took a cigarette from a packet on the table and sat opposite the woman. I heard them through the open window.

'So what are you doing here? You're a foreigner.'

'Yes, I'm from Wales. You know?'

'Ahh ... like our beautiful Rize, on the Black Sea?'

'Yes, just the same. I'm here to monitor the journalist trials. I go to court and write reports.'

'The crimes of the state! They are so many. Especially now,' said the man. 'You will never be out of work. They arrest more people every day. Some for having an app. Some for posting on social media. Some for talking in their own home. None of us are safe.'

The woman nodded. 'Yes. It's bad. I sit there, in the Palace of Justice, and listen to the will of one man, channelled through the judicial panels. It's a show. A very bad show.'

She turned her head and stared at the view of a concrete wall and the neighbour's backyard.

'But listen,' she continued, 'I would like to come back one day and interview you. About your life as a porter. My friend said that, once, she saw one of you carry a baby grand piano across the Bosphorous Bridge, on his back. Is that true?'

'Oh, easily true,' said the man, rolling the ash carefully off the tip of his cigarette and onto the inside of an ashtray. 'We carry 100 kilos without a problem. There were even greater porters, years ago. Armenians. Wrestlers. Giants.'

'So, what's the heaviest thing you've ever carried?' asked the woman.

'Me...?' said the porter, his voice floating away with his attention.

I served them tea as the woman said, 'Yes, you.'

'Well ... no.... Ask me another.' He laughed, nervously.

'I can pay you for the interview, when I come back,' the woman ventured.

'No,' the man raised his right hand. 'I won't accept your money. You are my guest.' He paused. 'It's just ... well ... the heaviest thing I carried?'

He looked away from her. 'I don't know if some stories should be brought back to life.'

'I am a writer, remember,' said the woman, stirring her tea and watching the sugar cube disintegrate rapidly at the bottom of the glass. 'The worse the story the better, for me. Come on. You must have seen some terrible things in 34 years.'

The man looked at her for a few seconds. 'Thirty-*five* years. And yes, sister, I have,' he began. 'But the worst one of all was also the heaviest job. A series of them. You see, I started this job when I was seventeen. Fresh from the village. I was willing to carry anything.

'I worked with a group of porters. Our chief was very fair and we were all paid the same at the end of a day, no matter how much we had carried.

'Well, this one day, the big Armenian – called Aro – was sick and didn't turn up. That never happened. There was a job for a client that only he dealt with. It was urgent, so they sent me.

'I was to carry a fridge from one restaurant to another. Both near each other in Taksim. Easy enough, normally. But when *I* arrived they were angry. They wanted their regular porter and said that the restaurants were owned by Madame Merih and that she'd make trouble with my boss for sending a new guy.'

'Madame Merih? Who was she?' asked the woman.

'A businesswoman,' he replied. 'A bit of a monster. She owned a string of dancing bars and restaurants. She's dead now. But in her time, she was very well known.'

'Carry on,' said the woman, nodding her head.

'Well, as I say, they were angry. I didn't understand their concern, until they loaded the fridge on my back. I staggered.

And I was strong. With only the little L-shaped wedge strapped to my back, I carried that fridge down the steps and onto the street. One of them ran beside me and whispered, "Be careful. We were short of time, so the fridge is still full of meat. Go carefully and get there in one piece."' The old man carried on. 'I ran down the road and onto the even steeper incline. I took a short cut through the residential street, where the road dips down to the expensive apartment building. And, with a lot of effort, I delivered it safely.

'After that, they used me regularly. Once every two or three weeks. It wasn't that often, but always, so heavy. On the last occasion, I took the same shortcut, but two fighting cats shot out under my feet just as I passed the turquoise house, and I tripped.'

He looked at the woman and nodded slightly, as if asking her to confirm the story, as if it was one she already knew. She stared back at him, so he continued.

'Well, madam, I fell hard. I twisted at the same time, so that I was not crushed by the fridge, which was already bigger than me. It hit the floor and the band that held it shut broke. It was a nylon one, just like you have with a seat belt...'

'Yes...?' said the woman.

'Well, the door fell open. And ... she fell out.'

'Who?'

'A dancer. Still in her bikini and shalvar. Tied with those scarves edged with coins ... and all her hair, lots of black wavy hair. She was face down in the street. I mean – she was very pale. And ... you know...'

'Dead?' ventured the woman.

I appeared at her side with a second glass of tea. She took it without looking up. Then she stirred the silver spoon, round and round, as I retreated to the kitchen. 'So, who was she? I mean, what happened?'

'You know what?' said the porter. 'She looked like my sweetheart. I swear to you. The same girl I left at home. Same hair. And when they moved her, the same face. I swear.'

'Who moved her? The police?'

'Oh no, madam. I was working for Madame Merih. Her men, they had followed me. Every time, perhaps. But they saw me fall and came running. Before anyone had seen anything from their windows, they'd bundled her poor body back in and shut the lid. Someone had to go back for more rope. And they made me carry on.'

'You had to go on? Knowing what was in there?'

'Yes, madam. No delivery, no pay. They told me to forget what I'd seen. Threatened me. And I never did that job again. But I never forgot what I saw. I can see her now...'

He looked down. There was a crocheted rug on the white tiles of the balcony. It was shaped like a yellow star with a purple centre. The porter shook his head. 'She looked just like my love. And I wanted to run back to my village.' He looked up and met her gaze. 'You know? To make sure she was still alive.'

The woman waited for a while, then asked, 'But who did it? Who killed the girl?'

'Oh!' said the man, lifting up his tea glass and swirling the remaining mouthful a few times. 'The ending of this story is really strange.'

'So, tell me,' the woman said.

'Oh no, that's not my job. I can't tell you. You'll have to ask the doctor.'

'Which doctor?'

'Old Doctor Bahadır Efendi. But we never see him these days.'

'Does he know who killed her?' asked the woman. She stood up with the porter, who was making to leave.

'I have to go home for my dinner, madam. Or my wife will be angry. We came late today. But if you come by earlier, say four in the afternoon, I will ask around and see if we can meet him. He will tell you. Maybe. But the end, it's not my story.'

'Well, thank you for yours. Thank you...' She fished his card out of her pocket, adding, 'Nuri Bey. *Noor-i alem.* The light of the world!'

The man's face lit up with a smile and he gestured for her to precede him, back through the corridor, past the phone shop and out into the ever-crowded street.

'Tomorrow at four!' she called to him and turned left, to ascend the road to Tünel. I collected their tea glasses on my small, silver tray and washed out the remains of sweet, red tea over the white porcelain sink.

2.

Nuri, the porter, and the foreign woman conducted their interview at four the next day. I followed them as they went to meet Doctor Bahadır Efendi for an early dinner.

They walked for twenty minutes through the maze of old streets, avoiding the main drag of Istiklal. Then, they came to Asmalı Mescit.

The woman walked slowly with her hands on her hips, 'All these streets seem to go up,' I heard her say.

'It's just up here,' said the porter. 'Istanbul is built on seven hills. And seven springs. Just like the other great cities. Washington, London, the Vatican. Come. They are my friends here.'

They walked into the hallway with its shabby red carpet and entered the two-person elevator. I waited until the button glowed red on the lift, and followed them up. The walls flew past as I ascended. I stepped out at the sixth floor and spotted them in the cosy roof-top restaurant. I liked this place with its dark wood, exposed beams and tables set in booths. I nodded at the owner, whose eyes widened for a moment, before he bowed his head. I began to polish some wine glasses that were set on a low table.

'Doctor Bey has arrived,' said the owner to the porter, after kissing the little man on both cheeks. He led them to a booth in the corner. Four other tables were occupied by couples and those who had left work early to take a beer.

'Doctor Bey!' called the porter, and introduced him to the woman. 'She has come all the way from Wales. She's keeping an eye on the courts and the state. To hear her talk, you'd think she was one of us!'

The woman and doctor exchanged pleasantries and sat next to each other on the bench seat in the booth. She told him about her work with imprisoned journalists. He told her he was retired, but that he'd once been the go-to man-on-the-street in Taksim. He always told people this story, especially tourist women.

'For years!' he said. 'I was the guy they called after fights, stabbings, accidents and not-quite-accidents.'

In between picking at the olives and mezzes already on the table, he glanced at her and squeezed his eyes half closed to emphasise a word here, a point there. There was glee in his hazel eyes and his movements were quick, like a squirrel's.

They ordered main courses and a large bottle of Rakı. The doctor and porter drank one-part water to one-part anis. The woman sipped her weaker version and listened as the doctor told her tales from the 1960s and '70s when Taksim was the wild epicentre of the city. The owner of the place played Arabesque and gypsy music, and after a few glasses of Rakı the woman swayed in time to the music and smiled as she talked.

Then, the porter winked at her. 'Ask him,' he said.

'Ask me what? Haven't I told you enough tales for all your grandchildren to come?' The doctor laughed, swigging his glass of Rakı and ice.

'Well, Nuri Bey, here, was telling me about some girls. Dancing girls and their disappearance.'

The stem of the glass in my hand clicked and broke. I laid the bowl and foot of the glass carefully on the deep-pink napkins, folded nearby.

I moved on to wiping tables. The doctor had put down his fork and was looking at the woman.

She prompted him: 'He was telling me he transported dead women in fridges and that you might know more.'

The doctor said nothing. He looked down at his plate and tore up some more bread. He pushed a piece around his plate, chasing the oil and dried tomato.

When he spoke, it was quietly. 'That too, was another time. It has no bearing on what we were talking about.'

'But he said you knew who had killed those women,' she pushed. 'Was it a serial killer? Was it Madame Merih?'

The doctor lifted his face and looked at her for a few seconds. 'Why do you need to know?' he asked.

'Well, anyone would want to know! Why did they have to die?'

'Madam...' the doctor began. His left hand was resting over his heart. 'One woman a day is murdered in Turkey.'

Then he continued, 'Why do you need to know about the old days? If you care so much, why don't you change your line of work and fight for the women's cause? The state does nothing to protect them. Our President said it was a man's holy right to kill his wife. One a day, madam. One a day.'

The porter was looking down at his plate. 'Well... I told her you would... I thought it would be...'

The woman lifted her serviette to her face, as if to wipe her brow. She kept it there.

'Look now,' said the porter. 'Look what you've done.'

'I'm sorry,' said the doctor, and lightly placed his hand on the woman's. 'I shouldn't have said it just like that. I'm sorry.'

She pressed the napkin tighter to her eyes and then lowered it.

'One a day?'

'I am so sorry,' said the doctor. 'I've been drinking and I get too excited. But, let me ask you,' he continued, 'does every crime have to be solved?'

At this point, he stared intently at the woman. Was he

expecting an answer to this question, I wondered, or was he just accentuating the drama of the moment?

'I mean ... isn't it better to face the source of our problems, not the outcome? To educate? To stop this constant battering of women? Why would you rather know about the crimes of a boy than of these men that do it every night at home?'

'A *boy*?' asked the woman. Looking at the doctor intently. 'You said, "a boy".'

I swept a few crumbs from the table to their left and withdrew to the low bench a few feet away.

The doctor lifted his glass, drank and then replaced it on the table, very slowly.

After a while, and without looking up, he began to speak.

'It wasn't just girls. He would also use their clients. Only a little at a time. But over weeks, or many evenings, there was a cumulative effect. Madame Merih blamed everyone. The chefs, the barmen, the drug dealers. Even the musicians. But the girls continued to get tired, depleted and the clients stopped coming. Some got very ill.'

'What was happening, doctor?' the woman asked, gently.

'I saw him do it, just the once. A very young boy who worked there. He'd run out for cigarettes, to fetch ice, run errands. He seemed to be everywhere. To have always been there. Like family. But I saw him, one night. He waited until the girls were high and sleepy and he massaged their feet. I saw him puncture the skin on their ankles and bleed them into a bowl. A carved, wooden bowl. Then he'd drink. It was all so quick. The blood would shoot out like water from a ground-floor tap! And, just as suddenly, he could shut it off. I don't know how.'

The doctor stopped speaking, and finished his drink. The porter was sitting very still, and made no move to refill the glass.

'When I examined one of the girls, it looked for all the world like a big mosquito bite, covered with green paste. Dry and crumbling. Then I would see clients, sitting on those low seats, watching the dancing and they would lean down and rub their feet, just above the ankle. I don't know how he did it, but... That's all. That's enough.'

They sat in silence for a while. The waiter came and removed all the plates, replacing them with a central dish of melon, watermelon and grapes.

'With our compliments!' he said with a flourish, but no one spoke. They all stared at the fruit.

The porter broke the silence.

'Some say he is the Impaler's six-year-old brother,' he said, quickly. 'When the Ottomans defeated their father and took all his lands, they brought both brothers to the Sultan. The older child grew up to claim back the lands, but they say that his little brother, Radu the Fair, is still paying for his brother's sins and is trapped here in Istanbul, unable to age or die.'

'Come on!' the doctor interrupted. 'Who says that, exactly? You're sharing gossip from the carpet shops. Nobody knows his story. All we know is what we saw, when we were both young men. That was over 40 years ago. That boy I saw was most likely...' He gestured both hands in the air as he paused, as if hoping to conjure the answer from nearby. 'Well ... a kid who got mixed up with...' He trailed off, then came back with, 'Nobody understands! Nobody knows!' He said it so loudly that customers on other tables turned their heads as they talked, then turned back.

The doctor ignored them and leaned his head towards the porter. He touched him on the shoulder and said, in a very soft voice, 'My brother, this city is made of story. It's all that holds it up. Story is what brings new people from outside every day, every week – in search of the life-changing energy of this city. But it's all just ... story. Speculation. That's all there is to it.'

'Well, every story has a purpose, truthful or not,' replied the porter, 'And you told me this one ... so I passed it on.'

'Yes!' proclaimed the doctor, turning to the woman and smiling broadly. 'And we've been good hosts, we've entertained! Now, let's not tire our friend here any further. When are you going back to your country?'

'Umm... Tuesday,' she replied.

'Well, Tuesday. I'm sure you'll have a lot of work before then. We will have this fruit and some coffee and then I will take this rascal and his stories back to his home and I'll board the ferry. Where are you staying?'

Their small talk carried the performance to the end of the meal and soon the woman was saying goodbye to the two old men on the street. She assured them that her hotel was nearby and watched them walk away, the doctor's arm around the porter's shoulders, face-to-face, debating amicably as they went. I waited in the dark of the doorway to see what she would do next.

3.

The woman turned and walked a few steps down the cobbles in the direction of her hotel. She edged into a doorway and began looking something up on her mobile telephone. Arabesque tunes were pouring down from the floor above. She stood there for a few minutes. Above her, in the first-floor window of a tourist restaurant, I saw the raised arms and fixed smile of a belly dancer, hip-swinging between the chairs as she moved.

The woman on the street raised her head suddenly and spun round. She began to run after the doctor and the porter. They were nearing a busy intersection of alleyways, still in animated conversation.

A moped swerved around them, casually, and a man from the expensive café with high windows raised his hand at them to wave them in. Both men tipped their heads back in a 'no' and opened their palms like stars, as was the signal of refusal in this place. Then, after repeated hugs, slaps on the back and kisses on the cheek, they went their separate ways. 'Allah open your path,' they said to one another. 'Allah travel with you.'

The woman waited a few seconds, then followed the doctor. He wasn't heading to the ferry, after all. He scythed through side streets, a little unsteady on his feet, back towards Galata. He was singing a folk song, softly, as he went and seemed to be gathering speed. The woman was out of breath and the doctor's route made no sense. He wound through the streets of Cihangir and Galata, up and down, never seeming to tire. After an hour of this, I saw him duck left onto the steep street leading down to the tower. I ran down the parallel alley and into a yard where the shoeshine man left his ornate seat and brass box of polishes. The seat was covered, as usual, in a dark red kilim, scratched by cats and stiff with age. I pulled off the kilim. Then I dragged the box and chair down the alley and onto the pavement.

The doctor was just reaching the clock shop, two doors down from where I sat. He looked around. Two cats disappeared over a wall. The street was empty as he pulled at the metal door.

The woman came next. She was gasping for breath and unsteady on her feet. She leaned a hand on the crumbling plaster of a souvenir shop and watched the doctor slip inside the doorway of the dusty clock shop. There, he resumed his vigil. His face was barely perceptible behind the unclean window of the tiny shop. His white moustache and clipped white hair appeared as dusty as the little plastic boxes of Seiko wristwatches in front of him.

His left hand was resting lightly over his heart. Floating there, like a bird atop his greeny-brown cardigan. Then, without removing his hand, he shuffled around to face the back of the shop and was gone from sight.

The woman stepped towards the shop and then looked around. *'Buyur abla,'* I said. 'Please sit.'

She mumbled something and sat down, heavily, in the chair. Its gold legs were sprayed unevenly and the red velvet of the seat and back were shiny with wear. The woman didn't take her eyes off the clock shop.

'He is waiting for someone,' I told her, as I rubbed her shoes with a dry cloth. 'He waits every night. Until the first call to prayer. Then he goes home.'

I lifted her foot onto the brass box and took out a brush. Brushing lightly at her sandal made of fine leather straps. I turned her foot in my hand and laid it gently back down.

'Where has he gone?' she asked. Her voice was faint.

'He's passed through to a small room,' I said. 'There is newspaper on the floor and a wooden cot set halfway up the wall. He will be smoothing down the blankets where the boy has been sleeping. Sit back.'

She sat back in the chair and relaxed, not looking at me once. In my small hand, her left ankle glowed like an orchid.

The Quiet

Diana Powell

It is the quiet you notice first. A quiet loud enough to be heard. It puts its gloved hands to your ears, and holds them tight, filling them with the purring of the sea found in a seashell. Except there is no sea here.

Another hand, velvet-clad this time, presses itself to your nose and mouth, soft, furring, trapping your breath inside, forcing it back down to your lungs, keeping it there. So that, yes, you are breathless, like the wood.

You shake yourself free, take in a gasp of air – what air there is – and listen. There must be something. Yes, there are reasons for the silence. It is a valley, after all, deep within the mountain walls, the sides rising high above it. The trees huddle close together, their canopies touching, like the heads of gossiping women. The road you came on dwindled to a rutted track long ago.

But still, there should be something. Birds. There should be birds. The trilling of warblers among the leaves, the tapping of a woodpecker, the shrill mew of red kites wheeling overhead. You saw enough of them on the way. But no, if they are here, they are all quiet, now.

The rush or babble of water. You know there is water here – a blue line runs through it on your map. A waterfall is marked.

Nothing...

People. Yes, you know there are people here, too. Not farmers, where there is no grazing. Or cottagers – too remote, their homes fallen into a tumble of stones. People of another kind. People who somehow exist here, without making a sound to break the silence.

That is why you have come.

You take a step forward...

And...

Sheep. For the last dozen miles all she has seen is sheep.

'They've got a lot of sheep there,' Nick told her. 'That's about all I know about it. Oh, and they play rugby. And parts of it are supposed to be quite cool. The coast. The mountains.'

He was right about that. After she had left the motorway and passed through the old coal and steel towns, the slopes changed to smooth green hills. Lakes glided by, a wide river seethed to her right. Trees. So many trees...

He was right about the sheep, too. They were everywhere. Playing 'king of the castle' on the rocks. Chomping at the side of the road. Looking at her as she passed. But what she wanted now was a human being. Someone to tell her the way.

The last person she'd spoken to was the teenage girl in the garage just outside a town that looked as if it were carved from the mountain it sheltered beneath. Grey slate from grey slate – the last sign of civilisation before she reached her destination. She had filled the car up, then gone into the shop to pay. The girl was sitting behind the counter, watching her with round, glazed eyes, but saying nothing.

She took her map out, asked if the route she had inked there was right. A slight movement of the girl's head. Did it mean yes or no? Perhaps the girl didn't speak English. This was Welsh-speaking country up here, apparently. But still, surely they all had to learn both languages?

She turned and headed back out.

'They don't welcome strangers there,' the girl called after her. 'They like to be left alone. In peace. But yes, you're on the right road.'

But was she still? After that last turning? She seemed to be heading into… Nowhere.

A 'nowhere' place, in the middle of nowhere. What else?

'Do you really think that's where Ailsa is?' Nick had asked. He had offered to go with her, but the trip would have to wait a few weeks, when he could have time off work. It had been too long, already. 'I mean, you know what Ailsa's like…'

Yes, she did know. She knew more than anyone.

Ssshhh… Ssshhh… A finger raised to smiling lips. The word unsaid, unnecessary. The same finger curling to beckon you on, showing you how to follow the sway of the branches, the give of the grass, so that they let you pass soundlessly. Showing you where to go.

Deep, deep, deeper into the wood, to the clearing, where the maidens were waiting for you.

That was how it began. That was what you wanted. That was what you'd been told. Silence.

Once upon a time, you liked noise. Loud voices, the hubbub of the city, of the cars, trains, planes. Muu-ziccc!!! The way it shook your head, heaved your body and stamped your feet as you danced.

You saw them dancing, first, when you reached the clearing. A different kind of dance from yours, their arms waving in time with the soft branches, their fingers trembling like the river water ran. As if it was the wood's music they danced to. Silent.

Once upon a time, you liked words, liked to use them, liked to hear them. Liked the way they sprang in your mind, then burst forth through the lips. People hanging onto them as they fell, wanting to catch them and do what they told. Now you know 'once upon a time' is only for fairy tales.

And then, after they danced, they sat in a circle around you, linking hands, looking at you, reading your thoughts. No need to speak to them at all. Silent.

...she was her sister, after all. A sister little more than a year younger. She had spent her entire life, from her earliest memory, watching what Ailsa did, wanting what she had, trying to keep up with her. Following, always following. But never quite catching. Not that it was Ailsa's fault that she was prettier, smarter, more popular. It was just the way it was.

Until... What?

Ailsa's first summer home from uni, she stayed in her room most of the time. No music blaring, no friends in and out, male or female, no endless phone chats. Just lying there.

One day, Em had found her in there, head under the pillow. 'Isn't it so much better like this?' Ailsa said.

'I'm not going back.' Something else Ailsa told them as the autumn term approached. Of course, their parents rolled out all the usual arguments about why she had to. And yes, at the end of September, they saw her off at the station, waving her back to London. Only ... she never arrived at her digs.

There is noise, now. You. Only you. The branches that snag on your shoulders, the blades of grass rustled by your boots. A path of sorts, something you are following... Only, it is made for lighter feet, for slighter bodies. Leaves turn away, like sulky teenagers, cross with your intrusion. Your breath... Your breath is louder than anything. Your breath, wavering between thick and heavy, with the heat, with the tension; or held. Nothing then. Back to quiet, then. As you stop and listen, holding your sounds to yourself. Nothing. You can hear nothing, again. You carry on, the path widening a little, you think. It will widen further, soon, to the clearing, turning it into 'somewhere'. It will be easier, then. Easier to be quiet, because your body won't fuss against the trees, the undergrowth; there will be more air, making it easier for hushed breath. *Hussshhh!* Is there something now? You stop again. The murmur of the leaves? Water? Laughter, gentle laughter... Surely... No.

But there is someone watching you, you are sure.

There were cameras at the station, showing Ailsa getting off the train. Then nothing. The police weren't interested, at first. Boyfriend trouble, drugs, something like that – the usual thing. Then, by the time they became interested, the trail had gone cold. If there ever was a trail. They had tried, themselves, contacting Missing Persons, scanning social media, searching here, there and everywhere that might have had some connection with Ailsa, some reason for her to go there. Nothing, always nothing.

This is how it begins, with you in the middle as they sit and stare. In, out; in, out, your breathing goes, as the thoughts empty from your head, into theirs. A word. A word hangs on your lips, wanting to be said. A shake of their heads then. No. No. No need for it to be spoken out loud. Bite it back, swallow it down, let the juices of your body dissolve it to nothing.

Let this dissolve it to nothing. 'Drink me' it gestures, the cup that is put to your mouth, the nectar that lies within. 'Drink it,' their kind, smiling eyes say.

And you drink it, the words float into the air, away among the trees, and soon your whole mind floats with them.

Something. 'Something must have happened in uni.' The friends she shared with agreed. Not boys, not drugs. 'We thought it might be because of her work, that it wasn't going well. She'd been called to the department a few times.' But the others on her course said they didn't know anything, and her lecturers, her tutor, they all shook their heads. Silence.

...tell your mind to rise above – this is what you tried to do. Something they tell you to do. Your body is a separate thing. Don't think about what happens there. 'Don't make a sound,' he told you. 'Or it will be worse for you.' His hand, one of his hands, saw to that anyway, tight across your mouth, keeping your shouts, or screams, or words in. Keeping your breath in, so that you could hardly breathe.

And after – 'Don't say a word to anyone. They won't believe you, anyway. Just think about that – who I am, who you are. Me – 'me', and you a little nobody, a first-year student. Your word against mine. So just keep quiet.' So you do, you do... you must.

'You must, Em. You've got to let it go,' Nick kept telling her. 'Even your parents...'

'They're just tired. It's too much for them. But not for me. I can keep looking. I *will* keep looking.'

'But what's the point when you don't know where? None of the sightings has turned out to be genuine. There isn't a single clue.'

And there wasn't, until Ailsa's rucksack turned up on some wasteland near Cardiff station.

'Cardiff? What was she doing in Cardiff? Why should she go to Wales?'

Whatever was in it had been scavenged a long time ago, except for, right at the bottom, a crumpled page ripped from a magazine. An advert circled in red pen.

'C-w-m ... Coombe? ... something or other. "If it is peace you are seeking, join us here."'

A valley, to the north of the country, according to Google. Deep in the mountains, the nearest town miles away.

'Do you really think Ailsa could be there?'

'It's the only lead we've got. It's worth a try.'

And so she'd gone.

This is how it begins... The eyes watching, the leaves parting, a girl, not much older than you, revealed. A finger, raised to her lips, her hand curled to beckon. This way, this way. And yes, the path widens, and yes, it is easier, then, because, just as you thought, the trees let you through, the air calms your breath. And more air now, as the trees move to the edges of a circle, and you watch, and wonder at what you see, there, where the maidens dance, their swaying arms making you sway, until they lead you in, and quench your thirst with their magic potion. 'Drink me!'

Once upon a time... You, as a child, lying quiet in your bed, while your sister rushed about; you, sitting in the corner with a book; you, listening, while words tumbled out of your sister's mouth, non-stop, so that, even if you wanted to, you couldn't get a word in, edgeways, or any other way. But then words stuck in your mouth, not wanting to come out, or stumbled over themselves and came out broken or muddled. 'Don't say a word, don't make a sound. There's no point, no one is listening to you.' 'Shut up, Em, no-one's listening.'

So you had, you do, you must.

And now, in this place where you are, you don't have to talk. You can be happy in the quiet, at last.

Sheep. He was right about the sheep. He's been driving all day and all he seems to see is sheep, mountains, rivers. What do they do for kicks round here, he wonders. In the one town he stopped in, there were no shops that he could see, and the pubs weren't open until twelve. There should be another town soon, a bigger place, the last before the valley. And there should be a garage. And yes, it's here, now. He fills up and goes into the shop. There's a guy there he can ask about the way, and about whether he saw Em when she passed through a week ago.

He shows him his map, the route he's planned. 'Cwm Key ... Kai ... Cun... Sorry, mate, can't say it properly!'

'Are you sure that's where you want to go? They don't take kindly to strangers, there – men, in particular. Funny lot... A "retreat" they call themselves. That's what my daughter says too. "Just a place to find some peace, Dad. Nothing wrong in that." She goes up there, sometimes. Comes back... Well, I'm saying nothing about that. Others around here call them one of those cults. But the police say there's nothing criminal to be proved against them, nothing that they can find.

'But, yes, that's the right way. And, no, sorry, I've not seen your girlfriend, or the other one. They could be there, though. It's young girls it's for.'

When he gets out of the car, the first thing he notices is the quiet. He's never heard anything like it before. He laughs at that. How do you hear 'quiet'? And yet it's like that – a heaviness around him. His ears strain for something. Anything. A bird's call; a distant tractor. The wind. No. He wants to reach back into the car, turn up the radio, just to have some sound, but the signal went, along with his phone's, a few miles back.

There's no sign of Em's car. Isn't this where she would park? There's nowhere else, according to the map.

No sign of anything to do with people. Just the wood, digging deep into the mountains. And still no sound.

Well, he can make a noise, can't he?

'Em!' he shouts, at the top of his voice. He expects the word to echo back and fore across the steep sides. But no. The word stops as soon as it leaves his lips, making him wonder if anyone in there would hear it. He tries again. 'EMMA! EMMA! AILSA!'

But it is the same. This time, it's as if they fall to the floor in front of him. Gone.

He tries the car horn, pressing his thumb to it, holding it there. 'Ha, that'll make them notice!' Someone will appear soon, surely. The clearing where the retreat is can't be far from here, otherwise how would visitors, deliveries and the like reach it? He waits. Nothing.

And there is no path that he can see for him to follow. Still...

He pulls on his boots, pleased with himself that he had brought them – and his rucksack, packed with a few bars of chocolate and some water. Enough for a few hours' trek. Locks the car, heads towards the trees... Where?

You lose the quiet, now. Your heavy feet trampling the thorns, your hands reaching to break the branches. Your shouts. Emma. Ailsa. 'Hellooo?' The huffing and puffing. Your muttering... Yes, you are doing that – talking, swearing under your breath, or louder... Yes, the words shouted, almost, when a bramble tears itself across your cheek, when a tree root twists your ankle. 'FUCK!' But then, when you stop to listen for some reply, for some human activity, it is there again. Silence. As if you, only you, are here. Yes, that must be it. Emma is not here, Ailsa is not here. Perhaps she never was; or perhaps she was and Em found her. Either way, Em, or both of them, have gone – moved to some other place, where there is still no phone signal, or the battery's gone, or there just hasn't been a chance to contact you, yet. Maybe Em's having a heart-to-heart with Ailsa, finding out what happened, helping her through with words, talking it over. Not like they do in this place... 'Silence' – a fucking stupid idea. If there is a 'place' here. Because you are not finding it. You find nothing but more trees, thorn bushes, nettles, tangled ivy, blocking your way, or sending you back where you are sure you have already been. Well, that's what you want anyway, now. You'll head back to the car, drive to the next town, and maybe get the police there involved. See what they say about what goes on here. Whatever that is. Yes.

But ... is this the way you came? Doesn't it all look the same? Because you can't see the mountain sides from down here. All you can see are the trees, always getting closer together, so that there is less and less light between them. As if night is falling. Night isn't falling, is it? You don't want to be stuck here in the dark... 'For fuck's sake, man, pull yourself together!'

A stream... You remember the line of blue on the map. A stream would flow down from the mountains, along the valley bottom, then out. All you have to do is find the flowing water. It can't be far, because where you are is at the lowest point. All you have to do is stop, calm your breath, and listen.

You stand there.

And yes... Isn't that some kind of murmuring, that could be water tumbling over rocks?

You follow the sound – if it is a sound – but there is no sign of any water. And aren't you climbing back up, deeper into the valley?

But ... isn't there something else, something other than the furious beating of your heart, your jagged breath? Another murmuring, which could be voices, couldn't it? It's them, isn't it, surely?

You hurry after it, the brambles thickening and ripping your flesh, the branches bruising your limbs. The sound is there, ahead of you, calling to you? Telling you, 'This way'. You carry on ... and on. But you never seem to reach it. And it is dark now.

Stop, for Christ's sake, stop, and listen properly.

In, out; in, out, your breath slows, your shoulders drop, your muscles ease. A pause. Good. Then... You tauten, strain, breath held, now. You raise your hand to your ear to stretch its range. You climb onto a fallen tree to raise your elevation. You turn your body this way, that, to take in all directions. East, west; north, south. All ways. Your whole body listens.

Nothing.

All you can hear is the quiet.

The Cats of Riyadh

Rachel Morris

Deryn looked out at the darkening landscape and thought how tired she was of looking at that desert. It was the same burnt-orange colour and pebbly, crusty texture from the boundary wall to the horizon. As was true of much of the desert she'd seen in this country – mostly from a moving car – the sandy earth, the earthy sand, was littered with discarded food and drink containers, strips of shredded vehicle tyres, and scraps of metal and plastic.

On this side of the ornate wall at the edge of the secure residential area, however, were colourful flower beds and bushes, and lush, pristine green lawns. Well, green lawns, anyway. Maybe not lush, really, except by comparison. The contrast made Deryn miss the generous green hills near her home village more than ever.

The men who tended the gardens were as dark-skinned as humans can be, looking even darker in their bright orange overalls. Deryn wondered if their skin was that dark naturally, or if working under that desert sun all day every day made it so. She wondered how they could work outside at all in that appalling climate. She wondered how little they got paid. There was plenty of time for wondering about things in this place.

The outside men weren't supposed to talk to you or look at you, but sometimes some of them did. They would say hello, or good morning, leaning on a hoe or other tool. She wasn't supposed to talk to them, either, but sometimes she would say hello back. Or nod, at least. They were human beings, after all. It seemed terribly rude not to.

It hadn't taken long at all, she hadn't lived there long, before looking at or talking to any men, anywhere, anytime, felt like a dangerous game. Except for the restaurant waiters. They were always from the Philippines, and she sensed that they were often or usually gay. They were always really friendly and she talked to them a lot, if they weren't too busy. Deryn missed talking to men.

Loads more men, hundreds, descended on the campus at night to do maintenance. All the women had to leave at a certain time, by late afternoon, so they didn't cross paths. The men had to leave by a certain time in the early morning, so as not to see the women. Deryn didn't really believe in those night men for a long time, the maintenance elves. Nothing broken ever seemed to be fixed. But then one afternoon she'd left work, already dangerously late, walked back to the residential area only to find that she'd left her keys and iPhone in her office. She could have found a residence manager to let her into her apartment, but without her phone her evening would be as empty as the view.

So, she trudged back wearily between the rows of date palms and rosemary bushes through the still-hot evening air, her heavy feet tripping on her dusty-hemmed abaya. And sure enough, there were hundreds of men everywhere, in bright overalls of different hues from the orange ones of the gardeners. One was sleeping on the sofa in the office next to hers. Another of them let her into her office, and accepted a KitKat as thanks. She kept little things like that in her office, for visitors. For snack attacks. Sometimes treats vanished overnight. She didn't mind. She needed that phone, though.

The desert caught her eye again. It often did. She wondered how it could catch her eye so easily when there was so little there for her eye to catch on. It just lay there, being empty ... aside from trash. The trash had probably blown there from the nearby highway. Everyone threw it out of their vehicle windows as they drove; soda cans and burger wrappers, ice-cream bowls and date boxes. Sometimes families parked their cars next to the highways, put rugs over the pebbly sand, and had picnics right there next to the roaring, badly-driven traffic. Perhaps some of the trash was from those picnics. Now and then, someone in an orange overall would venture out to the other side of the painted concrete wall and pick some of it up.

Half of a crimson sun was swiftly sinking below the far horizon, the sky a matching red there but changing to violet then indigo above, the first stars emerging. The call to prayer sounded. It always entranced, annoyed, and haunted her in equal measure. The man's voice was beautiful, but it was so very, very loud. Why did they always house the non-believers closest to the mosque's loudspeakers?

As the desert disappeared into night, slowly then quickly, Deryn noticed the dryness. It had been so long since there'd been rain. The stony sand was packed hard. If you jumped on it, if you could get outside the wall that is, it would break into sheets of cracked fragments, like the top of a crème brûlée.

When it finally rained again after many months of no rain, which it would, soon, the petrichor would be astonishing. The smell of earth after rain was glorious anywhere. But here, with the sand and earth giving up the aerosol of itself after so long waiting, it was as heady as a drug, acrid yet somehow also delicious. The raindrops would be huge, and shockingly, icily cold. Deryn would go up the fire stairs to the roof. If there were no women up there smoking – which there probably wouldn't be – because of the rain, she'd stay until she was soaked, and dance, and laugh at the lightning. No one would see her. There were walls. Always there were walls.

The desert had gone from view until morning now, the street lights were on, and prayer time was over. White-clad figures left the mosque, and black-swathed figures surged in and out of the small supermarket. Children ran and played and rode bikes all over the paths in their cheap sandals, some with coloured lights flashing in the heels, in the dark. Something flashed swiftly outside the wall, sometimes. Light reflecting off broken glass, perhaps, or the eyes of the stray cats she sometimes heard growling on the breeze.

Deryn realised that the coffee she was holding had gone cold while she watched, and wondered, in the air conditioning of her en suite room. She went to the kitchen to make another, and to put some pasta on for dinner. While she cooked, she wondered how many hours of her life she'd have spent staring out of her suite's window by the time she finally left.

There was a saying. You came here with two bags: one would fill with money, and the other with bullshit. You left when one or the other was full to the brim.

The morning started with a drama. Same old same old. Some students ran into Deryn's office to say their teacher hadn't turned up. Deryn WhatsApped a Coordinator to either find a cover teacher, or cover the class, then asked another Coordinator to track the missing teacher down and bring her in to explain her absence.

In the first term, there'd have been no cover teacher, they'd been desperately short-handed. The recruitment agencies always found too few teachers for the first term, too many for the second. It was always fucked up, and no one ever learned from any errors. That was just the way it always was here. The definition of insanity – doing the same things repeatedly while expecting different results – was just business as usual.

The women who learned to take things as they were, rather than as they could or should have been, settled in fairly well. Most didn't think like that, though. They'd turn up raging, or in tears of frustration, or both. Deryn would gently try to get them to see that they couldn't change what was, only their reaction to it. That their reactions were a choice, and ones they could change. That the wall they banged their heads against had been built by them themselves. The message rarely got through, though. Those women left when the money bag wasn't yet full, or after the darkness and madness they'd brought with them grew, until they were asked to leave.

Whatever you brought with you to this place was amplified, for better or for worse. It echoed and burgeoned in the empty, litter-strewn desert.

Two teachers were brought in for fighting, mid-morning.

Actual physical fighting. Nothing new there. One had pulled the other's weave partly out, one had left a raw scratch mark on the other's face. They agreed to stay away from each other, and went back to their classes. There would be bitching behind backs in staff spaces all over campus in the coming days, the taking of sides, the spreading of rumours, until another drama pushed it onto the back pages. Oestrogen and menopause filled the air until you could almost see them, shimmering down the corridors like a mirage.

Deryn then fielded a complaint of rudeness against one of the Coordinators. She knew what had really happened: the woman had caught a teacher out in some way. With an empty classroom, having allowed students to sign in then leave, so she could sit playing on her phone for a few hours perhaps, or with a classroom full of students playing on their phones. Either way, the teacher had pre-empted trouble for herself by firing a complaint off first, and higher up. The Big Bosses would take the teacher's side, the Coordinator would get a mark against her file and a talking-to simply for doing her job, and the days would roll on until summer break. The definition of insanity.

Two things always struck Deryn about here. One, that a place so infamous for restrictions against women was actually giving so many women a freedom they could get nowhere else. An escape from abusive and controlling relationships, a place to go after divorce, after the kids left home, after breach of mortgage agreements and house repossession. Women putting their kids or themselves through college, clearing their debts, ticking off their bucket lists. The pay wasn't as high as people at home thought, nor as it used to be, but you kept nearly all of it to do with as you wished.

Deryn also thought about Jungian philosophy, about the Shadow. There were great teachers here, terrible teachers, everything in between. Many were middle-aged, the time of life when the Shadow is to be tackled, confronted, and befriended, according to Jung. And here all these women were, cloaked in black abayas, walking around clad in shadows. You weren't allowed to wear them on campus, must wear them off-campus. The younger women, the students, liked to cheat the rules: wearing abayas on campus, but unfastened. They wafted through the hallways, clouds of rich perfume and glorious hair trailing in their wake, dark-lined eyes, like those of wild cats, narrowed in laughter, their flapping abayas giving the place the air of a desert Hogwarts.

An American Coordinator had tracked down the absent-without-leave British teacher, and brought her to Deryn's office. Her name was Lujain. Deryn made her an Arabic coffee, and sat regarding her silently. Lujain's eyes were red-rimmed, glistening with tears. She was very, very beautiful, which caused her some trouble. And she looked local, which caused yet more, especially as her husband resembled the orange-clad gardeners more than he did a local man. Other teachers spat jealousy at her, old ladies in the shopping malls spat that and a kind of classist-racist mix, and didn't understand why she didn't understand their angry Arabic even a little bit.

Despite all that, Deryn knew Lujain to be a kind soul, an excellent, reliable, and honest teacher. More than that: the sort who volunteered for extra work, and performed it well and cheerfully. A rare gem, then. They had shared an office once, a few years before, prior to Deryn's promotions. Deryn was more than a little surprised to find Lujain to be the culprit.

When the long silence between them became uncomfortable, Deryn cracked it.

'Lujain, I know enough of you to know that you will have had good reason to miss your class this morning. Do you want to tell me about it?'

Lujain shook her head. She pleaded with Deryn silently, with her huge, wet, dark eyes.

'Is it your husband? Kids? Another nanny who turned out to be a thief, or worse?'

Lujain kept shaking her head, staring at the damp tissue between her tense fingers.

'I hope you know by now, after all this time, that you can trust me. And you surely know that you have to say something. I have to write a report, of course, and I'm not going to just make something up to put in it. That wouldn't be fair. I also need to know this won't happen again. You know this, Lujain. Come on...'

Lujain nodded. The tissue was in sodden shreds. She stood up and dropped it in a nearby bin, then walked to the office door. Deryn had an open-door policy, but Lujain started to close it, before looking at Deryn questioningly. Deryn nodded her assent, and Lujain shut the door. She walked back to the desk and sat down.

'Deryn.' Lujain took a deep breath, like an inside-out sigh. 'Deryn, I think someone's been killed. Murdered, I mean.'

Although their work visas bound them to this one job, many teachers also worked as private tutors outside their working hours. Sometimes, if they could get away with it, during working hours. It tended to be for wealthy families, in palatial homes, well-paid and with an uplift to compensate for time spent in traffic. One of the family's drivers would collect the tutor, and drop them back at the campus residences later.

Lujain had been helping two teenage girls, sisters, to improve the science grades they needed to get onto university courses in epidemiology and dentistry. There were many young women in higher education who were just using it to kill time until they got married, to hang out with friends in a looser environment than at home, to get out of the house at all, to make out with other young women in unseen nooks on campus, or to make a little money, since they were paid by the government for their attendance. But some genuinely wanted a career of some sort, and the science-based courses were often highly competitive.

Ameesh had been Lujain's driver for this particular job for over a year. True to his name, he was an honest and reliable young man, similar in character to Lujain herself. At first the rides weren't enjoyable, stuck in traffic and full of awkward silences. Ameesh was afraid to speak to Lujain, both because she was beautiful and because he assumed she was local.

Eventually Lujain couldn't bear the discomfort anymore, and had asked him to at least play some music as they rode together in the high-end SUV. They got to talking about music, then other things. It turned out that Ameesh was from a part of India not too far from her husband's family. At first he couldn't believe that Lujain was married to someone so like him. She explained that her background wasn't what he thought, and anyway, things were different in the UK. Somewhat different, anyway.

Eventually they became, if not friends, circumstances not really allowing for that, then at least friendly. He always asked after her young children, by name. She always asked after his family in India by name. They would sometimes look at each other's family photos via the futuristic display in the car's dashboard. They would never share WhatsApp numbers, or birthday dates, or truly personal stories, but the rides were much more comfortable and, in this desert place, anything which bloomed even a little was welcomed and admired. Their conversations were little flowers emerging from cracked concrete.

One Monday evening, Ameesh was taking her home from a two-hour biology tutorial. The main roads were even busier than usual, but they weren't that far from her campus, so he got off the highway and took a back way. All the roads looked the same to Lujain, she didn't know how on earth all these men ever knew where they were going, but then she supposed you saw through different eyes as a driver than as a passenger. They zoomed up a small residential street, the houses on either side behind high walls, as always, looking unassuming or even unfinished, the complexity and richness of the interiors only to be guessed at.

As they turned a corner, a cat darted across the street, and the SUV rolled over it. Lujain felt the bump of it, and gasped. Ameesh was going to keep driving, but she begged him to stop, and clambered out of the high back seat of the car, careful not to trip on her abaya or allow her legs to be revealed. She bent down, and saw that the cat was crushed and dead, lying at the end of a sticky streak on the dusty road. She didn't hear the plaintive mewling of kittens behind an overflowing dumpster through her tears. He made her get back in the car, then pushed the cat's body nearer the dumpster before getting back in himself and driving off. Lujain cried quietly the rest of the way home. She didn't tell her husband about the cat, nor did she ever once mention Ameesh. It might have been misunderstood.

One Wednesday evening, the SUV pulled up outside her apartment building. The nanny had gone home. The kids were inside with their dad. It was warm but there was a pleasant breeze, with a hint of the rains to come on its teasing breath. The burnt-dark men in their Day-Glo orange suits were raking leaves, or resting on their rakes, looking like prisoners on work-release. An empty Twix wrapper blew along the pavement as she walked to the car door. A handsome, pleasant, honest-faced young Indian man came around the car to open the door for her. It was not Ameesh.

By now, Lujain knew that the family she and Ameesh worked for was large and complex, with at least four brothers and a powerful old matriarch. As far as she could work out from the things Ameesh or her tutees had told her, and what she'd seen herself, the multiple households of the family juggled ever-changing and unevenly distributed privilege and resources, based on the capricious whims of the matriarch.

Long-since widowed, and some variety of princess by birth, this unnaturally short and toad-faced old woman ruled her restrictive dominion with a hard, thin mouth, and a surprisingly deep, if querulous, voice. Walls within walls. Lujain had caught a brief glimpse of this petty monarch just once. But Ameesh had opened up a few times about his living situation, or rather his working situation, for they were one and the same. When he wasn't driving someone somewhere, on call 24/7, allowed under the terms of his visa to return home just once every two years, he slept on some sacks in a garage, next to the SUV, like a stable boy forced to live with the horses.

Lujain didn't ask the new driver's name, nor was it offered. When she asked where Ameesh was, the new driver just shrugged, though she saw in the rear-view mirror that his eyes flicked nervously towards and away from her. He spoke not a word during the entire journey to the tutees' house. Lujain asked the girls about Ameesh. They, too, shrugged. They claimed not to be sure which of the family's drivers Ameesh even was.

One of them laughed, and said, 'Maybe he went to the desert.'

The other shot her a look, and said, 'Maybe he went home. Maybe his mother was sick.'

Lujain drank four small paper cups of strong Arabic coffee while she related all this to Deryn. Deryn herself abstained from the coffee, as the cardamom in it made her tongue numb. While she was saddened to hear of Ameesh's situation, it was nothing she wasn't already used to hearing.

'Lujain, maybe his two years were up, or his mum *was* sick, and he did indeed go back to India. You didn't know him that well, don't know everything about him.'

'His mum is already dead, she died years ago.'

'Well, okay, his dad, then. A sibling. Or he found a better job. He's not going to ring you to say goodbye, is he?'

'If he was going home, he would have said. He would have been excited. I don't think they'd ever let him go, anyway. They had his passport. He'd been here about six years. I didn't get the impression he'd been home in all that time. And, the last time I saw him, he told me something.'

'What thing?'

'The old woman. He was driving her home from somewhere. They were stopped at some lights. He was daydreaming a bit, and tired because they'd had him driving all over the place all night, picking up and dropping off. His eyes wandered, and before he knew what he was doing he caught the old woman's eyes in the rear-view mirror.'

'So?'

'So she was furious! She accused him of staring at her. Giving her the creeps. He just took her home and nothing more was said. But he was really nervous. He said she's the sort who broods on things. And you just know that she's never once not had everything her own way, all her life. She's had the littlest things her own way, always and forever.'

'So are you saying she booted him out on the street? Is that where you were this morning, looking for him? How on earth do you think you'd find him in this city, Lujain?'

Lujain looked at her hands, tearful, once more. 'Sort of. I hadn't slept all night for worrying. I couldn't think straight. I realised Ameesh reminded me of my husband's little brother, who I love. He's simple, and good, and all alone. So I hid my phone, and told my husband I'd left it at the house the night before. He took me there, and waited in the car outside the family compound. I walked through their garden, and found one of my students, the one who wants to be a dentist, feeding peacocks, if you please.'

A tear rolled down Lujain's cheek, and she shook her head.

'So?' said Deryn.

There was silence for a moment. Deryn could faintly hear a teacher in the nearest classroom, begging her students to pay attention. The whirr and chunk of a photocopier. A Coordinator in her office, a few doors away, laughing at someone's joke. Pigeons trilling on a windowsill.

'So... I asked her again about Ameesh, said I was worried about him, asked for her help.'

Lujain took a deep, shuddering breath, swallowed back tears. She looked Deryn directly in the eyes for the first time that day. And Deryn realised that Lujain was crying, not just because she was upset, but because she was furious. Deryn only ever cried herself if she was deeply angry, so she knew the look; she recognised the glinting fire behind Lujain's eyes.

'I've always got on really well with those girls. I thought they were kind and lovely, before. But I won't be teaching them again. This one, Amal, she looked surprised at first, then she drew herself up really straight and looked at me with contempt. Utter contempt. And she said, she said, "I told you.

He went to the desert. Don't ask again." Then she turned away and carried on feeding those horrible, screechy birds.'

In the silence, a bell rang for the end of class, and the hallways filled with the echoing chatter and laughter of young women, headed for their next class or the food court or the place where they'd wait for their drivers to pick them up.

'Lujain, I'm sorry, I can't say I fully understand.'

'We can't do anything here. We can't do anything but shop, and eat, and raise our kids. We can't ask anything, or find anything out, or understand anything, or report anything, not really. We can't even drive ourselves. But me, I can pray, at least. That I can do. I will pray for him.'

Lujain stood up abruptly, went to the office door, and opened it. The sounds of shrieking girls and complaining, tired teachers clattered into the room. Deryn thought suddenly of mewling, hungry kittens behind a dumpster.

'I think you don't pray, Deryn. But if you ever do, then, well, please ... do. And what happened this morning, I'm really sorry, truly, and I promise it won't happen again.'

Without waiting for a reply, Lujain disappeared into the crowds of beautiful raven-haired young students in the hallways, looking just like one of them. The black hems of abayas floated about like magical cloaks. Deryn threw Lujain's empty, brown-stained paper cup into the bin, and opened up her ever-refilling email inbox.

Deryn couldn't focus on her work. It wasn't Lujain or Ameesh occupying her thoughts, but an evening she'd spent downtown with her friend Teesha the year before. Stopping to admire some street art, they noticed two teenage boys scuffing at the pavement next to them. Deryn had gasped, realising that they were kicking at a tiny black-and-white kitten. Not kicking hard, almost nudging, but still. The kitten was frozen in fear, looking like a china cat, or a paper picture in a Victorian scrapbook.

Deryn told the boys off and sent them packing, then stood looking at the kitten. It looked back at her. She'd thought through how she might take it home, to a residence where pets were forbidden. Then home again from there, some day, by plane and train, to what would seem to the animal a different planet. It seemed impossible, or very difficult at least. So, when Teesha had scolded her – that she mustn't even think about it, that she couldn't save everything in all the world, that she wasn't fuckin' Jesus, that they had to get to the gelato place before it closed for prayer time – she allowed herself to be pulled along.

Trudging home, long after the other women had left but before the maintenance men would see her, Deryn felt her eyes continually drawn to the decorative outer wall of the compound.

Out there, on the other side, were holy desert places honoured by an entire nation, by the world. Somewhere beyond that wall were camps to which families went from the city, and relaxed, with beautiful tents, carpets, and coffee pots, with their treasured children and camels and falcons. That was deeper in, where she'd probably never be able to go.

But out here, on the edges, to be stared at later from her fifth-floor window, was the burnt-orange crust of the desert's urban rim, littered with all the things people no longer wanted. She could see it, but she couldn't touch it, or reach it. The concrete wall was too high to climb, and had no gates except where it met the roads the drivers used. You couldn't get through the wall, and you couldn't climb over it.

Deryn didn't know when she might ever leave this place, and live at home again, away from the orange, amidst the green. She didn't know which of her two bags would be fullest when she did. But, when she did, she thought she might get a cat. A rescue one.

Pharricidal

E. E. Rhodes

The forecast was 5, increasing 6 soon, rain or slight drizzle, good. I turned the sound down until the old wireless was just a murmur of noise in the background. I pulled on an oilskin, against the inclement weather, and stepped out of the house into the already damp lane. Decision made. Certain now of what I was about.

The streets were almost deserted at this hour and I passed no one on my way down to the quay. I kept to the sodium shadows, puddles glittering, scattering diamonds of light as I misjudged a depth, or step, and sent up spray. At the bottom of the hill I checked again. Still no one else about, in this thin time between the pubs going dark and the pre-dawn workers at the canning factory going on shift.

I crossed the road and pulled open the heavy door of the public telephone box at the harbour's edge and dialled up the lighthouse radio. I spoke to the Second Keeper to let him know what I'd seen one evening a week or so back, just as the pubs were closing, in the ginnel behind The Lobster Pot where the empty barrels were stacked. He was quiet for a bit and then muttered his thanks. I was smart about it, using a scarf to muffle my voice. He didn't know it was me.

Gulls were screeching full throttle the next morning, disturbed by the flit boat that was already in from the lighthouse. The skipper had moored up at the jetty and the Third Keeper was being carried off the boat by four of the fishermen just in from their lines and pots. I could see that the Keeper's face was bruised, purpled and marshmallow-soft. The marketplace was alive with the gossip that he was seeing the Second Keeper's girlfriend on the sly.

I saw her then as she pushed past me to get to the stretcher. A pretty lass usually, though her face was marred by worry now. Anxiety weighing her down, scored in the downward curve of her neck and dip of her head. She followed close behind the men to a waiting ambulance, her fingers tying themselves into knots. The red and blue lights were a sickly strobe against the pale skin-blush sky of the incoming day.

I shouldered my old kitbag and headed for the flit boat myself; the skipper shrugged when he saw me and spat a stream of chewing tobacco onto the cobbles.

'All right then?' He asked. 'Trinity giving you the Relief?' There was a sharpened edge to his tone. His queries whetstoned on the quiet rumour and gossip that powered the social engines of the town.

Everyone knew that the Trinity Lighthouse Company wouldn't take me on as a full-time keeper. Somehow I was never good enough for that. Though they'd have me as a Temporary Relief when they were desperate. Oh yes. They'd expect me to drop everything, when it suited them. Like today. Though I'd been packed and ready for it. Just in case.

I nodded, handing him my bag as I stepped over the

gunwale, sitting with my back to him to avoid a conversation and so I had a view out to sea. The short crossing was smooth enough as these things go. Just a little white-edged bounce to the rollock of the waves.

As the jetty for the lighthouse came into sight I could see both the remaining Keepers sitting on the rock-hewn steps, waiting for me. Ready.

The Keepers were tough men, long custom and habit smoothing down only some of their corners and rough edges. We hadn't always had the easiest time of it in the past, but when I passed my bag to the Second, they both shook hands with me and seemed pleased enough that I was here now.

It was comfortable and familiar, and over the next few days we fell into a tidal rhythm of chores and downtime.

Three nights in, on my first night watch, I climbed the stone stairs to the lightbox to check the lantern and its workings. Everything was put away, clean and tidy, and there was no sign of any trouble. Across the bay I could see lights from lone houses and several villages dotting the coastline, cwtched in inlets and modest hills. The tiny panes of glass fractured the image when I stepped away.

The ink-washed sky above was clear and bright. Just a salt-spilled scattering of stars. If everything worked out the way I hoped, it would be just a temporary calm.

I looked everywhere for evidence of the fight between the Keepers that must have happened. One room at a time. One by one. Steady. Careful. I hunted for mended furniture, or chipped crockery, or anything with a fresh paint smell.

After a futile week of searching everywhere in the lighthouse itself I tried the old stores. It looked as though a recent storm had tumbled a corner of the building and the Keepers had put up a bit of canvas tarp to cover the gap. The bricks had been piled up neatly nearby, almost too neatly I thought, and took a closer look. I shifted them slowly, one at a time. Keeping an eye on the path that led back to the lighthouse. Making sure I was alone.

Finally, I found half a brick with blood curdling its crumbling edge. When I examined it more closely, I found there were also a few rust-coloured stains in the stitching of the canvas tarp.

I hid the brick carefully, folded the canvas away behind a barrel in the stores, fixed up the wall with some of the tumbled bricks and a different bit of tarpaulin and, from then on, was even more cautious around the other two men. I didn't deliberately avoid the stores, nothing like avoiding something to draw attention to the very thing you hope people won't see. But I did everything I could to avoid raising suspicion. I completed the scheduled tasks I was assigned, I acted normally, I did nothing to stir any argument or discord. Even I could see the irony when the Keepers seemed to warm to me a little, when both of them were friendlier than usual.

On the last late watch of my temporary relief, I waited until I was sure that both men were sound asleep, then I crept down the solid stairs from the fug of the kitchen into the operations room. I waited a while, letting the quiet settle round me like an incoming fret, just to be sure I'd be undisturbed, and then called the police on the lighthouse radio. I was careful about it, muffling my voice, simply leaving a message on a tip line about the brick and the canvas tarp, and where they could be found.

I went back up to the kitchen and saw that my hand was almost steady when I drank the tea I'd made. Up in the lightbox I did another round of checks, watching the lights wink in the distance. A rough kind of morse code that I decided not to parse. The Second Keeper relieved me in the early hours and I went to my bed. But I could only sleep fitfully, not my conscience disturbing me, more a sense of anticipation.

Just after the end of the next early watch the Permanent Relief came in from the mainland. The First was waiting with me, the two of us exchanging pleasantries, just to pass the time until the boat could dock. The jetty was at a difficult angle, meant to protect it from the worst of the weather that came in from the sea, and I could see the flit boat skipper gritting against the push of the tide.

The Relief climbed over the gunwale, we shook hands, and I took his place on the flit boat. The skipper nodded to me and I sat in the front of the boat. I faced him this time, looking beyond him and over the stern, so I could watch the lighthouse recede.

As we drew away from the island, I could see the Relief heading up from the jetty. The First had already climbed back up the steps and he and the Second Keeper were standing in front of the stores, hands raised in farewell, a contrast against the newly painted whitewash where I'd fixed the wall. I watched as the Second shook hands with the Permanent Relief. He and the First turned and waved again. I lifted my hand in my own goodbye. Like too many people before them, the Keepers thought the sea would keep their secrets drowned.

Ten minutes into the journey I suppressed a smile as the captain of the police launch from the town nodded to us as it passed on its way out to the lighthouse. He had two of the local constables with him, both of them like slabs of beef on the turn. Not everyone in this place of fish and slate had their sea-legs. Though they were ready enough with their fists if a fight turned bad, in The Lobster Pot or after a match, and they'd be good if this job turned as sour as I thought it might.

The skipper coughed to attract my attention and spat his tobacco into the waves. 'Marvellous innit? Don't know if they called ahead. Anyone tell you what happened?' I shook my head and he went on, a sour turn to his lips. 'The Third Keeper's gone and died.' He stopped for a moment and then spat again. 'What do you think? Reckon Trinity will want you now?'

I nodded as if in deep thought, considering the question. Down three men rather than one? There was every chance those bastards would come begging. They would have to call on me now.

'They'll probably need me...' I said, slowly, as though it had never crossed my mind, had never even occurred to me that time I'd caught a glimpse of the Third Keeper with the Second's girl, necking at the back of The Lobster Pot. Seen the potential of rumours... 'the forecast's promising storms.'

Docked

Philippa Davies

Call me innocent, but when I first visited the dock, it seemed something quite different from what it means now.

Spanish seamen with ponytails, earrings and come-hither dark eyes unloaded their catch; I got whiffs of sea salt, fish and rope at every turn. Old sea-dogs turned landlubbers, readily identifiable by their still-rolling gait and wistful gazes out to sea, walked their Staffies. And their lovers, now big-bottomed and heavy-limbed, ate chips and ice cream, while recalling the graft and grunt of fishing, and the broken-heart threat of no return.

Of course, every teacher must find the occasional student fascinating and attractive. It was my second job at Porthcleddau School and my first A-level class. Ceredigion born and bred, I'm far from an adventurous woman... Indeed, moving south to the more English Porthcleddau felt rather daring.

My mother, as mothers often are, was to blame for the infatuation. She loved Elvis, played his music relentlessly and constantly sang the praises of his winning combination of black hair and blue eyes.

'Stunning, that mix, cariad,' she used to say. 'Quite stunning.'

When she'd hit the sherry, she liked to belt out 'In the Ghetto', though it was an odd choice for a family such as ours, perched in a poky Victorian terraced house overlooking Llandysul. Mamgu joined in the singing too, but it was 'Love Me Tender' that made her cry.

Anyway, that was their Saturday nights, a talent show on TV then Elvis with the amontillado.

Mostly, I stayed in my room with my lead character friends when all this was going on. Georgette Heyer heroines, Anne of Green Gables, the twins at St Clare's: I gorged on them all. Thanks to the little torch from the kitchen, I would often read under the covers until the early hours. At school, I was known as 'swotty bot', and nobody was surprised when I was the first Prosser to go to university – albeit Aberystwyth – to read English.

While dealing with shock at encountering students who ate kiwi fruit and chicken satay, I hunted for, and found, my places on campus: the library and the university bookshop. Every hour I could spend in the former I did, and I got a part-time job in the latter. I rarely went home, even less after I overheard Aunty Blod, on the amontillado, ask my mother, 'Why is Mair so drab? She's inoffensive enough, but hardly going to set the world alight.'

Little did Blod know, the only world I wished to set alight was that of radical beat poetry in the jazz quarters of Paris and New York.

Anyway, a degree, masters and teaching qualification later I was forced to enter the toad world of work. To emphasise my introspection, I dressed in severe plain clothes, black, grey or navy, with the occasional white shirt, a grown-up version of school uniform. I developed a speaking style which was strongly Welsh, quiet and extremely precise. I faked shyness and sensitivity so people gave me minimal bother.

Am I putting you off here? So many people are virtue champions these days, it's become impossible to differentiate between true good and evil. I read somewhere that the best way to run anything is via an approach called 'radical candour', so that's what I try to follow. If aroused, sorry for your sensibilities.

When the internet arrived, that teeny-weeny interest I had in sex died altogether. The bookish potential of this new world, of Amazon, bloggers and YouTube interviews, had me captivated. When I wasn't teaching, I was online, making friends I knew I'd never meet but who were there when I wanted them. Chat rooms, forums, blogs, Myspace, Goodreads – I was in them all. My online name was @booknutz, and remains so to this very day, if you fancy a follow.

My worlds were neatly compartmentalised. During school hours and for a couple of hours after, as I marked, I was in Porthcleddau. The rest of the time I was in the bountiful global cyber playground. Yes, there was one nasty incident when I bumped into Jake Jenkins, head of chemistry, in a Creating Imaginary Worlds chat room, to both our embarrassment. For a couple of months after, he'd sidle up to me in the staff room describing ideas he'd had for fantasy novels. I entertained them and suggested he develop synopses. He never came back with a single one and I resolved to steer well clear of the less literary online locations in future.

In my seventh year at Porthcleddau School, MJ joined the sixth form. Like Elvis, he had black hair and deep-set blue eyes. A better-looking Matthew Rhys (my favourite ever Mr Darcy). The head said his mother had died, he was an only child and his father worked as a pilot in the docks, having previously been a ship's captain.

MJ was tall, lean and had a surprisingly deep and authoritative voice for such fine, chiselled features. He was my trump card in teaching *King Lear* as he read the lead role with empathy and aplomb. Listening to him deliver lines like, 'When we are born, we cry that we are come to this great stage of fools...', it was impossible to believe that he was just seventeen. Even the most distracted student sat transfixed. In one lesson, for instance, I noticed Rosie Price with a large glob of saliva at the tip of her chin, so rapt and engaged was her attention.

And yes, everyone knew he was my favourite, but no one seemed to mind. He took to staying on after class to ask me whether he could improve his work in any way, or to fret over some small aspect of an essay. He said he wanted to study English at university and maybe become an academic, while I plotted for him to apply – at very least – to the Russell Group, maybe Oxbridge. He was my project.

I pictured visiting him among the dreaming spires, perhaps for once abandoning my usual sartorial severity for something a little more floaty. We would sit and picnic on the riverbank, discuss Sylvia Plath and Samuel Beckett.

One afternoon, after double English on *Lear*, focussing on the 'Blow, winds, and crack your cheeks...' scene, when Lear is losing the plot on the moor in a storm, I suggested to the head that I took the A-level class down to the dock where there was an impending storm. He said he saw no harm in it, as long as no one got struck by lightning, and as it was after school hours it could be unofficial.

Each student was to generate their own, alternative version of Lear's imprecation, based on what inspired them, and then we would review and discuss their work when back in class. The storm was some way out at sea but the yellowish light, distant rumbles and ominous swell excited my students and they scribbled eagerly.

One by one they peeled off home as hunger and other competing ideas got to them. By Mackerel Quay, only MJ remained.

At the entrance to the dock, Mackerel Quay gives its visitors the best vantage point of the whole port, with the King's Arms and Marine Services shed on one side and the lookout station, with a VHF 14 Pierhead sign, on the right. (VHF 14 became our text alert to each other, when needed.)

You swivel to see more dock buildings, some yachts, the town behind them and then a wide expanse of water, open sea in one direction, narrowing into a river in the other. Even on the greyest of days, this panorama offers an uplift, helped by the bright-blue railings which lace the parameter with the sea. Not even the strange decision to break up some of the concrete ground with AstroTurf detracts from this effect. It is still a wide expanse of possibility.

MJ pointed at a small building. 'Dad's shed is over there,' he said, 'where pilots stash their kit.' He held his arms up to the sky and whirled around. 'But it's a circle of vision here. Three-hundred-and-sixty degrees. What a marvellous thing.'

'This is how I like to read literature,' I said, 'looking at everything with a circle of vision.'

'So who would you be, Miss Prosser, in the centre of a circle of vision?'

'Goodness, I don't know. A bookish spinster surrounded by school, literary interests and the internet.' I didn't feel comfortable with the way this was going, so I added, 'Anyway, I think it's more useful to put who we study in there rather than ourselves.'

'Yes, ma'am!'

The wind was picking up so I suggested MJ head home. Whatever possessed me, I don't know, but I swayed in that circle until the storm hit the coast, the rain stabbed my flesh and I returned to my flat, exhilarated and saturated.

A week later, I'd finished double English again and Rosie Price stayed behind.

'Sorry, miss, I just thought you should know.'

'What Rosie?'

'MJ, he's had mental health, like, you know, after his mother died.'

'Okay.'

'Just so you know, he makes stuff up.'

'Thanks, Rosie, I'll bear that in mind.'

Somehow, MJ and I slipped into a funny little habit of meeting maybe once every couple of weeks at the circle of vision. I gave him my phone number and he'd text me with small enquiries. 'Do you think I should apply for straight English at uni, or English and Creative Writing?' and 'If you could go to any university in the world, where would it be?'

I can't truly remember much of what we talked about during these meetings, but after we'd done a session in class on metaphor and cliché, I remember MJ loved to play with this idea.

When we met he'd ask, 'So, Miss Prosser, when we gaze into the glass that is the water here today, what do we see?'

I would try to come up with some surprising idea or a new image: an abandoned submarine, some locks of a deceased pirate's hair. He would add to these and elaborate on them. The submarine would have ghostly souls floundering within. The pirate would gain an eye patch or an earring.

Somehow, too, these meetings, often occurring at twilight, started to involve greater and greater disclosure. How MJ had sought solace and comfort in poetry after his mother died, or how, when his father was away at sea in his early years, he'd escape into a fantasy world of make-believe where he was also at sea, with his dad. He asked me about my fantasies too. Were there writers I imagined being? Or taking as lovers? What did I imagine about other students and teachers in the school?

I knew his father's job involved jumping onto ships to bring them in safely to port here. Their relationship was a good one, albeit rather distant and formal, given they'd been apart for long periods as he grew up. Clare, his mother, had loved gardening and after she died, his father had become consumed with this too, creating their extensive garden in tribute to her. MJ was close to an aunt who'd taken it upon herself to mother him, and his earliest sexual experiences had been with her daughter, slightly older than him and now studying marine biology in Bangor.

'I don't know why,' he told me, 'but that always makes me think she saw my cock in marine terms, like a razor clam, maybe, or a particularly long prawn.'

When he said things like this, I never replied, though I was amused. It was not a subject area I felt we should dwell on.

He said Rosie Price and he had sex sometimes, and that did not surprise me in the least.

The night he went missing, we'd had an English class outing to the Phoenix Bowl, located at the open sea end of the dock. We'd been considering British and US cultural influences in the writing of T S Eliot and, as this was a legitimate, health-and-safety-policed outing, the school minibus dropped us off near Mackerel Quay afterwards so we were able to walk to the bowling alley for games and burgers.

MJ sent me a text on the coach journey: *Do NOT want to share you this evening. If you can't find me, go VHF 14.*

I noticed he hung behind the rest of us as we left the coach and by the time we got to the bowling alley he was nowhere to be seen.

'Oh, MJ's got left behind,' I said. I checked the others in and instructed them to go ahead and start playing.

I jogged back to the circle of vision and found him leaning on the blue railings.

'Square with me,' he said. 'You want me, don't you?'

I was unable to speak, knowing myself to be like a lovesick teenager, craning for a sight of him in the school corridor, checking my make-up was perfect before his lessons, wearing stockings and suspenders under my plain skirts.

I leaned in to him and then cannot recall in the least what happened afterwards.

There are phrases that may or may not have been said. 'Like fucking my mother,' was one of them. 'I am so so sorry,' perhaps another. We may have been physically aggressive to one another, and somehow he slipped, or I may have left and then the accident occurred, and he toppled over the edge. Or me even finding him there in the first place might have been a trick of my imagination.

When I got back to the bowling alley, Rosie looked worried.

'He's still not here, miss. Any luck?'

'No,' I said, 'and it's dank and foggy out there.' I suggested he might just not have been in the mood and had probably walked home.

His body was found three days later, washed up, up-river. Rosie and I both told his dad, Clive, that we knew he could be depressive, and the head said MJ had spoken to the school counsellor. The dock webcams covered the gate entrance to the port but no wider, not to Mackerel Quay. After the police interviewed all of the staff, they decided it was a tragedy of a young male unable to fully articulate his feelings and express his need for help. I knew he would have hated this, but decided best to keep schtum.

Clive asked me to have coffee. He said how much MJ had admired me, and that he had filled poetry notebooks inspired by my teaching. Somehow, we started to meet every few weeks. He took me to the Royal Horticultural Show and various celebrated Welsh gardens. One day he said, 'Something that surprised me about MJ is that he never kept any notebooks relating to his birdwatching. He used to go and do that quite often at twilight.'

I suggested we might add that to our range of interests, but we never did.

Within a year, he asked me to marry him. Clive was organised, neat and respectful. Our sex life, while not exciting, was satisfactory. I put a photo of MJ in one of these internet sites that ages you, and Clive looked pretty much exactly like MJ was predicted to look in middle age. Clive also knew that I was shy, and he accepted completely that I preferred to make love with the lights off.

On our third anniversary we both had too much to drink.

'Can I ask you something, Mair?'

'Of course, cariad.'

'Have you ever felt like killing anyone?'

There was what felt like an incredibly long silence.

'Good grief, no.'

'Well I have. When Clare was dying, I never believed that someone could suffer so much. Time and time again I thought about Dignitas or mercy-killing her myself ... but then MJ would come into my mind, and how would he work that one out?'

I squeezed Clive's hand very hard and said, 'You made the right decision.'

That night I couldn't sleep. Image after image of the dock, MJ in the circle of vision with predatory birds pecking at his beautiful corpse flooded my brain. At first light, I dressed and went down there to talk to the spirit of MJ, which I know is there still. I whispered what the glass that is the water showed today and imagined how he would respond.

As I made breakfast and Clive enquired where I'd been, I said I was embarking on a sea-bird project, spotting as many as possible and sketching them in a journal. I found someone on the internet who I pay to send me unsigned bird sketches, which I put into convincing sketchbooks.

Now I visit the dock most days and Clive always tells people I'm obsessed with the place. The circle of vision calls me to it and I have no agency to resist.

I'm head of English at Porthcleddau School now, and Clive and I have established the MJ Foundation to send the poorer English students over sixteen to the RSC in Stratford once a year. We go too, of course, and spend much of our time there discussing what MJ might have become: an actor maybe, or even a director.

Some years after MJ's passing, at a school drinks do, Jake Jenkins took me aside.

'Do you know the police were wondering seriously about your relationship with MJ, before he died? I said there was no chance – you're hardly ever in the real world, let alone capable of any violent action in it...'

'Goodness... Thanks,' I replied.

But no doubt, *you* may feel you deserve some radical candour here, before we finish.

For any teacher of English Literature, death is a challenging but required subject of discussion. My own conclusion is that it's merely a loss of consciousness, similar to our non-experience before birth. If that consciousness was fully and vividly inhabited by an individual during their life, then that's all that matters – not the length of it. All the other stuff we do – the prayers, the rituals, the tributes, the fond memories – these are for those of us still conscious, so that we might feel better.

And this is what the dock means to me now. A place of death and rebirth, of arrival and departure, of gateways, flows and tides. A place where the glass that is the water, rather like people, is always open to interpretation. And every night I thank God that the tide can't share my secrets, but keeps me here in this dock, in thrall to them.

The Oba's Head

Claire Boot

Mrs Cadwallader found the head on the Captain's desk.

'Bloody thing,' she muttered.

The head was small and made of a blackened metal of some sort. It had rings around the neck and a cone-shaped cap on the top. Mrs Cadwallader didn't much care for it, nor for any of the Captain's foreign knick-knacks.

She skirted around the desk to the bay windows and hauled up one of the panes. The scent of lavender from the front garden mingled with the smell of last night's tobacco. She tried to ignore the head as she piled up half-empty teacups and stained saucers on the desktop, but when she moved a gravy-streaked dinner plate, there it was again, gazing blank-eyed from a sketch in a notebook.

Mrs Cadwallader huffed. The Captain must've taken the head from its usual place in the cabinet and not put it back. He'd been pleased enough with the likeness to sign it 'HCB, June 1911', though, to her mind, he'd not captured the nose well at all. She peered at the sculpture and detected a layer of dust on the ears. That wouldn't do. She flicked a cloth out of her apron pocket and picked up the head to give it a good polish.

She heard a tut.

Mrs Cadwallader looked up from the head in her hands and

saw, at the window, another just like it. Same colour, same nose, but life-sized and not made of metal. As she stared, the face outside the window cracked into a broad grin.

The housekeeper slept poorly that night. Gwen Cadwallader was not given to flights of fancy but she couldn't account for that grinning face. Her disturbed night risked making her late for work and she hurried from the terraced house she rented with her brother. It must've been a reflection in the glass, except how did it move? The main road rattled with carts and motor cars as Mrs Cadwallader passed dockers and shipping clerks on the pavement. Maybe it was some coal-hawker out on his rounds, playing the fool to impress his pals. She turned through wrought-iron gates into a narrow park alongside the railway line. Should she tell Captain Bevan? She didn't want him thinking she was skittish.

Mrs Cadwallader didn't notice the man sitting on a bench until she got within a few paces of him and he raised his hat.

'Good morning, sister,' he said, with a broad grin. Just like the face at the window. Same colour, same nose.

She backed off the path in alarm and stumbled onto the grass, for once not concerned about the mud. The man jumped up and stepped towards her, so she spun round and started for the road. He followed her, calling out that she was in danger and he wanted to help.

'It is the curse of the Oba's head!' he cried.

Mrs Cadwallader stopped.

'What nonsense are you talking?' she snapped, jabbing her umbrella at him.

The man held his hat to his chest and begged her to listen. He meant no harm but she was in danger. It was the head. Had anything bad happened to her since she first went near it?

She hesitated. There was that bad dose of flu over the winter, and only last week she'd dropped her best vase – her mother's favourite – on the kitchen tiles.

'Let me help you,' said the man. 'Leave the window open tonight and I will take it from your house and no more bad things will happen.'

Mrs Cadwallader set him straight. The house, and the head, belonged to Captain Bevan.

The man nodded. Had anything bad happened to him, her master?

'My employer, not my master,' she retorted. She had to admit, misfortune seemed to dog the Captain. His brother had died at Easter and he himself was frequently unwell, what with his malaria flaring up.

'Tonight,' declared the man. 'Leave the window open and I will save both you and him from the curse.'

Captain Bevan was delighted. A plot, a genuine plot. He'd never imagined that prim and proper Penarth could generate such excitement. Quite the thrill for a Thursday morning.

After her encounter in the park, Mrs Cadwallader had delivered the tale of the man at the window along with the Captain's morning tea and daily newspaper. She'd explained that she'd thought it best to let the man think she believed him, so he'd be caught red-handed.

'Most impressive,' said the Captain. 'Very resourceful. Shame I didn't have more men of your mettle in the field.'

The housekeeper offered to fetch the constable, but Captain Bevan wouldn't hear of it. He was an old Africa hand, he could deal with this miscreant. God knows, he'd dealt with enough of his kind before.

'Don't look so worried, Mrs Cadwallader!' He laughed. 'I'll wager you a day's pay that you'll come in tomorrow and find me right as rain with the thief all trussed up and ready for the magistrate.'

The Captain lost his bet. At a quarter past eight the next morning, Mrs Cadwallader found her employer dead in his study. The window was open and the head was gone.

Osawe Okomu burst out of the English Wesleyan Methodist Church and pelted down Loudoun Square, weaving around families in their Sunday best. He swung a right into Angelina Street, dodging three men sharing a cigarette on the corner, and sprinted along to number 13. He rapped on the door until the landlady's cook finally pulled it open, and then flew up the stairs, two at a time, to the top of the house. He barged into the attic room – prompting a loud expletive from his fellow lodger – and bounded across the floor. Halting at his bed, he carefully pulled a New Testament from his inside jacket pocket.

The book was a gift bestowed by the Reverend Walter Sutton, minister of the chapel in Loudoun Square. Osawe had met the Revd Sutton three weeks before, when he walked into the vestry with a letter of recommendation from the Thomas

B. Freeman Theological College of Lagos. The principal of the college warmly commended Osawe to any such Wesleyan Methodist minister as may feel moved to provide tutelage to the young man for a short period. Osawe had worked his passage to Cardiff, via Liverpool, on a palm-oil ship and wished to further his studies before returning home. Revd Sutton, touched by Osawe's eagerness, agreed to the arrangement on two conditions. The first was that he lodged with Miss Howell-Hopkins at 13 Angelina Street. She was both a very respectable member of the congregation and proprietress of a boarding-house of quality and distinction, in sharp contrast to the many lawless dens of iniquity springing up all around the docks. (Miss Howell-Hopkins had several conditions of her own, most notably that no lodger of hers was to utter the vulgar epithet 'Tiger Bay' in place of the correct nomenclature 'Butetown'.) Secondly, the Reverend requested that Osawe consented to be known as Thomas. This was in honour of the celebrated Wesleyan missionary to West Africa and founder of the college in Lagos, but also because Thomas was easier for the Revd Sutton to say.

Up in Miss Howell-Hopkin's attic room, Osawe slid the New Testament under his pillow. Revd Sutton had invited him to join the family on a jaunt to the seaside and Osawe didn't want to mislay his gift or get sand in the binding.

'Almost a month in Great Britain, Thomas, and you've seen nothing but docks!' the minister had exclaimed after the morning service. 'Come with us to Penarth, my treat – we're leaving in ten minutes. Mrs Sutton has already made the sandwiches.'

Satisfied that the Good Book would be safe until he returned, Osawe buttoned up his jacket and raced back to the chapel.

Revd Sutton, Mrs Sutton, the four Sutton children and Osawe bundled off the train at Penarth and followed the flow of day trippers down to the seafront. The beach surprised Osawe, covered as it was by grey rocks, muddy-brown sand and dark-green seaweed. Mrs Sutton spread a blanket over the pebbles and shared out the sandwiches. As the children gathered shiny stones and knobbly driftwood, Osawe amazed them with stories of tribes who used shells as money.

Alice, the youngest Sutton, poured all her shells into the lap of her pinafore and held it up by the hem.

'Look, Thomas,' she said, with glee, 'I'm rich!'

After lunch, they clambered off the beach and queued for the pier. Alice's brother teased her for being scared of the sea between the wooden slats beneath their feet, so Osawe assured her he didn't like it either and they could be brave together. Revd Sutton bought them all candyfloss – another surprise for Osawe – and they leaned against the railings to eat the sweet fluff and watch the paddle steamer depart for Weston-super-Mare.

Alice, her face pink and sticky, tugged her mother's sleeve. 'Why is that lady staring at us?' she asked.

Mrs Sutton shushed her daughter, but Osawe whispered that she was probably staring at him. He winked at Alice and gave the lady a broad grin.

The woman screamed.

She fell against the man next to her, shrieking about a thief and a murderer. He tried to hold her as she crumpled to the ground sobbing.

'Gwen? What on earth's the matter? Here, come to the bench.'

Revd Sutton leaped forward to assist, and Osawe did too, but that made the woman cry out even more.

'In God's name, grab him!' hollered the man. 'Can't you see my sister's terrified?'

Hands took hold of Osawe. He struggled to wrestle them off. By the time the pier-master came running, Osawe was pinned face down on the wooden slats, his shirt torn and his nose bloodied.

Chief Inspector Beresford came all the way from the divisional headquarters in Barry to question the suspect. He wouldn't normally bother with seamen from the colonies – deaths in dockside brawls were ten a penny – but the Bevan case warranted his attention. A respected military man, bludgeoned to death in his own home, for the sake of a mysterious African artefact. A victim of voodoo, claimed the more sensationalist newspapers. Rumour had it that even the Marquis of Bute had expressed an interest in the investigation.

Sergeant Griffiths opened the cell door. 'On your feet, darkie,' he chivvied. 'Look lively.'

Beresford watched as Osawe, wincing from the previous day's bruising, twisted off the bunk. 'Prisoner's name?' he asked.

The sergeant consulted his notebook. 'Oss ... Osserwee ... Oaker-mew?'

'Revd Sutton calls me Thomas, sir,' offered Osawe.

Methodist minister, Sergeant Griffiths informed the inspector. Chapel in Butetown. Already been up this morning wanting news of his student.

'Well, Thomas,' said Beresford, 'you are accused of theft and murder.'

Osawe shook his head. 'No – no – I didn't.'

Beresford raised his hand. Osawe had been explicitly identified. The woman who screamed at him on the pier was housekeeper to a man found dead two days earlier. She'd seen Osawe outside the victim's house and subsequently in Windsor Park.

'It was not me, I swear,' said Osawe.

'You'll have to do better than that, boy,' snarled Beresford. 'Wednesday and Thursday mornings – where were you?'

Miss Howell-Hopkins held a prayer meeting for her lodgers at eight o'clock every day, except Sundays, when they were expected to attend church (Methodist preferably, Anglican grudgingly, Catholic absolutely not). Osawe was sure she would tell the inspector that he was always there.

'We'll see if she does. And Thursday night? Still praying?'

On Thursdays, Osawe went with Revd Sutton to the seamen's mission for Bible study with the sailors. As usual, he returned to his lodgings, ate some food, and went to bed.

'Prayer meetings, Bible studies – very devoted, aren't we?' sneered Beresford.

'I can go now?' asked Osawe.

Beresford laughed. These natives were so simple, it was like interrogating a child.

'No. You'll stay here until I decide if you're telling the truth. And if I decide you're lying, you'll hang.'

The sergeant followed Beresford out of the cell and locked the door. Osawe sank onto the bunk, thinking of the New Testament he'd left under his pillow.

Beresford conceded that the prisoner must be telling the truth. Miss Howell-Hopkins confirmed that he faithfully attended her morning prayer meetings, which regrettably she could not say of all her lodgers, and was most affronted by a question about comings and goings after her door was bolted at half-past nine. She rather scolded Sergeant Griffiths for daring to suggest there could be any night-time shenanigans at her establishment.

The other occupant of the attic room, Ahmed Masih, also verified Osawe's story. The sergeant tracked him down in the Coal Exchange and spoke to him between deals. Yes, he was certain that Osawe was there all night on Thursday because of 'his bloody coughing'. Ahmed asked if the police could keep Osawe at least till tomorrow, just so he could get another decent night's sleep.

To the surprise of Sergeant Griffiths, Beresford dealt with Osawe's release personally. There were no grounds to detain him further, but it rankled to lose their strongest lead. Mrs Cadwallader had been so adamant. True, all women were prone to hysteria, yet the housekeeper struck him as the steady type.

'Mistaken identity, Thomas,' he said. 'Can't blame the woman. She's had a hell of a shock and you do all look the same.'

'I understand,' replied Osawe. 'Sir, if I can, I would like to help you.'

'Help me?' smirked Beresford. 'How?'

'The man who died, he collected many African things? If I could see what he had, maybe I could tell you why someone would kill him.'

Within twenty minutes the sergeant arrived on foot, with Osawe, at the Captain's house. Beresford was already there, thanks to the privileges of rank and the use of a police motor car and driver. He rang the bell.

Mrs Cadwallader opened the door and nearly slammed it again.

'I hoped we'd still find you here, Mrs Cadwallader,' said the inspector. 'We need to see the Captain's study.'

'With – him?' she stammered, jerking her head towards Osawe.

'Yes, Thomas is helping us with our enquiries. May we?'

The housekeeper stepped back and Beresford led the way to the study. At his orders, nothing had been touched. The desk chair still rested on its side. Dried blood streaked across the floorboards and clotted beside the bookcase. Only the window in the bay had been closed.

Osawe scanned the room. A leopard skin lay over an armchair and two wooden masks bookended the mantelpiece. A carved tusk stretched along a bookshelf, next to a string of red coral beads. On the Captain's desk, in the open pages of a notebook, Osawe found a drawing of an Oba's head.

'Do you know where exactly he went in Africa, sir?' he asked.

Beresford sent the sergeant to ask Mrs Cadwallader for the Captain's medals. He returned with a small tin. Beresford rooted through the contents and read out the inscriptions: South Africa, 1901 and 1902. Nigeria, 1896 to 1897. Benin, 1897.

Osawe tapped the picture in the notebook. 'He stole this.'

'Watch your mouth, boy,' barked Beresford. 'British soldiers don't steal.'

Osawe considered asking if the inspector would prefer 'looted' or 'plundered' to describe how the Captain gained possession of the head. Instead, he chose to explain that the sketch showed the bronze sculpture of an Oba, a king of Benin. It was hundreds of years old.

'And someone would commit murder to get hold of it?'

'If there was only one picture of your Queen Victoria, and somebody had it, what would you do?' shrugged Osawe. He surveyed the bloodstains on the floor. 'Was it the sword that killed him?'

'Not by itself. According to Dr Reynolds, a brick wrapped in sacking caused the main injury. A blow to the head while he sat at the desk, then several cuts to the body.' Beresford glared at Osawe. 'Who told you that a sword was involved?'

'Cuts from a curved blade, this long?' he replied, holding his hands half-a-yard apart.

'Tell me how you know about a sword,' demanded the inspector.

Osawe motioned towards three hooks in the wall near the desk. They were ideally set to display an ada, a ceremonial sword belonging to the Oba. Perhaps the Captain had taken the sword down ready to fight the thief and dropped it when he was attacked.

He beamed at Beresford. 'I said I would help you, sir. Find the head and the sword, and you will find your killer.'

Mrs Cadwallader pushed the needle into a stitch, hooked the wool, pulled it back, caught the yarn again, and slipped it through the loop. She shouldn't have to crochet her own shawl, not on her wages. She'd have been buying herself fine Nottingham lace if she didn't have her brother to keep.

Richard slouched into the kitchen and dumped the coal scuttle by the fire. He could never hold down a job, not with his shakes and headaches and quick temper. His sister's war widow's pension hardly covered his quinine, let alone his beers at the Station Hotel. The landlord's wife would come and settle up with Mrs Cadwallader whenever the tab got too long.

'The police came again today,' she said. 'With the thief.'

'Handcuffed, I hope,' frowned Richard, wiping his hands.

'Didn't look to be.' She flipped over her crochet and began a new row. 'They asked to see the medals, find out where he'd served.'

'You could've told them that.'

'I thought it best not to let on.'

The first time Mrs Cadwallader had seen the Captain he was wearing his medals. She'd gone to Cardiff, with Richard, for the unveiling of the South African War Memorial. She'd warned Richard against it – might set off his bad dreams – but he'd fought the Boers and had more right to be there than most. He kept himself calm, until the speeches got underway and the mayor invited Captain Bevan to address the crowd. Bevan, bloody Bevan, with his damn medals and sodding empty words about glory and sacrifice and those left behind. The bastard. Richard had started shaking and sweating and Mrs Cadwallader had pulled him away just in time for him to throw up in the gutter of City Hall.

She'd returned the next week, by herself, to find Bill's name on the memorial. 'W. Cadwallader, Royal Welsh Fusiliers'. Her husband and her brother's best friend.

'I'm off to the Station,' said Richard. 'Don't sit up.'

'Ten o'clock and no later,' she called after him.

She wasn't going to bed with the door unbolted. Not with that man running free.

Beresford stood on Holton Road and scowled at his timepiece. If he didn't walk briskly, he'd be late, and he didn't know which irritated him more: keeping Councillor Jones waiting at the Lodge or trotting through Barry like a common constable. Inspector Lloyd, that bothersome upstart, had filched the last police driver and God only knew where all the town's cabs were. Beresford elected to cut through the side streets, in hope of giving the impression that he might be on covert police business.

He turned off the main road and took a right on Castleford Street, passing women scrubbing their front steps and children playing hopscotch on the pavement. From the moment he crossed Dock Street, he knew he was being followed. He veered sharp left at Station Road, then immediately right into the alley, and tucked behind an open gate. As his tracker rounded the corner, Beresford darted out, grabbed the man and slammed him against the wall.

'Bloody hell, Thomas?' He let Osawe go. 'What the blazes are you playing at?'

'I am sorry, sir, forgive me. I have to speak with you, in secret. It *was* me at the window – the housekeeper, she was right.'

'You damn liar,' spat Beresford.

'I did not kill the Captain – I didn't, I swear.'

Dragging Osawe to the station by his wrists was Beresford's preferred option, but if the younger man bolted, the inspector realised he'd never catch him. No matter. Although Beresford couldn't outrun Osawe, he could surely outwit him.

'All that praying, making out you're such a good boy, and all along leading us a merry dance. Shall we ask Revd Sutton what word the Bible uses for scoundrels like you? Hypocrite, isn't it?'

The ploy worked. Osawe fell to his knees. He pleaded for mercy – a man was dead and he must clear his conscience before man and God.

'Get up,' ordered Beresford. 'The truth. Now.'

Osawe pulled his New Testament out of his pocket. He took a newspaper cutting from inside the back cover and handed it to Beresford. At the college in Lagos, students read old copies of *The Times* to practise their English, and Osawe had come across this article about the unveiling of a war memorial in Cardiff. It quoted the rousing speech given by Captain Henry Cecil Bevan, veteran of campaigns in Benin and Nigeria as well as South Africa.

'My grandfather was custodian to the Oba. He died when

the British attacked Benin City,' said Osawe. 'Many precious things were taken from the palace. When I read that this man had been there, I thought he might have something. Not for me – for my grandfather.'

'How did you find him?' asked Beresford.

'A sailor from Dahomey, in the seamen's mission. He said he'd seen an Oba's head. I went to look for myself and that's when the housekeeper saw me.'

'You're lying. Your landlady said you're always at her prayer meetings. She's a liar too, is she?'

'Miss Howell-Hopkins gets confused. Like you said, we all look the same.' Osawe smiled a little. 'I can help you, sir.'

Beresford snorted and shook his head, but Osawe persisted. The killer knew that Osawe was supposed to go back to the Captain's house, so they made it look as if he murdered him. But they didn't know that Osawe had confessed to the police. He could lead the inspector to the Captain's killer.

'What's in it for you?' retorted Beresford.

'It is simple. The killer has the head and the sword,' said Osawe, 'and I want to take them home.'

The knock at the door brought Mrs Cadwallader from the kitchen to the net curtains in the parlour. She crossed to the foot of the stairs and hissed Richard's name. He appeared on the top landing. She glanced towards the door and put her finger to her lips.

The knock came again. Mrs Cadwallader pulled back the bolt and opened the door to Osawe.

'Good evening, sister,' he smiled. 'May I come in?'

'You're not welcome.'

'We need to talk business. Better inside the house than on the street, yes?'

She pointed to a chair beside the fireplace and closed the door behind him. Osawe sat down but Mrs Cadwallader remained standing and folded her arms.

'I have been very helpful to you,' he said. 'A man comes to the window of your master's house. He asks you to help him take something. Now the master is dead and the thief must have done it.'

'Exactly,' said Mrs Cadwallader.

'Except we both know he didn't.' Osawe sighed. 'I don't care who did. The Captain killed many people in war, now he is dead. All I want is the ada, the sword. You know where it is. Give it to me and I will go and say nothing. If you do not, I will tell the police everything.'

'Hasn't he learned a lot from the coppers?' Richard stood at the foot of the staircase. He held a long sword with a curved blade. 'They should make you Chief Constable in Bongo-Bongo-Land. You can lock up the monkeys for stealing your bananas.'

Osawe rose to his feet. 'Let me have the sword and no one will know anything, I swear.'

Richard sniggered. 'Nah, blackie, we're keeping this. It's our insurance.'

'Then I will tell Inspector Beresford.'

'He won't believe you over us,' interrupted Mrs Cadwallader. 'Not after you forced your way into the house and threatened a defenceless woman with that awful weapon.'

'Thank God I was here to get it off you,' added Richard. 'I

dread to think what you would've done to my poor sister otherwise.' He lifted the sword and advanced into the parlour. Osawe backed into the corner behind the chair. 'Best get the constable, Gwen. Quick as you can. Don't know what I might have to do in self-defence!'

Mrs Cadwallader pulled open the front door and discovered Chief Inspector Beresford, Sergeant Griffiths and two constables ready to rush in.

'Morgan, upstairs. Harrison, the kitchen and yard. Griffiths, see to Thomas.' Beresford held his hand out to Richard. 'Mr Roberts, I'll take the sword, if you'd be so kind.'

'We were fearing for our lives,' exclaimed Mrs Cadwallader. 'Thank heavens you were outside, the brute could've killed us both! First the Captain, now us. Is no one safe in their own home anymore?'

Harrison returned to the parlour with a small bundle. 'In the yard, sir, with the coal.'

Beresford unwrapped the sacking and held up a small black metal head.

Mrs Cadwallader gasped.

'What the hell is that?' spluttered Richard.

'It's the head – from the Captain's house, but we never had it – he took it!' cried Mrs Cadwallader.

Beresford directed Sergeant Griffiths to arrest her for the murder of Captain Henry Cecil Bevan.

'You've got it all wrong! He's right in front of you, the man at the window!'

'This way, Mrs Cadwallader,' said Beresford, opening the door.

'Let her go!' demanded Richard. 'She didn't do it.'

'All the evidence says she did,' replied Beresford. 'Know something different?'

Richard tightened his grip on the sword's handle. 'I did it. I killed the Captain.'

'Don't listen to him, he doesn't know what he's saying.'

'You'll hang, Gwen! It was me. She told me about the man who wanted to steal from Bevan and I knew it was my chance to get the bastard. He left us for dead at Colenso. Came back a hero. You know how long it took Bill to die? Two days.'

'Mr Roberts—'

'Keep away!' he shouted. 'I killed him, but I'll not swing for it!'

Harrison lunged for the sword. Richard thrust the blade at the constable and sent him crashing over a side table. Before Morgan could reach him, Richard scrambled for the kitchen. He wrenched open the door to the yard, dashed for the gate, and stumbled into the lane.

Standing before him was a man with a face like the Oba's head. Same colour, same nose, and brandishing a long pole with a knife lashed to the end.

'What the devil – you can't be – how the hell did you...?'

The man grinned.

Griffiths struck Richard with a truncheon across his back. Morgan knocked the sword from his hand. Harrison kicked his legs from under him. By the time the officers handcuffed Richard and hauled him to his feet, the man who couldn't have been Thomas was gone.

Ekiuwa Okomu sat in the courtyard of her second son's home, shaded by a mango tree. He did well to re-build it, though it was not as beautiful as she remembered. None of the houses in the city were, the palace least of all. The British had sent the Oba into exile and some said he would never come back. They laughed when Ekiuwa said she still hoped to see an Oba in Benin City.

But today Ekiuwa was laughing. Laid on the floor at her feet was a magnificent leopard skin. On it was a necklace of red coral beads, a curved ceremonial ada, and the bronze head of an Oba, with rings around the neck and a cone-shaped cap on the top. Beyond all these treasures stood her grandsons, Osawe and Obosa.

Ekiuwa made them tell her again how they did it – how Obosa convinced the housekeeper that the head was cursed, how Osawe coughed all night to annoy Ahmed. Who, she wondered, was the Dahomey man who discovered the head?

'No one. Revd Sutton led us to it.' Osawe smiled. The minister had spotted a talk advertised in the circuit magazine – 'My African Adventures' by Captain Henry Cecil Bevan – and asked if Osawe wished to attend. Osawe declined but, of course, Obosa went and followed the Captain home.

'I slept in the garden that night,' grumbled Obosa.

Obosa saw the head on the desk and the sword on the wall through the window. He spoke to the housekeeper in the park and returned to the Captain's house as planned.

'But he was already dead?'

Obosa nodded. 'I could smell blood. I didn't see his body. There was no ada so I took only the head.'

The brothers guessed that the housekeeper knew where the sword was. To retrieve it, they decided they must involve themselves in the investigation. Osawe handled Beresford, while Obosa hid the head in the coal shed and confronted Richard Roberts in the lane. 'As the Good Book says, "The fool shall be servant to the wise of heart,"' said Osawe, with a chuckle.

'Thanks to us, the police found the head and the sword and the killer,' said Obosa. Beresford, keen to assume the credit for single-handedly solving the case, encouraged Osawe to leave Cardiff as soon as possible. 'He let us take whatever we wanted from the dead man's house. Whatever Osawe wanted – he never knew about me.'

Ekiuwa laughed. 'Your grandfather can rest now,' she said.

'We are not finished yet,' replied Osawe.

'No,' agreed Obosa. 'We want to go to London.' The brothers grinned at their grandmother. 'We need to pay a little visit to the British Museum.'

Strike Weather

Louise Walsh

Strike weather, they called it. Later, people would say that the weather wasn't as good as the miners recollected in 1926. It only *seemed* hotter and brighter because it was the first whole summer the colliers had spent above ground in a great many years. But that day – the day of the Coegnant carnival – the sun blazed and burned in a bottomless blue sky.

Noah had cycled miles to Coegnant, travelling west. Had the carnival been closer, his wife and two young sons would have accompanied him.

He spent the day enjoying the tug of war and watching the fancy-dress competition. They had a few variety acts and a comedy football match.

The humidity buzzed and shimmered around the families of the striking miners. The lazy bluebottles seemed bigger and the sun was as sharp as a circular saw. Noah repeatedly wiped at his forehead with his neckerchief.

By the afternoon the puffy cream clouds, which in the morning seemed to have joyfully exploded in the growing heat of the day, like corn popped from kernels, grew dark and stale. In the south, thunderheads the colour of wild woodland mushrooms began to build and the clouds above Noah took on a choppy, serrated look. A warm wind picked up and caused random quarrels to break out in the treetops. Overheating, red-faced and hungry children fretted and cried.

Noah, like most miners, enjoyed the open air, where no pockets of poison gas pooled around your boots or above your head, but he was concerned to note the birds appeared to have stopped singing. Whether down a mine or out of doors, the sudden cessation of birdsong never signifies anything good.

Heading for home, his ancient bike caught a puncture. When the storm front caught him, he abandoned his bike and cut across the fields, using the trees for shelter.

Still miles from home, darkness fell and the rain fell too. When the deluge turned to a brief burst of hail, anger at his difficulties motivated Noah to keep going at a great pace. He inhaled deeply, smelling the electricity on the air and the sweet tang of wet grass.

He decided, in the end, the time had come to stop stubbornly pressing on and find temporary shelter. Just then, a fork of lightning lit up across the sky and illuminated the fields as an inky line-engraved landscape, cross-hatched by rain. In the middle of the field, he saw a great upright stone. Sheltering behind its leaning protection, Noah ran his hand over it in disbelief.

As lightning shot in blinding branches across the sky, Noah's eyes remained fixed on the stone. Slicking his hair from his forehead, he saw the tell-tale speckles of quartz. The wet crystals sparkled in response to every crackle of high voltage above. This was a bluestone – a standing bluestone – seemingly studded with needles of reflected light. The hairs on his arms stood on end and Noah gazed out into the field.

He counted between the thunderclaps, waiting for the lightning. It was six seconds before the lightning came again and he swallowed and blinked in hope as he waited for the next burst. Huddled against the stone, in torrential rain, he saw in the field the outline of a large stone circle or, rather, he saw shallows where the great stones had stood. Only someone with an eye for these things would have seen it at all.

Later, Noah would relate to his curious listeners that it wasn't as outlandish as it sounded. Noah was a man familiar with the rock and stone in the darkest and most dangerous of worlds. Miners knew one black rock from another, hundreds of feet underground in the Garw mine.

Noah had to get a higher vantage point. Ignoring the inherent danger of trees in storms, he scrambled up into the knobbly branches of a great sycamore on the field boundary. Wrapping his arms around the trunk, he pressed his feet into a tight fork and clung on, grateful for the small shelter the wide, waxy leaves provided.

The rain fell so heavily that pools of water were filling up all over the field and when the lightning came again, it confirmed what he already suspected. The individual puddles of water formed a pattern: a mighty circle.

The storm lit the field in just the right way to reveal its secrets. He saw more than a long-dismantled standing-stone circle. His mind brought forth Salisbury Plain's Stonehenge. Noah knew the Stonehenge stones were Welsh but, until that day, had never considered that the site might have been dismantled from his part of the world, before being moved and reassembled on what was now English land.

Noah had nothing on which to record his discovery, other than to try and measure out the circle in steps. He did his best to commit the site to memory, but the reality of his situation crept in. Shivering and soaked, he ordered himself to find his way home and then determined that, at the first opportunity, he would return to prove his hypothesis.

The moon was high when Noah arrived home, feverish and excited, rambling incoherently about Stonehenge and stone circles. His wife, Ellen, knew at once that he was seriously ill. She stripped him of his clothes, arranged a bath and helped him to bed, where he remained delirious, on and off, for the best part of three days.

He alternated between shaking with cold and sweating under a raging temperature. Twice Ellen felt her heart turn to stone in fear her husband had stopped breathing. For days, Noah was a deathly, greasy sallow-grey.

Noah slowly recovered, but it took a full month before he could strike out once again to find the field, with an extra jumper tied to his waist in case he caught cold.

The strikes continued and it was at the Garw valley communal canteen, rather than a formal miners' strike meeting, where Noah decided to share the idea he'd formed during convalescence.

Not wanting to feel like charity cases, the miners had spruced up their soup kitchens in mimicry of fine dining establishments. They had gramophone records playing, tablecloths and jars of flowers in front of every third place-setting. At the end of this particular meal, of a pea soup so thick you could slice it, Noah lifted the needle, interrupted Chopin's 'Impromtu' and addressed the room.

He told them that he had an idea. He didn't know how many of the assembled knew it, but Stonehenge was Welsh. He said some attributed the stones getting as far as Stonehenge to natural phenomena. But many believed the stones had been transported by men using wooden sledges and rollers. He told them that he believed this second account. Stonehenge was originally *their* monument. Not the Sarsen stones, but the great ring of bluestones. That was *our* Stonehenge. This was a Welsh monument and a Welsh feat of engineering and logistics. He said *they* – the English – had long claimed it as the most famous historical site in all of England. The listeners nodded, encouraging Noah. He said that the miners displayed their solidarity and strength in many ways – their kitchens, their carnivals, their fundraising – but he called on them to do something even more extraordinary.

Noah got to the point. They should come together, steal Stonehenge, bring it back to Wales and reassemble it where it had originally stood.

They didn't take him seriously at first, but Noah explained that he just had to locate the original site once more and, when he did, he would speak to them all again. He said it could be done and would make them infamous. The entire world would talk of the south Wales miners. The operation would demonstrate that when workers unite in common cause anything is possible.

It took the miners a week to agree, and they did so simply because the audacious idea took their minds off their troubles even more than the fancy dress, jazz bands and local carnivals did. Some of them cautioned it was probably treason to destroy a national monument, but the idea had taken hold. The anger of the strike had fuelled it.

'They've stripped enough of *our* rocks and minerals. I say we take some of them back,' shouted one soup-kitchen diner. 'I say we're entitled.'

'Let's treat them the way they've treated us – by not giving a damn about *their* history and heritage. Let's see how they like it,' shouted another.

At mealtimes, they amused themselves by ruminating on the details. Since the army had been training on Salisbury Plain since 1898, they decided that, if they did go through with it, they should dress as soldiers. Many of the older men still had at least part of their First World War uniforms.

Transport gave them a headache. None of them had any money, let alone the petrol money for ten or more trucks, even if they could scout out farm vehicles on loan. By this time, the women were scouring the countryside for anything they could find to fill their families' stomachs, such as nettles and berries. Men fished and poached rabbits. But, as resourceful as they were, nobody had discovered a way to forage for petrol – other than to siphon it out of someone else's vehicle by sucking it up a tube.

Plaid Cymru, founded the year before, quietly promised them the use of one truck and a full tank of fuel – though nobody could figure out how they came to know about the secret Stonehenge plan. The miners decided on a test mission – accepting the offer of the truck. A small party would recover one stone to Wales. Then, if it all went well, they would return for another and another, storing them somewhere until Noah found the original home of Stonehenge. They laughed together as they speculated how long it might take the English to notice the slowest robbery of pre-history in history.

The miners had to get around the fact that the Stonehenge site had been intricately recorded by archaeologists on numerous occasions over the years, but then one of the youngsters had a bright idea. The trick was not to initially remove any of the stones out of the ground because this would leave a tell-tale sign – as obvious as a missing tooth in an otherwise perfect mouth. He suggested that they take one of the lintels. The lintels were smaller and, practically, it was far easier to pull something down than to pick something up. Gravity would do the hard work for them. Consulting the plan in their library book on Stonehenge, they settled on the smallest lintel sitting atop stones six and seven of the outer circle.

Ten of them left on the first full moon after the summer solstice, eight of them in the back of the flatbed truck, two in the front, dressed in the uniforms of the Welsh Regiment.

One of the men had said he'd heard that the Beachley to Aust ferry was operating again and this would shave hours off their journey.

When they got to the Beachley ferry, they realised that they had underestimated several things: firstly, their collective weight made it dangerous; secondly, none of them knew how to operate a ferry; and thirdly, the non-swimmers panicked at the high tide.

Without a word, they got back in the truck, taking a 60-mile detour via Gloucester. With so much time wasted, they didn't get to Stonehenge until the early hours of the morning.

When they got close to Stonehenge, they fell silent. Cold, tired and watchful, it felt as though they were alone in the world as the wind tumbled over the vast pre-dawn plains, empty save for the crows and their guttural glottal-stop cries.

Noah watched as his friends took off their caps in respect and drifted silently, in awe, gazing up at the enormous megaliths.

He could almost feel the weight of those great stones rooted reassuringly to the ground. It seemed to him that this monument, without doubt, represented a community in rock. He wondered what *his* community would look like in the same medium and concluded they too would form a defensive, protective circle. They too would have their arms around each others' shoulders, in the same way the lintels linked the ring of stones together.

'Are we going to see this through?' he asked the group.

Noah convinced himself and the others that the builders of Stonehenge – their forefathers – would understand. From the back of the truck, reversed into position, the miners hurled the ropes with grappling hooks over the 'six and seven' lintel. The endeavour was akin to reeling in a great stone sea creature. The stone finally plopped right onto the back of the truck, putting a dent in the floor and just missing Noah.

'No going back now,' Noah said.

They would never get it back up onto the vertical stones. With the flourish of a magician about to make something vanish, Noah covered the lintel with three Welsh wool blankets.

They arrived back at the village to find that, as dawn broke, their petrol ran out. They jumped from the truck, watching as the cool red and grey clouds of dawn reflected in every village window as though the same fire burned in every home. The priority was to hide the lintel. One of the miners lived in the next street and so the lintel found itself temporarily stored in his garden, camouflaged by rotting wooden doors and his wife's plant pots. Plaid were contacted to collect the truck.

For months, the Garw miners scoured the papers. They waited for a knock at the door. Nothing appeared in print. No cars parked up. No police officers called. No questions were asked.

They never did go back for any more stones. Things got tougher and, in the end, the strike was over. They had to go back to work, and for longer hours and less money. But they laughed amongst themselves about the theft of the stone. They enjoyed the secret. The lintel stone itself regularly moved hiding places over the years until the miners found a place to hide it for good.

As the years dragged on, old Noah was viewed by younger generations as a lost and obsessive dreamer, spending every minute of his spare time trudging the countryside in search of his vanished stone circle. His steps became slower. He began to walk with a stick. Names and places faded from his recollections, but the field of post holes was always lightning bright.

His sons rolled their eyes, talked of nostalgia being an escape.

'I gave them something bigger to dream about than carnivals,' Noah said, shaking his white head. 'And, before I go, I want to show them I was right.'

The old man maintained to the end that archaeologists would find the empty holes where the bluestones once stood in Wales.

When he passed, nobody commented on the unconventional thickness of his headstone in the cemetery. The metal plate fixed to it bears simple, raised lettering:

In loving memory – Noah Owen, 1896–1955 and his wife, Ellen Rose Owen, 1902–1964. What you leave behind is not what is engraved in stone monuments, but what is woven into the lives of others (Pericles).

Time and weather have given the metal letters a white bloom around them – a chemical reaction to the elements.

The effect – strangely – is that of a ransom note.

The Pigs in the Middle

Kittie Belltree

'Owen! Wake the fuck up! It's the police! For Chrissakes, Owen. The feckin' police!'

It was like waking up on *Megaphobia* – tossed from warm sleep-flush to cold, hard fear in a microsecond, my guts stuck on the up-chuck, my head imploding on impact.

Eden was on top of me, shaking me furiously. 'There's a man from Housing with them. They know, O! They know about the fucking grow!'

I flung off the duvet, the slap of morning air sending further vomit-inducing shock waves through my flesh and bones. Then there was a rush of raised voices in the hallway, the fizzle of white noise and me stumbling about in my underpants like a fart in a jam jar while Eden sat on the bed rocking backwards and forwards, face in hands, sobbing.

I closed my arms around her. 'Look, I'll just say it was me, all right. That you knew nothing about it.'

'Don't be *twp*, O. They'll never buy that. The whole bloody street can smell it. Besides,' she squeezed my hand, 'we're in this together.'

My thumbs traced the knots where rheumatoid arthritis had gotten to her finger joints. 'But … it's your place. You could lose the flat. Because of me.'

'It's not because of you, you moron. We're in this together. We said so from the start.'

'Sir. If you wouldn't mind...' It was one of the *dic pwdins* outside in the hall.

We gawped at each other, hands over mouths, stranded in a state of post-detonation Whisky Tango Foxtrot. Eden wiped away a string of snot with the sleeve of her dressing gown. Then there was an exaggerated cough from outside. So, I gulped and stepped into the hallway to face the music and dance.

The two coppers looked at me like a shit stain smeared on their new size tens. I was wearing Y-fronts and my second-best grin. The police deserve no better.

'Look, my wife's disabled, all right. Just let us get dressed and get her sorted will you?'

'Miss Green, I really must speak with you.' It was a short-arse in a Bri-Nylon suit, who I assumed must be from Housing. He elbowed past me and cracked a knuckle against the bedroom door. 'Miss Green? I believe you may be acting in breach of your tenancy agreement. This is PC...'

Yeah, that's right, I thought. You friggin' cowards. Go for the woman, the disabled woman. I was feeling pretty pissed off as well as freaked as fuck.

'Look, just give us a bloody minute to get dressed.' I manoeuvred my naked torso past Housing and slammed the bedroom door.

Eden was slumped on the floor like a crumpled dish-rag, clutching a pillow to her chest. Her dressing gown had fallen loose so's I could see her knees, the joints taught and swollen.

I knelt beside her. 'Ede? You're burning up and shaking like shit. Are you okay?'

'Of course I'm not okay. We've been bloody busted for fuck's sake.'

'I mean are *you* okay? You're not having a flare or something?'

'I dunno. Yeah. Maybe,' she blubbed. 'Oh God, Owen. What are we gonna do? What the hell are we gonna do?'

I plucked a T-shirt and jeans from the pile on the floor. 'Look, I don't want you getting ill over this. I'll just give it to them straight, like. Tell 'em the truth. Tell 'em it was my idea and I did it cos of your arthritis. I did it cos there's nothing the fuck wrong with it. I just planted a few seeds. A few fucking seeds. It's them that's—'

I was ranting and the spooks in the hall could hear me for sure, so Eden quite rightly told me to shut the fuck up.

'Okay, but I'm getting your chair. You need your chair.'

'Don't you tell me what I need, you—'

'Together,' I interjected. 'Now's no time for a bloody barney about shit and hassle.'

Eden's wheelchair was all that stood between the plods and the door to the cupboard where our plants sat in pots, awaiting their fate, like murderers pending the electric chair. Just a few more days. A few more fucking days. Fuck. Fuck. Fuck.

First, she'd been dead against the idea. Not just for the obvious reasons like getting caught, but, because the way Ede saw it, the only thing I'd ever managed to grow was mustard and cress on soggy blobs of cotton wool back in primary school. But it didn't look too difficult, I'd pointed out as we'd argued the toss in one of our all-nighters. And with the lights I'd unearthed at the car boot, we were halfway there. Just order some seeds online and get growing. The upshot of it was, by the time I'd heard the clink of the milkman picking up the empties, she'd come round and we'd decided to have a crack at a grow. I was buzzing afterwards. I mean, you couldn't tie me down I was that bloody excited. The thought of self-sufficiency was like the pot of gold at the end of the rainbow.

The seeds sat soaking in a jar of spring water before we put them into pots, which initially we just kept on the windowsill. The spring water was Eden's idea. She thinks the stuff that comes out the taps is full of toxic waste and they're trying to poison us, and by the way it tastes these days, I'm starting to think she might be onto something. A couple of days later, the first tiny shoot popped up. I was gobsmacked. Like seeing something for the first time. That secret spike of green that – until then, until I showed Eden – no one else had ever seen.

Seeing two teeny leaves uncurl from each shoot, separate then fan out into four, I was euphoric, bristling with an unprecedented verve and vitality. Most of my life I'd been bumbling about not thinking any further than a week's wages and what to do with them at the weekend. But after popping the beans, my thinks were all about budding, bursting forth, branching out. More than that. I had a mission. A purpose. A duty. It was like the only way was up.

They grew fast. Really fast. Within a couple or three weeks they were nigh on a foot, so we stashed the Hoover in the kitchen, set up the light in the hall cupboard and settled the plants into their new home. Seeing them flourish filled us both with the joys of Mother Nature and those couple of months passed in a blur of sex and drugs and rock and roll. Well, not really like, cos we had to eke out what little smoke we did have, meaning we didn't exactly blow our minds. And there wasn't any rock and roll either because Eden prefers listening to the blues, so there was just lots of sex, really. Pretty soon we had six four-footers and some fruity little buds starting to form.

Another thing we'd begun to notice, alongside the increase in size, was the smell. At first, we just put it to the back of our minds. You could write down what I know about women on a Rizla and still have room for a phone number. And learning about living with a wheelchair user was like landing on Mars. We'd had our altercations. But since the grow, things had been going great between us. It felt like nothing could bring us down. Looking back, we were just kidding ourselves when we'd agreed we'd just light some joss sticks for any unexpected visitors.

It was a week or three later when it became clear that whiffs of weed were wafting out from under our front door and into the lobby area shared with three other flats. I'd been fumbling for keys after a night on the lash when my nose detected that delectably distinct aroma. We panicked at first, but after some sniffing experiments we came to the conclusion that you could only *really* smell it if you were stood on our doormat, and managed to convince ourselves that nobody else would really notice. To be on the safe side, I stuffed a towel under the cupboard door, spritzed some air freshener about the place and just carried on as if nothing were happening.

Nothing did happen. I was convinced we were home and dry and looking at a bumper crop for Crimbo. My head was fizzing with ideas for festival edibles – Rum and Cannabis Butter on my Christmas pud perhaps, a Ganjabread House, or Canna-Chocolate Brownies? A few weeks later, Eden had taken the car to her mam's so I was catching the bus home. I was about to get off when the driver asked did I live in Allt y Bryn.

'Reckon someone's growing in your block, butt. *Mŵg drŵg.* You can smell it all over. Honking, it is, mun.'

Pins and needles danced across my forehead. Then a hammer thwacked me in the chest. It kept on pounding the wind out of me. All the way back to the flat. Inside, the place felt dense and strange, like someone had left the gas on. I sat in the kitchen, staring at the ceiling, rehearsing how I'd break it to Eden and what the fuck were we gonna do? Bits of dust clung to the Artex in a thin, grey haze like mist rolling over the sea. We'd nattered a bit about re-decorating in the new year. Only Ede'd fancied Purple Passion while I'd wanted Woodland Sage. But what did any of that matter now? If the Housing found out, we might not have a roof, let alone four walls to fight over.

But when I broke it to her, Eden was adamant that we were in this together. We did consider chopping the plants, but agreed we were so nearly there. Surely, our luck would hold. So next morning, I nipped to Spar, bought a load of masking tape and a bottle of Zoflora, sealed up the cupboard with layers of tape, wedged a blanket against the front door and set up a fan heater on cold to blow the smell backwards into the flat. At nights, I took to sneaking out and sprinkling

Zoflora around the lobby like holy water to mask the aroma. It reeked like my nan's outside loo and I was sure it would do the trick.

It didn't. But we were barely three weeks away from harvest. Some inexplicable madness had taken over and we absolutely just could not believe that our luck would not hold. We rigged up a multi-socket extension lead in the hall, loaded it with Glade plug-ins and determined to keep going. A fortnight passed and I was in Spar stocking up on air fresheners when the girl on the till asked, 'Who's growing killer skunk in your block then? Fuckin' stinks, it does. You can smell it in Becky's...'

'Eh?'

'Fuckin' hell! Can't you smell it? First it was like, only when you turned the tap on. But now it's all the time. Humming, it is.'

I coughed some excuse about having a cold and shot out like shit through a goose. Becky's flat was directly above ours. But we were barely a fortnight from cropping. We'd already trimmed the smallest plant. The other five were looking lush. Just a few more days. A few more days...

Another week and we'd chopped our second biggest plant and hung it up to dry in my wardrobe alongside the first. We were chuffed to beans because, by all counts, we were looking at a possible seven-, maybe eight-ounce yield on our first grow. By the middle of next week, we'd be in the clear.

'We have reason to believe you have been cultivating cannabis and are in breach of your tenancy agreement. Miss Green? Is there any cannabis on these premises?'

I nudged the *lembo* from Housing aside and lifted the catch on the cupboard door.

The coppers' faces lit up like Blackpool illuminations.

I almost felt proud. Fuck it, I did feel proud as they clocked my four girls: lofty, luscious, loaded with buds. Then the fuzz's radios buzzed like Black and Deckers crossed with bluebottles and there was all this talking, and noises outside: a car. A van. And a greasy-looking sergeant come to have a chinwag with his porky pals.

The Housing dolt was like a dog with two dicks, clicking the end of his biro with his thumb and barking on at Eden about the terms of her tenancy.

'Look, just leave it with the Spanish Inquisition, will you?' I said. 'Can't you see you're upsetting her? She's still in her dressing gown for fuck's sake.'

The sergeant spoke. 'Normally, we would just issue you with a notice to appear at the station. But under the circumstances—'

'What circumstances? We've done nothing wrong.'

'You have been found to be in possession of a Class B drug contrary to section 6.2 of the Misuse of Drugs Act 1971,' one of the coppers piped up, brown nose and smug grin smudged over his face.

'As I said, what with you acting aggressively towards Mister Goronwy-Jenkins here and ... er ... your wife's ... um ... condition, we'll need to interview you straight away.' The sarge turned to one of his bobs. 'Get an ambulance.'

'What do you need an effing ambulance for? No one's been hurt.'

'It's for your wife, sir. As Mister Goronwy-Jenkins says, she is the tenant. Isn't that right?'

'Yeah, but she doesn't need a bloody ambulance.'

'Calm down, sir. We just want to make sure that she gets to the station safely. A police vehicle isn't the best place for someone in her condition.'

'Stop talking about my wife like she isn't here, you ignorant prick. If she's going anywhere, she's going with me, all right?'

'O, just leave it. Just do what he wants, okay.'

Ede looked white as a fish's belly. Her arthritis had gotten bad again after weeks of hardly needing the chair and she'd been having more sleepless nights. I just wanted this shitshow to be over for her. For us both. So I shrugged my shoulders and shut up.

After the sarge okayed me helping Ede get dressed, she explained how she'd gotten up early and was making a brew when she'd heard the door. The knocking went on and on and, in a sleep-deprived discombobulation, she'd just opened it. Next thing, the rozzers were in the flat and it was game over.

Outside our block a gaggle of grannies had gathered, shaking heads and tutting, '*Diw, Diw.*' Some other plods appeared out of nowhere, as they do, and made busy loading my plants into the back of the van. I politely pointed out to the paramedic that I could manage Eden's chair fine, thanks. But the cocky git said I'd got to go with the Five-Os.

To piss them off, once I'd been clocked in at the cop shop, I asked for a copy of the Bible. They had to make a special trip to WH Smith's, but I was well wound up – pacing the cell like a bull in a cage. So, when they offered me a solicitor, I refused cos I just wanted to get things over. It wouldn't be any use trying to deny the grow. I was planning I'd just admit it, hoping for a caution, a fine. Surely, I wouldn't get time? Not for four plants and a first offence? I told myself I'd keep it squeaky, bite my tongue if necessary. But the longer they kept me waiting, the harder it was not to worry, especially about Eden.

It was five hours before the cell door clunked open and I was ushered down a corridor into a windowless room smelling of armpits, where a second badge was already sat behind a table, waiting. He started the spiel about recording, evidence, and was I sure I didn't want a brief and whatnot. A spark of recognition crackled against the backs of my eye sockets. I've been collared a couple of times. Once for handling stolen goods when I was hobbling for a dodgy removals firm. Breach of the peace. A few speeders. A drunk and disorderly... I felt sure I'd crossed paths with this oink before.

'Your plants are some of the best-looking I've ever seen, Mister Edwards and, believe me, I've seen a lot. How long have you been growing?' It was the first flat-foot's turn to try and make me shit bricks.

'No comment.'

'Have you ever given any cannabis to any friends?'

'Nope.'

'So, you've never shared a spliff with a mate?'

'Never.'

'Does Miss Green smoke?'

'No comment.'

'Has Miss Green ever watered your plants for you?'

'Look, I'm not answering any questions until you tell me what's happened to Eden, all right?'

The pork chops swapped smirks. 'Miss Green has signed a full confession stating that you masterminded the operation and that she knew nothing about it,' chirped blue number two.

'Masterminded? That's clean off! It was just a few seeds, fuck's sake. You don't have to be a bloody mastermind to do that, you...' I swallowed back a string of expletives.

'Nonetheless, we have Miss Green's signed confession that you were growing cannabis with intent to supply,' said One.

'Bullshit. Eden would never 'fess anyone up.'

Two swivelled some papers on the table then jabbed a finger where, to my fucking horror, Eden's signature jumped out at me.

I looked from one ugly mug to the other. 'That's bollocks. All right, I've admitted it. I was growing. But it was just a bit of green for my missus. She's got rheumatoid arthritis and I done what I done cos she's in pain. Now, I want to know if she's all right.'

'So, are you denying the fact that you were caught producing cannabis for profit?'

'Look. It's like I told you. I was growing to help my wife. Any decent person would've done the same. It's got nothing to do with fucking money.'

'Then why did our officers find scales at the premises?' said the first streaky rasher.

'Oh, for fuck's ... because my missus likes baking cakes.'

'These weren't kitchen scales, Mister Edwards. These were specifically for the purpose of weighing cannabis.'

'Oh those. I got them to check the weight of the stuff I was having to buy from dealers. There's some unscrupulous types about, you know. Now, tell me what's happened to Eden.'

'Miss Green has been released without charge after making a full confession. We may still charge her at a later date, pending further enquiries,' said gumshoe two. 'You may as well tell us your side of the story because we have here her full confession and as soon as you start to cooperate, well, the easier it will be for everyone, including Miss Green.'

'I've already given you my side of the story. I got the gear at a car boot and, like I says, I did it to help my wife, all right?'

'We know everything,' said Two. 'Miss Green has told us all about how much and who you've been supplying, so you might as well do us all a favour by coming clean. Believe me, if you do, it will be better for you ... both ... in the long run.'

'Suck my balls.' I knew I should've held back, but this pair parleyed like they'd pinched Ronnie Biggs for the Great Train Robbery.

'Interview suspended at fifteen forty-two hours...' The coppers got up, chairs grating against the floor, and left.

I heard the metallic bite of key catching against lock.

What was this bunk about intent to supply? Surely Ede would never bubble? The streaky rashers kept me swinging for nearly three hours before they returned with a vending cup of lukewarm brown liquid, started the twin decks and tried it on from another angle.

'How long have you been out of work?' asked One.

'I'm not out of work. I'm a full-time carer for my wife.'

'Must be a bit tight for you both, money-wise?'

'We're doing okay, thanks.'

'Yes, but what about those little luxuries that women like? It must be hard with Miss Green's condition,' said Two.

'Yes, it is. So, if you don't mind, I'd like to get back to her. If you're gonna charge me, just get the fuck on with it.'

Two cleared his throat. 'Owen James Edwards. You are charged with production of cannabis with intent to supply contrary to section—'

'Intent to supply! Why don't you catch some real criminals, you effing wasters?'

'We have your wife's full confession... If you want to help her, it would be best if you just admitted the offence,' quipped the first fed.

'Look, I've held up my hands. I've said I was growing, all right? But that's it. If you want to try and pin anything else on me, then I want a brief. End of.'

'But as you've already said, the duty solicitor could be another two, three, four, I don't know, five, maybe six hours. Are you sure you want to wait that long?'

'Of course not, you idiot. I planted some seeds for my missus. Anyone with a shred of compassion would've done the same. Now am I free to go or what?'

'So, you admit that you were producing with intent to supply?'

'I didn't say that.'

'You just said you were going to supply Miss Green.'

'Go piss up a rope.'

I was photographed, fingerprinted and told I'd have to front the Maggie's down the line. Ede was sitting in the dark when

I finally got back to the flat. It turned out that, after a brief chat, the bacon had just brought her home. She hadn't been charged. But, because the scuffers had found the roots and stems of two cut plants still in their pots, the stuff drying in my wardrobe and a bag of trim, they'd decided to do me for production, not cultivation. The brief'd said it was all about seizing the proceeds of criminal lifestyles. I told him my criminal lifestyle amounted to sharing a spliff on the sofa, and he'd agreed, reckoning they'd likely drop it and just charge me with the cultivation.

I got us together some tea and toast while Ede scanned the papers from the gendarmes. 'But they're charging you with intent to supply. They can't do that, can they?' she blinked.

'The dibbles told me you'd 'fessed, Ede. They showed me your signed confession.'

'They what?' She tried to get up but slumped back into the sofa, her face a contortion of pain. 'Owen. I never did. I don't know what they're talking about.'

If there was ever a time I could've done with a J, it was now. 'Ede, they showed me your signature. Your full confession. That you'd told 'em I'd been dealing.'

'But I didn't say that. I swear. I'm telling you.'

I was on my feet, pacing the sitting room. 'Ede. You're not well, Okay? I know what they're like, the jumped-up little shits. Did they get heavy with you?'

'No, O. I didn't say anything, all right?'

'Well, you must have said something ... in your statement, like? Didn't they read it back to you first? It's all right Ede, I'm not blaming you or anything.'

Eden narrowed her eyes. 'I'm not that bloody stupid. They tried getting me to agree it was all your idea and that I knew nothing about it, but I just said "No comment, no comment," whatever they asked, all right?'

My problem was I had zero respect for them, meaning the bacon butties always wound me the fuck up. I hadn't realised Ede could be such a cool customer, what with her being so hot-headed with me so much of the time.

'Didn't they go through your bag and get you to sign for stuff in your pockets and that?'

'No, I had nothing on me, not even my purse or my meds. Only, when I got out of the ambulance, the paramedics asked me to sign something, but that was before I spoke to the police.'

'The lying, cheating, cunting bastards!' I kicked the coffee table, sloshing tea all over the plods' paperwork. 'They waved this feckin' piece of paper at me. Showed me your signature. Told me it was your full confession. The little shysters.'

'Tell me you didn't swear?' Eden's mouth quivered like a condemned building about to topple.

'So what if I effin' swore at 'em? They had it coming, the crooked bar-stewards.' I was tamping. 'It was cos they wouldn't tell me about you. My swede was cooked and I just wasn't thinking cos I was so worried about you.'

'Don't you try and pin your filthy gob on me.'

I was too knackered for any of our usual chopsing. 'Look hun, I'm sorry. It's just we haven't even got a single fucking joint to take the edge off this shit. Why don't I run you a bath or something?'

She mumbled something about washing the day off and I

thought it wise to slosh in a bit of extra Radox. While Eden immersed herself in bubbles, I was blobbed on the sofa, wallowing in a different kind of stew, when I had a brainwave. I leaped up, grabbed the cushions and chucked them on the floor in front of the telly. There was a thick layer of fluffy brown grit with two twenty-pence coins, a couple of paperclips, one of Eden's silver moon earrings, some sweet wrappers and stuff embedded into it like flies in a web. I got down on my knees to sift through it. On close inspection, I discovered a few flakes of green clinging to bits of matted hair and gunk, and began pulling them apart, picking out the specks with my fingernails. Pretty soon, I'd scraped together enough for a wimpish-looking one-skinner.

I brought it triumphantly to Ede and we tried to draw as much out of the limp little rollie as we could: Ede, wringing-wet and thanking God; me, sat on the pan, holding the end with a pair of tweezers so's to pull every last drag out of the thing.

The waiting was the worst part.

Because Eden hadn't been done, the Housing sent a warning but weren't going to chuck her out. It was a huge relief. My biggest worry really. As long as Eden wasn't going to lose her home. But I still had to wait nearly nine months before it all went to court.

The trial was a pantomime. I was determined to hang my balls out in the dock. I had nothing to hide after all. But Ede and my brief persuaded me that banging on about Big Pharma and my God-given rights to plant seeds would only wind the

Madge up. The filth had dropped the production but were sticking with the intent-to-supply charge, although the probation'd done a tidy job explaining about me being a carer and Eden's condition and all that. The brief argued I'd just took a wrong turn. An all-round good guy who'd seen the error of his ways and was determined to stay out of trouble. Figuring that a few minutes eating humble pie was better than a few months' porridge, I went guilty, said I'd regretted the whole thing, hardly smoked meself and only grew for Ede because we couldn't afford to buy from dealers.

I got away with a fine and 120 hours community service: 200 quid, plus 80 costs and a 120-pound victim surcharge.

'Who's the bloody victim?' I called out.

The Madge ordered me out of the courtroom before she could reconsider. The brief rolled his eyes and Eden shot me a look like she'd slit my throat.

Afterwards, she gabbed on about putting it past us and just getting on with our lives. But for me, it was never over. I'd done this to help her RA. Yes, I'd ended up making the whole situation worse. But that was, like, normal for me. No one was hurt. I'd got a slapped wrist and we'd had some dust-ups, what with waiting it out and Eden's RA flaring up and her getting sick with the side effects from all the pharmaceuticals she was having to take.

Nah, I wasn't giving up. I was determined I'd get her the very best medicine. It was the law that was wrong. Not me. Not her. We weren't criminals.

We drove home in silence, Eden flicking through her phone, me pretending I was concentrating on the road. Really,

I was weighing up the options in my head. What's that old chestnut about falling off a horse? It was time for plan B. A guerrilla grow. I'd already scouted a possible site near a lay-by off the A487.

With Both Eyes Closed

Tracey Rhys

1 October

My love is jogging, bare-backed and sun-kissed. I've never seen him looking such an Adonis, not even in those early days in Greece when a fortnight was forever and we couldn't bear to come home. Here we are though. He's on his way to speak to the man who's been sent to check the water levels in the reservoir. I watch as they shake hands. I know what Isaac will be saying, although their voices won't travel. Next, he's pointing towards our little brick house on the roadside above, bringing him in for a drink.

The floor inside our kitchen is red. I remember the first time we viewed the place; we yanked the carpet back from the corner, forcing the grips, and underneath were the original quarry tiles, worn and cool, dirty as any stone. We scrubbed and scrubbed that first week. It was back-breaking stuff, but worth it for how they look today. I love them in this sun, and what sun it is! It's all we've had for months, not a drop of rain.

Isaac and the man from the Water Board are in the room now. They're drinking mugs of tan-coloured tea, even though the weather's too warm for it. I'm back to my paints, wiping my hands on Isaac's old shirt that I wear as an overall, brush in hand.

'October and still 30 degrees,' Isaac is saying. 'No one expected this. It's killing us, isn't it?'

The visitor is telling us that most reservoirs to the east have dried up completely. We shake our heads in sympathy. I am suddenly aware of the water sprinkler running in the back garden. In the middle of a hosepipe ban. In the middle of the worst drought in decades. It's suddenly loud, like rain falling on a caravan.

'Do your best to keep track of the water level,' says the man with our mug, jerking his thumb towards the window where the reservoir used to fill the pane.

Isaac shrugs. 'I don't work for the Water Board, mate. We just live in the house.'

'We could wander down?' I offer, as convivial as you like, though I don't intend to.

'That'd be great. Just let us know if it shrinks lower over the next 48 hours. What do you do out here then?'

Isaac nods vaguely towards the other room, where canvases are laid out and stacked in various stages of doing and undoing.

'Artists, are you?' the man asks, surprised.

He looks at me for a moment, then up at a print on the wall. Neither of us did that one but we don't tell him.

'Very nice,' the man says. 'I'm a dabbler myself. Portraits, mostly. Paintings of the grandkids and that. Hey, we've got an art society in town! Perhaps you could come down and give us a demonstration?'

We nearly fall over each other trying to refuse.

'There's a fee, obviously.'

Isaac shakes his head.

'Too big for us are you?' the man booms, laughing. 'Hang on! I expect I'm embarrassing myself by here! You're famous artists, aren't you?'

'Oh my goodness, no!'

'Look at her! She's gone all shades of red. That's it, isn't it?'

He hands the mug to me, makes for the door. 'I've got your number! You're incognito.' He is tapping his nose and chuckling. 'Listen, there's a mountain fire about fifteen miles to the east. Smell it? Burning since yesterday. The road is closed.'

'Is it clear up to Llangynnar?' Isaac enquires, just to fill the air with this normality: the roads, the heat.

'Well, that's the way I'm going.' The man shrugs, then he taps the roof of his van with his keys, gets in and goes. I stand there watching the car drop over the hill, the mug still in my hand, the sprinkler hissing away just behind me and the reservoir down below, half-dry.

In the evening, Isaac and I sit in a cool bath together with big bubble-bath beards. The mobile rings at nine and it is Gino telling us to put on the TV.

'Hey listen, I don't know whether you've seen but they're evacuating whole villages down west. The police might come around to speak to you. Prepare your stories.'

'Shit!' I blurt, getting out of the bath.

'Gino,' Isaac says calmly, 'nothing will go wrong here. If anything can put out a fire, it's a reservoir. There'll be no police, don't worry, my friend.'

The phone slips from his wet hands, skitters across the tiles.

By the time he gets out of the tub and puts it to his ear, Gino's gone.

'Do you think it'll be all right?' I say. We're both standing on the wet floor.

'God, yes,' he says. 'Look, hardly anyone knows we're even here. And even if the police do come, they won't come inside. But we should work fast now. We've work to do. I'm going to paint tonight.' He kisses my nose.

Isaac's speciality is the work of William Mackie. He enjoys the sex and drama of Mackie's work: the domestic noir. Men in suits, women half-undressed perched at their dressing-table mirrors; the moments before things get steamy, that's what he loves. I liked them more when I was younger, when I wanted to be the girl being ravished against a wall. Now they bother me, those supine brunettes.

'I've modelled her on you!' he likes to tease when he's sculpted a particularly pert breast sweeping out from a blouse.

'You did not!' I laugh. Not in my current incarnation anyway.

Isaac can churn them out though: *with both eyes closed* is his favourite boast.

Gino takes Isaac's Mackie pictures and sends them out into the world as the real thing, to the auction houses of Italy, London and the States, where the artist is most in demand. Not the finished paintings of course – no, they're all accounted for – but as the oil sketches that flooded the market in the eighties. And so we get away with it, little by little.

'Not a fortune but a living,' Isaac likes to say.

And it is. It's a life. A nice life.

4 October
The electric was off for two days this week. Tonight it came back on so we watched TV. Now I remember why I avoid the news. All those people in the south carrying their children to the beaches to escape the flames, the sky lit up orange.

I've been painting with cadmium orange today and it's all I can think of as I watch. The chair and its amber wicker, the sky and its orange glow. It's all over my skin. I'm painting a picture of an old kitchen chair on our tiled floor. Not to be underestimated, the still life. It's more of a portrait really: whose chair is it? But after that news story tonight, I don't know. Something made me want to stand outside and exhale, get the orange paints out of my lungs.

5 October
I am making a Van Gogh. Did I mention that? Well, I am.

I know, it's insane. It was Gino's idea. I wonder whether he talked the client into it or they him. After years of the quiet life, here we are risking it all for money. The deal is this: Gino knows a family in the south of France who once owned a Van Gogh oil sketch. It's long gone now, sold on the black market to pay debts in the early part of the last century, but they are hoping that no one knows that. The family had a close connection with the artist Émile Bernard, a friend of Van Gogh. Along with Gauguin, the three used to exchange what are known as the 'friend portraits', and somehow, Gino's client ended up being gifted one of them. A rustic chair. A version of the chair at least, without pipe but with spring onions in a box and tiles on the floor. It's fully documented in letters, ready for the experts to pore over.

When I've painted it, Gino will deliver it to France and the family will let it languish in one of their extensive attics for a couple of years before 'rediscovering' it and auctioning it for millions. By which time we will be living somewhere far flung and lovely, miles away from anywhere.

'Just one last job, darling.' Gino smiled in that lip-curling way of his, flirting with anything and anyone, regardless.

'You make me sound like a getaway driver on a last heist,' I told him over champagne in Sienna.

'Only you can do it, darling,' he purred. 'I won't entrust it to anyone else.'

No one else was vain enough, I guess.

8 October

Send me rain. I can't paint in this. I can't sleep either. Nothing works except lying naked on the kitchen tiles, feeling the cool of the earth beat through.

'What are you doing down there?' Isaac is always sniffy when I do stuff like this.

'Cooling down.'

'You need to do some painting. Time is ticking, baby.'

The grass on the hills is yellow now, as if starved of every drop of nitrogen. And I can see smoke funnelling above the forestry over to the east.

'There's a fire again,' I tell him.

Isaac isn't interested. He's getting ready to package his work for Gino. He's done two this time. They're a bit predictable for my liking, but then that's the point.

'Studies in blue,' he tells me. 'You like this one?'

'I'm doing studies in orange.'

'You're doing studies in zero.' He opens a beer.

'It was a stupid idea,' I say.

'What was?'

'The Van Gogh. So stupid.'

'I didn't make you agree to it.'

'You did.'

It's too hot to sit indoors so I move to the bench in the front garden, batting away midges and watching a sheep rub herself against the drystone wall.

'Get some clothes on,' he says without looking at me.

'No one can see me.'

'I'm not comfortable with you sitting there like that.'

'I'm not comfortable with you.'

The wall is crumbling at its lower edges where generations of sheep have used it as a scratching post.

'Do you remember what you said to me, the first time we saw this house?' I ask. He doesn't reply, so I expound: '"Baby, it's a sign", you said.' He's still silent, sipping his beer. I can see his Adam's apple moving as he drinks. '"Van Gogh's chair already in the kitchen!" you said. "Take the job!"'

'I wish I was doing it,' he says, quietly.

'What is that supposed to mean? You think you're a better artist?'

'Shit! It means you... You aren't even trying.'

'I'm doing nothing *but* trying!'

'You don't need to channel the dead artist, you know. Just paint the chair, for Christ's sake.'

10 October

At 4.20 a.m. this morning I had a penny-drop moment.

'Hey, Isaac! Isaac, wake up! Did you know that Van Gogh was really into Japanese art? He had this huge collection of ukiyo-e prints, which were these cheap colour wood-block prints. He would copy some to get the feel of them. The greens against blues in *The Bridge in the Rain (after Hiroshige)*. And that rain! What we would do for a downpour like that, right?' I shook him. 'You know what he liked most about their style though?'

Isaac put a pillow over his head.

'The return to nature! Isn't that great? The return to the simpler ways of life. He called it a new religion. My God!'

11 October

'What the hell is that?' said Isaac this morning.

I thought he was talking about the mess I'd made, coffee grounds spilled on the floor, but he shook his head like a spinning top.

'No, not that. The painting.'

'Hush. It's getting there now.'

'Are you crazy? That's nothing like it!'

I take a step back. 'It is,' I say. 'I'm happy with this.'

'Have you taken leave of your senses? You've painted a bridge.'

'In the Japanese style,' I agree. 'I got thinking about what you said about channelling the artist.'

'I said you didn't need to!'

'No, but I think you're onto something. That's what's been

going wrong. I've been trying to emulate him. I need to reach him.'

'Oh, good God!'

'Don't laugh at me.'

'We are in massive trouble if you can't get this right. I mean *massive*.'

'I know.'

'Try prison. For decades.'

He has me by the throat.

'Ow! What are you doing?'

'It has to be faultless.'

'Look at yourself!'

'Well, do it. Get it done. No more messing around.'

12 October

I think Isaac is losing it. He doesn't know what to do with himself now the Mackies are finished. I overheard him talking to Gino last night. He told me he was going to arrange a pick-up for his paintings but I heard the tone of the conversation, the whispering travelling through the floorboards from upstairs. What the hell is he saying about me? I texted Gino myself afterwards: *All is ok. Don't listen to Iz. He doesn't understand my methods*. At midnight Gino sent a heart sticker back. Make of that what you will. I painted until morning. Slept on the sofa for three hours. Dreamed of being lost in a chair shop.

13 October

This morning I woke late and opened my eyes to the most bizarre view. The fire is close. I can see the tips of flames licking the top of our mountain. Fire engines are sounding in the distance. I've got dressed and have dragged the dreaded chair outside to sketch the black smoke creeping from the trees. I use charcoal, which seems horribly appropriate yet in bad taste somehow.

'Don't sit on the thing, paint it!' Isaac rages when he sees me. He looks sweaty already, a river streaking down the middle of his back like a flume at the fair. 'The chair, the chair!' he yells, hoisting it out from underneath me. 'You've a deadline in days and you're sat on it. Get up!'

I tussle with him for it, but he manages to stick his hand through the middle trying to keep his grip.

'Fuck!' He raves in my face, as if I've done it.

'Fuck you,' I scream back, and storm off to get away from him.

It's actually quite a long walk down to the reservoirs. The top lake is completely dry now, save for little patches of mud. The arch of a bridge is visible on the western side: *from the old village* I recall, remembering our little encounter with the Water Board worker the other day,

'Woah, that's a sight, isn't it?' comes a call behind me. 'Hope you've turned that hose off!'

Damn, damn, damn. It's only the same stupid guy again. He is breathless and jogging down the steep hill from the road above.

'Um, hi.'

'In another day or two, you'll see the old school. Can you see that there, sticking out of the water? That's the school bell. Or maybe it's the church.'

'Well, I have to be off.'

'Do you think I could trouble you to fill up my water bottle?'

'What?'

'Thirsty work.' He shakes it at me; it makes a tinny slosh against the aluminium.

'Oh... Yes. Give it here. I'll bring it back down to you.'

'It's all right, I'll call in at the house when I'm finished.'

I am flummoxed again. 'No... Isaac's working. He doesn't like to be disturbed when he paints.'

'Oh, right. Well, I won't be a minute. I'll just take some samples quickly and...' He dips some tubes into the edge of the lake. 'You can have a lift back if you like. Save you walking in this heat. I won't come in.'

I don't know what to do. He's smiling at me all expectantly.

'I'm not a maniac, mind,' he quips, 'but you're right to be careful. We're an 'orribly friendly lot round here.'

I don't know which would be worse: Isaac being home alone when the Water Board man comes snooping about, or me driving up to the house in his van. At least this way I can make sure that he stays put while I dash inside with his bottle. I agree and jog up the hill to the roadside where he's parked. While he climbs sluggishly behind me, I text Isaac: *With Water Board guy. On way back home in van. You are WORKING. He's not coming in. Wants a drink.* I press send.

'All right?' he puffs as he walks around to the driver's side. 'Jump in.'

I grab the newspapers and snack wrappers covering the seat and stuff them in the footwell.

'Sorry about that.' He chuckles. 'How long have you lived here then?'

Not now, I think. I'm not in the mood for questions.

'I've lost count,' I say. 'The fires look close by, don't they? Do you think we're in trouble?'

He ducks his head under his visor to take a better look. 'Kids set this alight originally, you see, forty miles away. Little sods. Are you renting or did you buy your place?'

'What?'

'Your house.'

I glance at him. Is it better to say we rented? Perhaps. He doesn't wait for an answer.

'That was a Water Board house originally,' he says.

'Was it? I'm worried whether we'll be burned in our beds.'

'Oh, I shouldn't think so. It's a hell of a mountain, that. It's actually miles away. Even the fires in the villages tend to stop dead of the homes. Always a first time though, I suppose!'

I smile weakly. We pull up in the yard and he gets out as I do. I cut him off where he stands.

'I'll get your water for you,' I say, laying my hand on his arm. 'You can sit here on the bench, if you like.'

'Thank you. Yes, as I was saying, this house goes way back. It was derelict. Did you see it then? A wreck it was, but you've done it nice.'

'Nothing special,' says Isaac, appearing in the doorway. He is wearing his work jeans, covered in oils.

'Oh, I didn't mean to disturb you.'

He waves his hand as if it's no trouble which prompts the Water Board man to stand up and come closer.

'Working, are you?'

Isaac purses his lips to show that he is mildly annoyed, and nods. I'm watching this through the kitchen window, running the tap.

'Lovely view, isn't it? You bought it, did you, this house?'

Isaac nods again.

'Who off, if you don't mind me asking?'

Isaac is instantly defensive. 'What do you mean?'

'Well, it's never been for sale, so... Who off?'

Alarm bells are suddenly clanging away like cymbals in my head. I run outside into the blinding white sun. 'Here's your water.'

'Thank you. I was just saying, this house... It's never been for sale, see.'

'Yes, it was,' I say, but it's weak-sounding, like the lie it is.

'No, it wasn't,' he says matter of factly, making his way over to the window, peering through the dark glass. 'Ask me, go on.'

'What?'

'Ask me how I know it was never for sale.'

I feel cold and hot at the same time. Isaac is directly behind him, looming and ashen.

'Because I own it.' He laughs. It sounds like a bomb going off. 'And technically, because you don't actually rent it, I own everything inside.' He strides into the lounge. 'Bloody hell, you're a messy pair of buggers.'

There are rags and plates, cups of turps, brushes soaking, clothes strewn everywhere and the coffee grounds still all over the floor from the other night.

'You need to open a window. Tidy up a bit.' He makes his way to the studio. 'But this is what I really came to see.'

Isaac's paintings have been neatly packed away somewhere. There is just mine: a dozen attempts at the chair, a copy of *The Bridge in the Rain (after Hiroshige)*.

'I own these,' he says.

'You do fucking not,' says Isaac, his voice shaking.

'You're not a hard-man. Listen to you! I'm a hard-man. We're all hard around here. You're a soft arty bastard.' He turns fast and pins Isaac to the wall by his throat. His hands are large and capable, like firm shovels. Isaac's neck disappears inside them, his face reddening to a Primary Magenta.

I pick the chair up and ram it down on Isaac's head. The blood blooms into his face like a rose.

'What are you doing?' Isaac wants to say, I can see it, his eyes as big as a caught fish, but the Water Board man holds him firm.

'Do it again,' the Water Board man says, so I do.

Isaac struggles a lot, then he comes to rest, breathing like a drain. I gather up my paints.

The Water Board man says, 'You like Van Gogh, do you? You've used my chair, I see.'

Growing Pains

Delphine Richards

Tia, the counsellor, makes me laugh sometimes. Not out-loud laughing because she doesn't do it intentionally. But I have to bite the inside of my cheeks and look down, like I'm thinking about stuff.

The thing with her is that she's quite old – about forty I'd guess – and she tries to be cool when she's talking to me in our sessions. She tries to use words like *scrote* and *wanker* when she wants to, like, *connect* with me! But whenever she says one of those words, her face looks like she's tasted something nasty and her cheeks go a bit pink. That always cracks me up. One day, I'm hoping she'll drop an F-bomb to impress me. That would be *epic!* But I suppose she just can't bring herself to say a word like that. Fair enough. There are words I can't bring myself to say out loud either. Words like 'killing' and 'death'. Uh-uh, not a chance. Tia says I have to let my guilt go and move on, but it's not happening any time soon. I just blank her out when she tells me that crap. Though I guess I must have listened to her at some point because it pops into my mind occasionally. Tia says I've got nothing to feel guilty about but what does *she* know?

It was two days after Easter Monday that Kelly told me she was going to kill Robbie Harris. We were both at her house and we'd been trying some cans of cider that her mum's boyfriend had left there. It was minging stuff! But the more we swigged, the better it got. I had never tried cider before. My parents are totally uncool – fourteen is too young for alcohol, blah, blah, yadda, blah.

Kelly said she'd first tried cider when her mum brought home a Chinese takeaway for them a few weeks earlier. She said her mum had told her she had to drink it because it made the takeaway taste better. I used to think Kelly's mum was cool. I don't think that anymore. Obviously.

We'd been at the fairground before going back to Kelly's, saw a load of people from school: Emily, Tara, Jessica from my class, few others too. We all hung out together doing stupid things. Then Doob and Gary turned up. Doob is Emily's brother and everybody knew that he wanted to hook up with Tara. Doob and Tara were just talking to each other while Gary mucked about with a silly trick he could do with his wrists. He had been trying to show Kelly how to do it when we heard a shout. We didn't take any notice at first because there was a lot of shouting and music at the fair anyway. Then it got louder and I saw it was Robbie Harris with some of his mates. Robbie was grinning and shouted, 'Hey, Gazz, what you doing with the Kleenex Kid!' while his mates snorted and giggled.

Gary just laughed and told him to fuck off, but Kelly went really red and her eyes filled with tears. She pretended to, like, lace up her trainers and kept her face down, but not before I had seen how upset she was.

When she had sorted herself out and Robbie had mooched off again, Kelly stood up and said, 'My mum says I have to be back soon. Something she needs me to do...'

'If I come with you, can I borrow your science notes?' I asked.

I had been off school with chickenpox before Easter and I was trying to catch up with all the boring school stuff. It was, officially, the only reason I had been allowed out to the fair. My mum had said I had to get up to date with schoolwork during the Easter holidays, so I said I could meet up with Kelly and the others to pick up stuff from my missed lessons.

So that's how we ended up drinking cider in Kelly's house. Kelly's mum was out when we found the cans so we took them up to her room. We tried on a new nail colour too, and talked about stuff.

Then Kelly said, 'Robbie Harris is a shit!'

I didn't know exactly what she meant so I just sort of screwed my face up as if I understood. My birthday isn't until the end of August so everyone in my class is fifteen except me and they always try to say things that they think I won't understand. I carried on doing my nails, though it was getting difficult to concentrate, what with the cider and listening to Kelly.

Then she said, 'I've decided I'm going to kill him.'

I shrugged a *whatever*.

'Did you hear what he called me earlier?' she asked.

'Not really. Sounded like Kleenex or something,' I said, sounding bored.

'He's been spreading minging rumours about me. I'm going to kill him!'

'Yeeesss!' I said. 'Make a doll and stick pins in it!'

'Or stab him with a barbecue fork!' she responded.

'Blow him up in a gas explosion,' I suggested.

By then I had nail colour on the sides of my fingers, my eyes felt funny and thinking of ways to kill Robbie Harris was much more entertaining than making a mess of my nails.

'Don't be a numpty, Tash,' she said, laughing. 'It's got to be something ... doable.'

'Run over him with a bus then!'

'I can't drive a bus either!'

'You could if you wanted to kill him that much!' I said. I was trying to practise staying in control of my eyes and my voice before I had to go home and face my parents. 'What's he done anyway?'

To my horror, Kelly burst into tears and hid her face in her hands. I didn't know what to do. I thought about giving her a hug, but I didn't really know how. We don't do that hands-on shit in our house. I sort of stroked her arm instead.

'He's just a baghead,' I said. I'd only just found out that baghead meant 'drug user' and was quite pleased to get a chance to use it and show I was cool. It was no secret that Robbie used drugs. He'd been excluded from school before Christmas when he and his skanky mates had been caught with some stuff.

Eventually, Kelly stopped crying and blew her nose.

'You really haven't heard what he's been saying about me?' she asked.

'No!'

'I went out with him on Monday,' Kelly glanced up at me to see how I was taking that news, 'after Club. On the way home we were ... you know, snogging and stuff.'

'You didn't...?' I was really blown away. Robbie Harris was a real creep as far as I was concerned.

'What? Oh no, not like that,' she said. 'He just put his hand up my top.' She started sobbing again. 'I keep my tissue tucked into the top of my bra, you know. There was nowhere else to put it. He just...'

I could guess the rest. Kelly was really weedy and thin and I'd heard some of the bitchiest girls in our class saying that, because she had no boobs, she stuffed her bra with socks and tissues to pretend she had something in it.

Everyone else knew she did it too, but no one had ever said it to her.

'He just pulled out the tissue and looked at me as if I was dirty. Then he said... Oh, God.' She broke off again, sobbing. 'He said he didn't go out with girls with no tits.'

This time she really did let rip with the crying and I patted her arm again.

'Don't let it upset you,' I said, 'What he thinks is not important.' (That last bit was a gem straight from my mum's bank of sayings. Even Tia has never resorted to that one!)

She gulped, then said, 'It was awful, yesterday, I bumped into a few of them and they started laughing and calling me "tissue tit."'

She started crying again. It certainly sobered me up. My eyes still felt a bit weird but apart from that I was okay. I just felt relieved that it hadn't been me who had been humiliated by those creeps.

Before long we heard the front door open. We heard Kelly's mum laughing and a man's voice talking. Kelly went into a total panic.

'Don't let her see I've been crying! I'd rather die than have to tell her,' she said. 'Just go and talk to her or something. Ask for a glass of Coke.'

I dithered a bit. I didn't really know what to do, but Kelly was desperate and tried to push me out of the door.

I went to the top of the landing and called, 'Hi, Mrs Duffy, could I be a pain…?'

I continued down the stairs and she came out to meet me. I thought she looked really cool and had great gear on. Now I can see that she just looked tarty.

'Hi, Tash. Wot's occurring?' she said. She always used to say the right things too. I didn't know the man who was with her but he gave me a welcoming grin.

'Could I have a … a sticking plaster, please?' I said. 'This spot on my arm is sore.'

'Course you can, babes,' she said. 'Mind you don't scratch at those spots. Chickenpox can scar you for life. Get Kelly to fetch you one from the bathroom cabinet.'

'Okay, thanks,' I said, not sure if I should leave them yet. How much time did Kelly want?

They both looked at me as if I was going to say something else. I was afraid to say too much in case they could smell the cider on my breath.

'Okay, then?' said Kelly's mum. She was obviously waiting

for me to go, so I mumbled a thanks once more and went back upstairs. Out of the corner of my eye I could see the strange man groping her and heard her laughing.

I went into Kelly's room and said, 'I asked for a sticking plaster. You'd better get me one or it will look suspicious.'

Kelly got to her feet reluctantly.

'It's okay,' I said, 'she won't come up. She's got a visitor. A man with a shaved head.'

'That's Phil,' Kelly said. 'He's nice. She dumped Terry. That's why I knew it was okay to drink his cider.'

She went to get the sticking plaster and I gathered up the school books I needed.

We both headed cautiously down the stairs. The living-room door was shut and we could hear Phil's voice.

'...but Kelly's got none of your looks, has she?'

'She's got it all upstairs though,' said Kelly's mum. 'Like her father, he had it all up top too.' She snorted laughter. 'And not much downstairs!'

They both laughed in a really disgusting way. It was gross, having to listen to oldies flirting!

'I think someone must have swapped babies with me in the hospital when Kelly was born. I was never a late developer like her. She hasn't even started her periods yet! What is she like!'

I could feel my face burning and I dared not look at Kelly.

'Gotta go or I'll be grounded,' I said and almost ran the last few metres to the door. 'See ya!'

I must have jinxed myself, because when I got home my folks

smelled the cider on my breath and I *was* grounded, and for the rest of the Easter holidays. I didn't see Kelly until the weekend before we started back at school. She had messaged me to see if it was okay to call by for her school books and my mum was cool with that.

When she arrived, she had a backpack with her.

'Been shopping,' she said. 'If I can hang out here for a while, I won't have to go clubbing with my mum tonight.'

I thought there could have been lots of worse things than going clubbing with Kelly's mum. Going clubbing with *my* mum, for example. Now that *would* have been embarrassing!

When we put the school books in the backpack later that evening, I saw that Kelly had some really weird things in there. There was a box with 'Handshake Shock!' written on it. I could see a warning on the side: 'May interfere with pacemakers and similar devices.' I couldn't see a picture so I had no idea what it was and Kelly didn't mention it at all. I could also see a set of barbecue utensils – the kind that come in one box and have stuff like a pair of tongs, a spiky skewer-type thing and a heavy-duty fork as part of the set. There was also a leaflet about a product called 'Rat Out'. I didn't really think about it at the time because people are always handing out leaflets in the shopping centre. In fact, I didn't think about it at all until after everything went bad. (I just can't bring myself to say the word 'death'. Tia says that's okay.)

Life just went on normally for a while after that. Doob got together with Tara. Then Tara dumped him. Emily was caught shoplifting and was given a warning. Our maths teacher had his car stolen from outside the school. Just normal everyday stuff.

About a month later I was at Club, with Kelly and the others, when Robbie Harris strolled in with his usual cling-ons. I thought Kelly would just leave before he could see her, but she gave him a little wave. He ignored her.

Later I heard one of the girls say that some of the boys had bottles of vodka outside. I guessed that Robbie Harris would be one of them and I really didn't want to be involved in anything he did. Kelly rushed up to me and said that she had to run home for something but that she would see me later. I guessed she was getting more vodka or cider.

I didn't see Kelly until much later that evening when I went outside to message one of the other girls who had chickenpox and who wanted to know what was happening at Club. As we messaged back and forth, Kelly appeared from nowhere and grabbed my arm. She was crying so much that I could hardly make out what she was saying.

'Oh Tash, please help me. Oh God, what have I done? I didn't really mean it. Oh God.'

All the while she was dragging me around the back to where the recycling bins were kept behind some wooden-screen fence panels.

I just kept saying 'What? What?'

It was dark, but at the back of the bins I could see a shape on the ground.

'Oh God, I've killed him,' she said. 'I swear, Tash, it was just meant to hurt him. I know I said I was going to kill him but... Oh God!'

'Shit!' I shouted. 'What have you... Get some help. What did you—?'

'No!' she shouted at me. 'You can't drop me in it. He asked for it. You've got to help me! Just say you and me went early or something.'

I inched nearer to Robbie Harris's body. I could hardly bear to look. I had never seen a dead body before and I wished that the faint glow from the lamps would go away so that I couldn't see Robbie's. I started crying.

'Ssh!' said Kelly. 'We've got to get out of here.'

Still crying, I leaned against the wall and slid down. My legs wouldn't hold me up and everything seemed to be far away and unreal.

'Come on, Tash,' urged Kelly. 'We have to go. Now!'

It was a really weird feeling. I knew what Kelly was saying, but I just couldn't make my body move. Everything became even darker and I thought I was going to faint. Then I felt nauseous and dry-heaved a couple of times. I was aware of Kelly standing over me while I wiped my mouth and my eyes. When I looked up next, she had gone.

More crying noises came out of my mouth again and I stayed crouched on the floor. I sounded like a small child. A sniff, a splutter, a hitch of breath, a moan.

But it wasn't me moaning.

I stopped crying and listened. The moaning was coming from Robbie's body!

Panic instantly told me to run like fuck, but the body began to move. And then it said 'Shee-eet...' in a long groaning voice.

Somewhere deep in my mind, instinct told me that the

undead don't moan out words like 'shee-eet'. From my ready-to-run position, I turned and saw Robbie sitting up. He saw me.

'Oh shit!' he said again.

'Are you okay?' I asked in disbelief.

'Help me up!' he snarled at me.

He rubbed his head and I went to his side and tried to help him. I put one hand on the floor by his leg and felt something wet.

'Oh God, are you bleeding?' I asked. I put my hand on his jeans. They were soaked.

Robbie felt along his legs and then he started crying – a long, low-pitched, bubbly noise. I had never heard a sixteen-year-old boy cry before. It was really weird.

'Please don't tell anyone,' he begged.

I realised that Robbie had wet himself.

'What happened?' I said 'Do you want me to fetch someone. An ambulance or—'

'No!' he almost screamed at me. 'I don't want anyone to know. Okay?' He stared at me in the dim light. 'Your psycho friend tried to fry my nuts,' he snarled. 'She had something in her hand. I didn't know what she was on about at first. We were just ... messing around, doing a body job. She said that she'd wanted to kill me but that she'd changed her mind. I thought that meant she liked me, but then she said that she was going to hurt me.'

He made a half-laughing sound which took me a moment to realise that he was crying again.

'You can't tell anyone about this,' he said fiercely. 'You'll have to help me out here. Otherwise I'll...'

He didn't need to finish whatever threat he had in mind.

I got up quickly, intending to leave him there, but he grabbed my arm.

'I'm sorry, I'm sorry. Okay? It's just ... I haven't had one of those fit things since I was six years old. Everyone will think I'm a freak. Will you help me?'

He looked up at me with snot and drool swinging from his chin and I couldn't see why anyone had thought that Robbie was good looking. He looked like a toddler. And there was a strong smell of pee.

I sighed and helped him to his feet.

'You gotta check if anyone's around,' he said. 'Come back and tell me if it's clear.'

I started out towards the road and then he added, 'And for fuck's sake, don't come back in here if someone sees you! Just wait for them to go!'

I went out to check. 'There's nobody there,' I told him. Then my phone rang. 'It's Kelly,' I said, reading her name on the screen.

Robbie grabbed my arm. 'Don't answer it! No way can she know what she's done to me.'

'She already knows, you numpty!' I said before realising that he probably meant about wetting himself.

'Just don't answer the phone or speak to anyone. Please?'

'Okay, okay. Now come on!'

We got out to the roadside with me slightly ahead of him to double-check if anyone was around.

He stopped suddenly.

'What?' I said.

'Give me your jacket,' he said.

I hesitated for a second, then took it off and gave it to him. Then he did something really gross – he tied the sleeves around his waist so the body of the jacket partially hid his wet jeans. I just hoped I could get home and put it in the washing machine before my parents noticed.

We had a long walk ahead of us. Robbie refused to go on the bus or have anyone pick him up in case they saw his wet jeans. And every time we saw someone walking on the road, he pulled me into doorways or alleyways and pretended we were snogging so that we would be left alone. Being so close to him nearly made me puke – the smell was gross, but he got totally frassed every time he saw someone.

Kelly tried phoning me three times while we walked to Robbie's house, but each time he begged me not to answer.

Eventually, we reached his house. He quickly untied my jacket, threw it at me and disappeared into the darkened building.

Although I was cold, I couldn't bring myself to put the smelly jacket on, so I turned it inside out and draped it over my shoulders. Then I tried ringing Kelly's mobile. It went to voicemail straight away. I tried six times before I saw the voice-message icon on my phone.

It was Kelly. She still sounded really upset. There was a lot of background noise and I couldn't make out all her message.

'Tash ... believe it ... what to do. I called Phil ... would help me ... you later.'

I replayed it several times but it didn't get any clearer. I tried her phone again, but either she was ignoring my calls or had the phone switched off. I found out later that she couldn't hear it ringing.

On my way home, my parents rang me to see why I was late. I pretended that the signal was, like, iffy and by the time I got home, my parents were really *extra*! They shouted and took my phone off me and said that I would never be allowed out again. I shouted that they hated me and that I hated them. Then I ran to my room and cried.

By the next morning I hoped they would have chilled out a little and, to start with, things seemed hopeful. Then, by about mid-morning, it all went bad. The police called at my house and wanted to speak to me. Mum came to get me from the utility room where I was putting some washing in the machine (my jacket hidden amongst my dad's work clothes). She stared at me with a hateful expression and said, 'I never thought I'd see the day when you brought trouble to our house, Natasha.'

I'd never seen her look so angry. I wanted to hate her, but I was frightened too. Had Robbie Harris ratted on Kelly?

I went into the sitting room with Mum. Dad was already in there. He had his car-washing overalls on. He looked worried and angry.

Mum stopped looking angry as the reason for the police visit became clear. Instead, she sat beside me and hugged me.

Kelly's body had been found a few miles out of town at the old industrial site. She had been strangled. 'Brutally raped and strangled...' is how the newspaper headlines put it when the story broke. In her pocket was a 'Handshake Shock' joke device and a dead mobile phone.

Since then, the trial has happened and Phil got life for Kelly's murder. In the end I didn't have to give evidence. I'm glad about that.

I've learned to keep my mouth closed. I haven't told anyone about the incident with Kelly and Robbie Harris either.

Tia says that the person responsible has been punished, but that's bullshit.

Okay, I know Phil is where he deserves to be, but he isn't the only one to blame for Kelly's ... murder (there, I said it out loud).

While I listened to Robbie begging for help, I could have been supporting Kelly and none of this would have happened. Tia doesn't know about Robbie, but she's always telling me that I've done nothing wrong.

I think I owe it to Kelly to finish what she started. I've already looked up 'Rat Out' on the internet. And I know where to get a bottle of vodka. Robbie Harris is too full of shit to stop drinking any free booze I give him just because it tastes funny. I'll make sure the bottle I drink from is safe.

One of my mum's sayings is, 'You may as well be hanged for a sheep as a lamb.' It's some kind of oldies' way of saying you'll get punished the same whether you go big or not. I know I'm partly guilty for Kelly's death anyway. What have I got to lose?

Maybe that's not what Tia meant when she said I should move on. But if it goes some way to paying for Kelly's murder, it works for me.

The Ship

Eluned Gramich

The boy with the bagpipes stands up and gives us his rendition of 'John Anderson my Jo'. He's halfway through when DI Medi Joan – Joanie – orders a pint of Black Dragon at the bar. We didn't notice her come in. She's always been a sly one for creeping up on you, unannounced.

The boy with the bagpipes takes his seat again. The pub goes quiet. We're sitting tight together in a little circle at the back, hot and flushed, not noticing the strong smell of ale and sweat. We're all watching DI Joanie. She sits at the bar, looking straight ahead, drinking the golden liquid in long sips.

It's been six weeks since the death and she looks shit: face like a crumpled plastic bag, her eyes swollen with lack of sleep. Her hair's showing wide streaks of grey. She usually goes down to Williams Sisters quite regularly, like the rest of the ladies, to get a cut and colour. But she's not been for a while. She looks over 70, not the 50-odd she really is.

The silence goes on. We wait for Joanie to join us. Old times, like. But she doesn't.

It's the business with the boy that's got her like this. Twenty-first of September. A Sunday. They had the whole story in the paper as soon as it happened. One journalist even added a timeline – the police complained about that. It should have been top secret, but it wasn't. The whole town knew.

Riley Evans dropped his little boy, four-year-old Jac, at his mam's house. They'd been on the beach all day, father and son, enjoying the Indian summer. He'd had a lot of ice cream, because dads who only see their son every other weekend buy a lot of ice cream. Jac was pink from the sun, too. By the time he arrived home to his mam, Jac didn't feel well. Lottie gave Riley a telling-off. He swore back at her, but nothing too bad. Par for the course with them two.

The evening was ordinary, more or less. Jac was too queasy to eat his dinner. They watched cartoons together, and he fell asleep around seven. Owain, Lottie's fiancé, came home late with a takeaway he'd picked up on the way back from the office. They ate, watched telly, and went to bed at eleven.

In the night, Lottie woke up with 'a bad feeling' and went to check on Jac. She found him sprawled on the floor, halfway between his room and theirs, as if he'd collapsed trying to get to them. He was struggling to breathe. She phoned an ambulance, and they took him to Bronglais. The boy died before they arrived.

There, sitting on the right, is Vera Llanfair's husband, Stuart: the man with the belly stretching out a grey T-shirt. He plays the recorder with us some nights, although he doesn't last too long these days as he runs out of breath. Good man, he is, but his wife's an angel. A nurse at Bronglais, she's been working there close to 30 years. When she got home after her shift that night, she was in tears.

'I've never seen her cry like that,' he told us, in confidence. This was the Monday after. We didn't play any music that night, just sat at the back of the pub together and tried to get our head round the news. 'Vera's seen it all, you know? Looked after plenty of sick children in her time, but they've always been moved down to Cardiff when the going gets tough. She's never had an ambulance open its doors to a ... a...' He put his hand up to his eyes; Stu's a real softie.

'It doesn't say what was wrong with him,' Carys said, paper in front of her.

Stu ignored her: 'He was that pale. They tried to resuscitate him on the ward but after a while you've got to stop, she said, because their bodies are only small. He wouldn't have been able to take much more.'

'Pale skin. Septicaemia.'

'Might have been. They've sent him off for a post-mortem. The police were called in.'

'That explains Joanie.'

Joanie was usually with us on Mondays and Wednesdays: for the music, mainly, and the cider. She played violin – when she bothered to bring it.

'Vera said that everyone was devastated. Like I said, a four-year-old, that small and sweet, just lying there, and there was nothing any of the doctors or nurses could do, you know? Two of them went away to have a cry. Vera said the doctor just looked like he was going to be sick.'

'You'd think they'd be used to it,' we said.

'Yeah.' Stu took a swig of beer.

'What about Lottie Thomas?'

'Yeah, she was there. Owain too. She'd gone in the ambulance, and he'd driven behind in the car. They had to help her down. Her legs were like jelly. But...' Stu paused. Looked up at the ceiling as though he were remembering something.

'But what?'

'Vera said it was odd, you know, because once they'd been told the news, Lottie just sat there, not saying anything. Owain was the one breaking down.'

'Owain?' We couldn't imagine it: Owain was our Member of the Senedd. (His PA, Rosie, used to play flute with us, which was our claim to fame for a while.) A proper, neat politician; the industrious, church-going kind. A man so together you couldn't imagine him swearing at a rugby match.

Stuart nodded. 'Well, Owain and Jac were close, weren't they? Like father and son. He got a call from work, and his voice was shaking, explaining everything.'

'Lottie didn't cry?'

'Vera said it's normal. The shock. But then,' Stuart cleared his throat. 'They had a job persuading her to sit with him. Sit with Jac. Usually mams – they can't let go. Want to stay with the body for hours and days. Lottie didn't want to look at him.'

'She'll regret it if she didn't.'

'That's what Vera said. Only Lottie was that determined not to see him. She said she'd ... well, top herself if she had to see the body. Owain just drove them home.'

Stuart went quiet then. We knew he had more to tell, only he was weighing up whether to tell us the whole story or not. We got him the next round, played 'Calon Lân', and waited.

'Vera said,' he began. This was during their long conversation in the early hours, Vera unable to sleep, lying flat on her back on the bed and staring at the Artex ceiling. '...it wasn't septicaemia or food poisoning or meningitis. It wasn't an illness. When they were working on him, trying to get his little heart to start, they all saw the bruises. Red bruises they were, which means they were new. That's why they had the police there, see, because they couldn't be sure where the bruises came from. But don't tell anyone else, all right?'

Vera wasn't the only one on duty that night who couldn't keep what they saw to themselves. It was too momentous somehow; it wasn't a private medical matter – the information belonged to everyone in town.

Wednesday night, two nights after the death, DI Medi Joan joined us again. Only she didn't bring the violin; she didn't say much at all. This was in the early days, of course, when her eyes were bright, her back straight; when she seemed to be gathering everything in, every look, every line of conversation.

'Have you come here to spy on us?'

She shook her head. 'I want to ask some questions.'

We laughed at that. She wouldn't get a straight answer from us, two sheets to the wind, half-nine on a Wednesday. 'What do you know about Riley Evans?'

We could write a book about Riley Evans. 'What do you want to know?'

'How would you describe him,' she said. 'If you were to introduce him to someone who'd never met him, I mean.'

Bitter. Volatile. Unlucky. A sad man, we told her, even

though she knew herself what kind of man he was. We'd all been to school together at one point or another, although Riley didn't last long in education. His mother left when he was a teenager to live with her new husband in England. Riley stayed behind with his granddad on the smallholding outside Llanon. He was seventeen when he started going out with Lottie. They married young and moved into town where he worked as a night porter in the various hotels while Lottie joined the Williams sisters as a junior stylist.

That was years ago now.

'They'd been on the rocks for a while,' said Carys Daniels. She worked as a nail technician in the salon opposite. 'You remember what happened with the glass door.'

We all remembered what happened with the glass door. But there was something else, before that, in the murky middle period of Riley and Lottie's marriage, years before Jac was born. A night out in Yoko's that ended with Riley punching Nate James in the stomach and throwing a plastic beaker full of beer at his head because he'd been flirting with Lottie.

'He was the jealous type.'

'What did he do anyway? He never had a proper job.'

'Nate James had to go to hospital to be checked for internal bleeding.'

DI Medi Joan brought the cider to her lips, her head tilted, listening, a slight smile on her face. We couldn't tell if this mattered to her or not: the fight at Yoko's with Nate, the fact that Riley would have been happy to keep Lottie under lock and key. Joanie knew the story as well as us, so what was she expecting?

'Tell me about the glass door,' she said.

Carys leaned forward, importantly, tucking her hair behind her ears. 'I was there,' she said. 'You know I used to work at Williams.' Everyone knew. 'It was Christmas last year. Lottie missed a few days of work. Then she came in to speak to Evie, that's our boss, privately at the back, but there's nowhere really private in the salon, so we all heard. She'd met someone else. She was divorcing Riley, but he wasn't having it. She'd been trying to get him to leave the flat for months. She ended up phoning his granddad down at the farm and he came all the way to pick Riley up. Told him to have some respect, collect his things. That's why she'd had to miss work. She got the locksmith in because she was scared Riley was going to come back.'

Joanie tilted her head the other way. The half-smile remained: her demeanour seemed to say, *impress me*.

'Evie was fine with it. Happy he was gone in all honesty. No one really liked him. So anyway. Lottie went back to work and everything was fine until two days later when he was spotted walking down the street. Actually,' she coughed, 'I spotted him when I was out on lunch. I legged it back to the salon and I said, "Riley Evans is on Darkgate and looks like he's on his way straight here." Evie had the door locked quick as a flash. It was just in time, because as soon as I'd said it Riley was there. It was like a scene from a horror film, I swear. He was rattling the door, banging it down with his fists, shouting for Lottie. Luckily, we only had one client in. It was old Mrs Thomas and she shouted straight back, "Get away you devil!" And Evie joined in, "Piss off or I'll call the police." Lottie, well, she was standing right in the middle of it all, scissors in her hand, like a rag doll. I tried to steer her to the staff room, but it was like she was stuck to the ground. Riley was effing and blinding, calling her all the names under the sun. Evie goes to phone the police. He sees her and starts properly kicking. That's when the door shatters.'

Carys took a breath, savouring the tension in the air.

'What happened then?' DI Medi Joan asked, softly.

'He got a few cuts and bruises, you know, from the glass. The police arrived.'

'But before we arrived,' Joanie said. 'Did he go through the broken door?'

Carys nodded slowly. 'Oh, yeah. It was gross. He put his bleeding hand through and unlocked the door. He went up to her. She had these scissors in her hands. She was gripping them tight.'

Joanie's eyes shone. The only sign that the story meant anything to her. 'Did they speak?'

'Yeah, actually. It was weird.' Carys shrugged. 'He just said he was sorry.'

Four weeks ago, the results of the post-mortem came back: death by blunt force trauma to the stomach, chest, and back. Trauma consistent with fists. The results of the post-mortem were a secret, of course, but DI Medi Joan told a few of us, here and there, and from then it was only a matter of time before the whole town knew.

Why had she told us?

Joanie leaned back into the red settee. She came in later and later, and there was always someone calling her from the station, so she had her phone face-down in front of her on the sticky pub table. 'It's no use keeping things under wraps when the answer to what happened that Sunday evening is here.'

'What? At The Ship?'

Joanie smiled. 'Yeah, I think so. In one form or another.'

We didn't know what to make of that – did it make us important, or complicit? We were frightened then. There was still some hope that Jac's death had been some terrible accident – an insidious infection or a fall down the stairs. Fists. It was too gruesome to contemplate. We had cwtched Jac: he came to the café by the seafront and crawled onto the high plastic chairs and called, 'Ice cream!' He chased the pigeons outside the new shopping centre, clapping his small hands in excitement. When he crawled onto your lap, he smelled of the salon where his mother worked, ylang-ylang and lilac. Sometimes, on sunny, rockpool-exploring days, he would smell of the sea, of salt and algae. When we passed him in the street, he would turn and wave. He could say hello and goodbye in two languages. He let dogs lick his face and he tried to lick them back.

We didn't like to think of his body. We didn't like to think of him as dead. Instead, he was simply away for a while, and when the culprit was found, Jac would be magically returned to us: whole and unblemished, like the ancient Welsh soldiers who emerged from the cauldron of rebirth.

They brought Riley into the station for questioning. They went over the weekend, again and again. They'd spent Saturday on the farm and then drove into Aber for Sunday lunch and an afternoon on the beach. It was good weather. Jac ate two ice creams; Riley admitted he'd forgotten sunscreen. He let Jac play despite the weather.

'When did Jac say he wasn't feeling well?' DI Medi Joan led the interview, in her black jacket, navy shirt, black slacks from Marks and Spencer. Hair pulled back tight.

Riley had been wearing the same clothes for a week. His odour filled the interview room – animal feed and sweat. 'I don't know.' He shifted in his seat. He seemed not to like hearing his son's name. 'After the Magnum. It was a caramel one. It was probably too much. Lottie...' he choked on the name, 'she doesn't like giving him sweets, so when he's with me, he goes to town.'

'And on the Saturday. I imagine there's all sorts of dangerous machinery on a farm...'

'I don't let him out of my sight,' Riley said. 'I only get two days with him. I don't let him out of my sight. Not ever.'

'But you forget the sunscreen on a scorching day.'

'Yeah. I'm not so good on the details,' said Riley. 'I'm not so good at things generally. But I keep my eye on him, always. If he'd been with me...' He stopped, looked at the ground. The thought hurt; there was pain all over his face.

'What do you think happened, Riley?'

'Ask Lottie. She should be in here, not me.'

'Could you describe your relationship with Charlotte Thomas?'

'We don't have one,' he said.

'You were with him the whole weekend. You dropped Jac

off at five o'clock. Six hours later, he's dead.' Riley shook his head. 'Some people might think you killed Jac to spite your ex-wife.'

Nothing. He didn't move, staring at a stain on the ground.

DI Medi Joan stretched her arm across the table, as though to touch him. 'Riley?'

'I don't know where to start with that, to be honest.'

'A yes or a no will do.'

'No,' he said. Then he seemed to gather himself. 'Jac's the only thing in my life that matters. She's taken him away. She's taken everything away from me. Everything.'

Sitting in a room with Riley was like sitting with a man who was watching his house burn down with his family inside. That's what Joanie said to us later in The Ship. We weren't sure; he was the sort of man who would be sorry after he'd punched you in the stomach, we said. The sort of man who would beg your forgiveness only to hit you across the face again a few days later.

'Maybe,' said Joanie.

The station received an anonymous tip-off. We knew that person was Natalia Paluszek. She'd been down in Cardiff, shopping for her wedding dress in the arcades with her mother and two bridesmaids when she'd spotted Lottie Thomas in the John Lewis department store.

'Is she even allowed to leave the county?' we wanted to know.

'I don't know,' said Natalia. 'But she was there. She was at the beauty bar, getting a full face of make-up done.'

'How do you know it was her?'

'Hundred per cent. I was so shocked when I saw her, I took a picture.'

We all looked over at DI Medi Joan. She was on her way out of the door, phone by her ear, when she turned and yelled, 'Nat. Send me that photo, okay?'

'Okay.'

Then Joanie vanished into the dark streets and didn't come back for five days. She was seen leaving the town in her red Nissan Micra in the early hours of the morning.

Riley's grandfather phoned the police because someone had thrown a brick through the window. He didn't know who it was; Riley said it was his ex-wife. He didn't know she was at the station when it happened.

'Charlotte Thomas.'

DI Medi Joan had returned in time for the interview. Her Nissan was parked outside, running low on fuel. She'd come in wearing some kind of lounge suit she'd seemingly slept in. Lottie, however, was wearing a sea-green dress – Ted Baker. Her light-blonde hair fell below her shoulders, and there was a pink shimmer on her cheekbones.

We'd gone over it the night before at The Ship. Joanie wasn't with us, but she would have the same information to hand, the same grainy memories of Lottie as a young girl at Penglais. Thin, wiry, brown-haired she was then. Riley was an angry adolescent, but what did that make her? She *chose* to be with him. They were together because they had so much in common – rebellion, frustration, a shared sadness. Lottie didn't get in trouble at school and she was bright, but she somehow messed up her exams. There was a crisis when she started dyeing her hair every other day and stopped eating. This lasted a year. Then she got the job with Evie Williams.

'Can you describe your relationship with Riley Evans?'

'He's my ex-husband,' she said. With Riley, his accent was strong, Cardi. Lottie could speak like a woman off the radio when she wanted. 'We were married eight years.'

'Why did the marriage end?'

'He was possessive. I couldn't handle it anymore.'

'What do you mean "possessive"?'

'You know what he did to Nate James. I told you the last time,' she said. 'Do I have to go into it all again?'

DI Medi Joan shuffled her papers together as if deciding. 'How have you been feeling recently, Charlotte?'

'What do you mean? Pretty shit, obviously. What sort of question is that?'

'Pretty shit,' said DI Medi Joan. 'Can you give us a bit more detail?'

'Can't sleep. Can't eat.' Lottie sighed, pushed her chair away from the table. 'I'm fed up with having to talk about it all the time. I want to grieve in peace.'

'What's your relationship to Owain Hughes?'

'We're engaged. We live together.'

'When did you start living with him?'

'Spring. End of March.'

'How did you meet?'

'At the market. He invited me for a coffee.'

'And when was that?'

'February.'

'You moved in pretty quickly, then.'

'It felt right,' she said. 'It wasn't like he was some stranger. I'd seen him around town for years. I'd heard him give his speeches and things. He popped into the salon to chat to Evie a couple of times about the business.'

'Can you describe Owain's relationship with Jac?'

'Oh, he loved him. He adored Jac. Ask anyone. Ask Rosie. He'd always wanted to be a dad, but it had never happened for him. It's part of why we work, you know? Because Owain knows we're a package, me and Jac, and he loves us both.'

Lottie sobbed; put her hand over her mouth.

'Take your time,' DI Medi Joan said, pushing the tissues towards her.

She pulled her shoulder back, lifted her chin. 'I don't want to. When's this going to be over?'

'What about your relationship with Owain? Any arguments or fallings out?'

'No. Why do you ask?'

'It's part of my job to ask.'

'It's Riley you should be asking. Jac was feeling sick *before* he arrived at ours. Don't you see? Riley's trying to frame us because he hates us. He hates me and Owain and Jac. He doesn't want us to be happy. He's ... he's deranged.'

'Maybe,' said DI Medi Joan. 'That was another question I wanted to ask you. What did you do after Jac arrived?'

Lottie rolled her eyes. 'I've told you this before. I offered him dinner, but he didn't want any. We watched TV then I got him ready for bed.'

'Did he go to bed with his clothes on?'

'No, of course not. I changed him into his pyjamas.'

'Okay. You changed him,' DI Medi Joan said. 'Didn't you see the bruises?'

Lottie let out a noise that was halfway between a sob and a laugh. 'I was in a hurry! He was tired and I was tired and I just wanted him to get into bed. When you change a kid's clothes twice a day, you're not scanning his body for bruises.'

'You noticed the sunburn,' said DI Medi Joan.

Lottie looked as if she was going to cry. 'The sunburn was just on his arms and face. He was wearing a T-shirt.'

'Okay. But the bruises were quite substantial.'

DI Medi Joan had her hand on a sheet of photographic paper, as though about to turn it over.

'Please don't,' said Lottie, putting her hand on Joan's arm. 'Please don't.'

DI Medi Joan let go of the photograph. 'You said you were engaged.'

'We wanted to get married in the summer. The Conrah Hotel.'

'Do you know Owain Hughes is already married?'

Lottie laughed. 'Owain? Not likely.'

'He is. I visited his wife last week. She lives in Woking.'

Lottie dug her manicured nails into her arm, just below the wrist. 'Where the fuck is Woking?'

'South-west of London. Don't worry, they don't have any children. His wife didn't know about you and Jac, but she does now.'

'You talked to her? Who is she? What's her name?'

'I'm afraid I can't divulge that information. But I thought I'd let you know he was married. It seemed the fair thing to do.'

They sat in silence. A full five minutes. Lottie had her legs crossed and her arms crossed; her eyes seemed unfocussed, as though a thousand thoughts were assaulting her at once. DI Medi Joan, on the other hand, looked as though she were listening to a Sunday afternoon play on Radio 4.

'Do you have anything you want to say, Lottie? About Owain?'

Her eyes sharpened. 'No,' she said.

At the end of every night at The Ship, after too much to drink, too much stupid conjecture, we think of the boy. We think of the boy on the cold mortuary table. We think of his little body, the soft curls; how he'd greet each one of us in Welsh and English. The smell of lilac and seawater. The sand he kicked up as he pelted towards the water.

A woman comes into The Ship, wearing an anorak and worn trainers. Late forties. There's something familiar about her that we can't pin down. She sits with Joanie at the bar. She perches nervously, looking over her shoulder at the door.

'It's okay,' Joanie says. 'You're with me. What will you have?'

'Nothing.'

'You'll have something.'

'Diet Coke.'

'Do you drink?' The woman nods. 'Then we'll get you a proper drink. Whisky.'

'I've left the dogs with the kids,' she says. She tries to whisper it, but we can hear her.

'It'll be over soon,' says Joanie. 'What time did you say again?'

'Nine.'

'It's nine now,' says Joanie.

The woman looks at the door again. 'What am I meant to say when he arrives?'

'Nothing. Just let him talk. You don't need to do anything. They're recording it all, my colleagues out in the van.'

'Where will you be?'

'I'll be in the back room. He won't see me if you stay in the main room, and he won't want to go near *them*.'

We start up the next song – 'Myfanwy' – just to remind them that we're here. Joanie picks up her half-drunk cider, and heads to the narrow storeroom behind the bar where they keep the spare bottles and enormous packets of pork crackling. The woman looks terrified. 'Wait,' she says, but then the door swings open.

Owain doesn't look at us, even though we've reached the chorus, and Stuart's baritone is flooding the pub. He nods at the woman and sits down at the furthest table, not ordering anything. He doesn't take off his long black coat, one button closed across his grey suit.

It's only when the woman joins him that we realise who she is: Rosie Eliot, Owain's PA. We didn't recognise her without her make-up and a good, wool jacket. She nods at us but seems too distracted for anything more. She hasn't brought her flute.

The song dwindles; we keep up the soft melody, just enough to make them think we're not listening.

'Have they called you in?' he asks. His voice is severe, quiet.

She nods.

'And? What did you say?'

'I said what you told me to say.'

'Which is?'

'That I don't know anything.'

Owain seems to deflate with relief. 'Good, good. What did they ask?'

'Nothing special. They wanted to know about your relationship with Lottie and... Yes. That's all really.'

A long silence follows. It's so long that it seems all is lost; that Owain is going to get up any minute and go home without speaking.

Finally, Rosie clears her throat. 'How is Lottie?'

'She found out, you know, about Yvonne.'

'Yeah, I did warn you about that,' says Rosie.

'She'll get over it. She loves the house too much to leave.' He smiles, weakly. 'You won't say anything, will you? If you say anything it's your job on the line as well as mine.'

Rosie shakes her head; brings the whisky to her lips.

'Good, good.' Another pause. 'I don't want you thinking I'm a monster, Rosie. I really did ... I really did love him.'

'What happened?' she whispers.

He shakes his head.

'You've dragged me into this so I think I deserve to know.'

'I can't say. It's not fair on you.'

'I heard it, Owain. I was downstairs in the office, working through the *fucking* weekend as usual.' She looks away, exhaling slowly, calming herself. 'I know I didn't see it, but I heard it. Him. So tell me what happened. Was it an accident?'

Owain nods slowly.

'Did you hit him?'

Owain stills, his gaze fixed at us, in the musicians' corner, as though waiting for us to play his favourite tune. We play 'Dafydd y Garreg Wen'. 'Yes.'

Rosie instinctively jerks away so that she's sitting with her body sidelong against the table. She can't look at him. She downs the rest of the whisky.

'Why?'

'I don't remember.'

Rosie crosses her leg, leans towards the bar, away from him, as though her whole body is repulsed. 'Something must have caused it.'

'He said something to me. I wanted to teach him not to say anything like that again.'

'What did he say?'

We've reached the last verse of 'Dafydd y Garreg Wen'. There is no song on earth that can follow this one. The sudden silence seems to unnerve Owain. 'I'll be off,' he says, gathering his big black coat and getting to his feet.

Only he stops in his tracks. DI Medi Joan is sitting at the bar with a new pint of Black Dragon and an open packet of pork scratchings.

'Evening,' she says.

Owain darts at Rosie, grabs her coat and drags her off the chair. By then DI Joan's got her contraption out.

'Don't do anything stupid, now, Owain,' she says, her voice low, holding the taser to his chest. 'Let's stay calm.'

Rosie runs towards us. We sit her right in the middle of our circle to keep her safe.

'Sorry. Sorry,' he says, his hands up. His face folds; he begins to cry. 'Sorry, sorry,' he keeps saying.

'Keep your crocodile tears!' shouts Carys Daniels.

'Scum of the earth!' shouts Stuart.

Joanie shoots us a look and we clam up quick. 'What's this about something Jac said?' she asks as she gets the handcuffs out.

Owain's sobbing – great, dry heaves they are. He has to lean back against the table when the handcuffs are put on him. 'I should say, you know, that you should be careful what you say because it could be used against you in court. But I am curious.'

'He had the best day with his dad,' Owain manages to say between the chest-racking cries. 'The *best* day.'

'That doesn't seem so terrible to me,' says DI Medi Joan, pulling Owain onto his feet, even though he was about a foot taller than her.

A long stream of snot hung from Owain's nose. 'He didn't love me. He only loved his real dad.'

'Well, he was right, wasn't he?' Rosie shouts from the back. 'He was right not to trust you.'

'Did Lottie know?' we ask Rosie.

'She was upstairs with him. She put Jac to bed. She put Jac to bed and did nothing.'

'We didn't think he was so poorly,' Owain says. 'We didn't know.'

DI Medi Joan has had enough; she's muttering into her phone and then, a moment later, Officer Davies and Officer Byrne are in the narrow doorway of The Ship. They take Owain away, his cries carrying along the night-time streets.

We are at a loss now. There's not a single tune anyone wants to play. We don't even want to drink anymore. We feel both light and heavy, relieved and burdened. We want to sleep and run at the same time. It's a strange night, because, for the first time since we can remember, we all decide to go home before closing time.

Contributors

Kittie Belltree
Kittie Belltree grew up in south London and now lives in St. Dogmaels, Pembrokeshire. She received a Literature Wales Writer Development Bursary for her debut poetry collection, *Sliced Tongue and Pearl Cufflinks* (Parthian, 2019) and her short stories, poems and reviews have appeared extensively, both online and in print. This includes work in the anthologies *The Brown Envelope Book* (Caparison, 2021), *Heartland* (Parthian, 2019) and *Cut on the Bias* (Honno, 2010). Alongside her writing, Kittie is also a Creative Practitioner and Agent for Change, delivering bespoke creative learning projects in schools and community settings for Arts Council Wales, Literature Wales and Disability Arts Cymru. She works as a Specialist Tutor for neurodivergent students at Aberystwyth University where she has recently completed a PhD examining linguistic representations of trauma.

Claire Boot
Claire Boot was born in Cardiff and raised in Penarth. She studied English Literature at the University of Birmingham, completing a Masters in medieval drama. Claire volunteered as a writer with a charity in West Africa before returning to Birmingham to write for a theatre-in-education (TIE) company. She moved to London, where she wrote for community groups, conferences, TIE companies and new

writing events, and came back to Wales in 2017. Claire's recent commissions include an audio play for Sherman Theatre, a site-specific audio walk for Barry Island, and a series of creative writing videos for Literature Wales. Her scripts have twice featured in SEEN at The Other Room in Cardiff and she also writes for Big Start Assemblies. Claire's prose fiction has been published in National Flash Fiction Day and Bath Flash Fiction Award anthologies. As a Welsh learner, Claire enjoys the challenge of writing *yn Gymraeg*.

Ellen Davies
Ellen Davies is a writer from the Rhondda, south Wales. She has a BA in English Literature and an MA in Creative Writing from Cardiff University. Ellen is primarily a poet – her pamphlet, *Accent*, was published by Cinnamon Press in 2015 and her poems have appeared in *Mslexia*, *The Lonely Crowd* and *Popshot Magazine*, among other publications. 'Simon Says' is her first crime story.

Philippa Davies
Philippa Davies is almost a nun. After expulsion from the Brownies for showing off, she lives a life of penitent contemplation in the deepest west-Wales sticks. Additional crimes include tabloid journalism, spin-doctoring and irreverent podcasting. She clings strongly to her belief in the power of redemption.

Eluned Gramich
Eluned Gramich is a writer and translator. Her memoir of her

time in Hokkaido, Japan, *Woman Who Brings the Rain*, won the inaugural New Welsh Writing Award in 2015 and was shortlisted for Wales Book of the Year in 2016. Her most recent novella, *Sleep Training*, is a lockdown ghost story that received *The Ghastling* Novella Award 2020. She lives in Aberystwyth with her partner and two-year-old daughter.

Maggie Himsworth
Maggie Himsworth was born and brought up in Pembrokeshire. She has a degree in English Literature from Aberystwyth University. She was a social worker for over 40 years, in Wandsworth, London, and in the family courts in Wales. She is married with three grown-up children and now lives in north Pembrokeshire. 'Play It For Me' is her first published work.

Sheila Kitrick
Sheila is a Londoner with Welsh (Richards and Lloyd) and Irish (Regan) bloodlines. She is married with two children from a first marriage. She left school at fifteen and returned to school aged thirty, graduating from City University, London with an honours degree in Psychology. Post-graduation she worked as a research psychologist in pharmaceuticals with a secondment to the London Hospital, St. Clements, to research drug therapy in community-based chronic schizophrenic patients (published). Sheila remained in pharmaceuticals, transferring to Paris, France for two years before studying for further qualifications in London. She set up in private practice as a psychotherapist in 1993, specialising in work with children and young people. She moved to Wales in 2010 and has

continued to practise part-time whilst devoting more time to creative writing. Sheila is also a contributor to the Honno anthology, *Painting the Beauty Queens Orange*.

Alison Layland

Alison Layland is the author of two psychological thrillers: *Someone Else's Conflict*, a compelling narrative of storytelling and the aftermath of war, was featured as a Debut of the Month on the LoveReading website, and *Riverflow*, a story of family secrets and community tensions against a background of flooding and environmental protest, was a Waterstones' Wales Book of the Month. She also writes short stories and flash fiction, winning the short story competition at the National Eisteddfod in 2002. She is the translator of a number of award-winning and best-selling novels.

A member of the Crime Cymru collective, she is actively involved in the First Novel competition and the Gŵyl Crime Cymru Festival.

When not writing, at home on the Welsh borders or in her caravan in the countryside of mid-Wales, she is an environmental campaigner, and involved in various local community projects focussing on sustainability and the natural world.

Rachel Morris

Rachel Morris is Welsh and Canadian, and has a PhD in Law from Cardiff University. She ran a research unit there on law and policy relating to Gypsies and Travellers, and was nominated twice for the Liberty/Law Society Human Rights Award for her work promoting equality and fighting discrimination.

She then worked in South Korea, Thailand, and Saudi Arabia, teaching and training on and managing education programmes. She's a member of Crime Cymru, the Crime Writers' Association, and the Society of Authors. In addition to law publications, her non-fiction, journalism, and creative writing have been published in *Red*, *Womankind*, *Byline Times*, *Visual Verse*, and *Globetrender*. Rachel is a digital collage artist/illustrator, founder of the annual prompt project #Marchollage. She is working on the second novel in a crime series. She founded the writing group Write Now Llangollen in her hometown in Denbighshire, North Wales, in 2013. You can connect with her at https://linktr.ee/FiveByFiveCreativity and https://www.fivebyfivecreativity.com/

Louise Mumford
Louise lives in Cardiff with her husband and spends her time trying to get down on paper all the marvellous and frightening things that happen in her head. Discovered at the 2019 Primadonna Festival, her debut book, *Sleepless*, a 'frighteningly inventive' speculative thriller inspired by her own experience of insomnia, was published by HQ Digital in December 2020. It has reached the overall Top 50 UK Kindle Chart and has been optioned for television by a Californian production company. Recently, *Sleepless* was the Karin Slaughter July Killer Read in UK Asda stores nationwide. She has contributed to LJ Ross's *Everyday Kindness* charity anthology and is a proud member of the Welsh crime-writing collective, Crime Cymru. Louise's new thriller, *The Safe House,* is out in May 2022.

Katie Munnik

Katie Munnik is a Canadian writer living in Cardiff. In 2017, she won the Borough Press Open Submission, and her debut novel *The Heart Beats in Secret* was a *USA Today* Bestseller. Her prose, poetry, and creative non-fiction have been published in magazines, literary journals and newspapers in the UK and Canada. Her second novel, *The Aerialists*, will be published by the Borough Press in April 2022. You can find her on twitter @messy_table

Tiffany Murray

Tiffany Murray's novels are *Diamond Star Halo*, *Happy Accidents* and *Sugar Hall*. She has a series of short stories on BBC Radio 4, 'Huldur's Café', and she is currently working on a crime novel, *The Girl Who Spoke to Birds*. Both projects are set in Iceland. Tiffany is also completing a memoir, *You, Me, and The Rock and Roll Cook*, about growing up in Monmouthshire with rock stars in the kitchen. She is a recipient of the Roger Deakin Award for nature writing from the Society of Authors, and she has been an International Hay Festival Fiction fellow, a Fulbright scholar, and a Senior Lecturer. Tiffany founded and runs Hay Festival's development program for Welsh writers, 'Writers at Work.'
https://litshowcase.org/writer/tiffany-murray/

Diana Powell

Diana Powell's stories have won, or been placed in, a number of competitions, including the 2020 Society of Authors ALCS Tom-Gallon Award (runner-up); the 2020 TSS Cambridge

Prize (third place) and the 2019 ChipLit Festival Prize (winner). They have featured in several anthologies and journals, such as *The Best (British) Short Stories 2020*. She has also been nominated for the Pushcart Prize by Arachne Press. Her novella, *Esther Bligh*, was published in 2018 by Holland House Books. Her short story collection, *Trouble Crossing the Bridge*, was published by Chaffinch Press in 2020. She is the winner of the 2021 Cinnamon Press Literature Award, and her novella, *The Sisters of Cynvael*, will be published by Cinnamon in 2023. Diana was born and brought up in Llanelli, south Wales, and now lives with her husband in beautiful Pembrokeshire.

Julie Ann Rees
Julie Ann holds an MA in creative writing from the University of Wales Trinity Saint David and is studying towards a PhD at Swansea University. Her short stories have been published both online at horla.org and in print with Parthian Books (*Heartland*), Sliced Up Press (*Bodies Full of Burning*), Black Shuck Books (*Dreamland: Other stories*) and forthcoming (*Cryptids Emerging: Silver Volume*) anthology with Improbable Press. Her first book, a memoir entitled *Paper Horses*, was published by Black Bee Books in February 2022. She works as a librarian and is a single mother to a teenager, two horses and a fiendishly spooky cat.

Find her at: https://www.facebook.com/julieAnnRees and https://twitter.com/JulieRe36071199

Tracey Rhys

Tracey Rhys lives in Bridgend, south Wales, where she works as a freelance writer and editor. Her first poetry collection, *Teaching a Bird to Sing* (Green Bottle Press), was the result of a Literature Wales New Writers Award. Tracey has worked in professional theatre, writing poetry as performance monologues for Winterlight Theatre, with a special interest in the representation of autism. Her art, poetry and essays have been published in journals and anthologies. Tracey was a winner in the Poetry Archive's WordView Competition in 2020. 'With Both Eyes Closed' is her first short story.

E. E. Rhodes

E. E. Rhodes is an archaeologist who lives in Cardiff. She writes a range of prose and prose poetry, is widely published and anthologised, and has been placed in dozens of competitions.

Her polyphonic flash novella, 'Sextet', won the 2021 Louise Walters Books 'Page 100' competition and her CNF manuscript, 'My Family & Other Folklore', was longlisted in Canongate's 2021 Nan Shepherd Prize; she won the 2021 Elliott & Thompson 'Spirit of Summer' Flash CNF prize; The Phare's 'Write Words' Short Story competition; and the Intrepid Times 'Reunions' Travel Writing Prize. Her chapter on a pilgrimage to Bardsey, 'All Among The Saints', appears in the 2022 Parthian Press 'An Open Door' Anthology of New Travel Writing From Wales.

She's the prose editor at Twin Pies Literary, co-leads 'Friday Flashing' for Retreat West and regularly runs workshops on creative non-fiction at festivals and for the Crow Collective.

Delphine Richards

Delphine was raised on a small dairy farm in Carmarthenshire. As an avid reader of Enid Blyton mysteries as a young child, it was almost inevitable that she developed a taste for crime thrillers as she grew up. Following a career in the police force, she turned to writing – both as a freelance feature writer (with a long-running column in a local paper) and dabbling in fiction. Several competition wins fuelled her determination to continue. Since then, she has written two novels, a special interest book, was a joint author of a humorous memoir, and has been a contributor to other anthologies (including the previous Honno crime anthology *Written in Blood*). A third novel is close to completion.

Katherine Stansfield

Katherine Stansfield grew up on Bodmin Moor in Cornwall and now lives in Cardiff. She is the author of four novels and several collections of poetry. Her latest novel is *The Mermaid's Call*, third in the Cornish Mysteries series. Katherine's latest poetry collection is *We Could Be Anywhere by Now* which was awarded a Writer's Bursary from Literature Wales and was selected by Wales Literature Exchange as a 'Bookcase' title: a book from Wales recommended for translation. Alongside her independent writing projects, Katherine co-writes with her partner David Towsey under the partnership name D. K. Fields (political fantasy trilogy *The Tales of Fenest*). She teaches for the Open University and the School of Continuing and Professional Education at Cardiff University. She works as a mentor for Literature Wales, a Writing Fellow at the

University of South Wales, and has been a Royal Literary Fund fellow.

Katherine is a member of Crime Cymru: a new collective of crime writers with a connection to Wales. She is also a member of the Crime Writer's Association.

Caroline Stockford

Caroline Stockford is a poet, translator and human-rights activist from Barmouth in North Wales. She gained an MA in the History of the Turkish Language from SOAS in 2000 and has worked most of her life in translation and in the voluntary sector. Her poetry, essays and translations have been published in *Sharp as Lemons, Into the Void, Gard Şiir Magazine, The Sultan's Seal, Burning House Press, Make Time for Aberyswyth, Assaracus Journal, The Gay and Lesbian Review, Kalyna Journal, Virus Magazine, MPT* and *The Berlin Quarterly* and in the recent poetry anthology, *A470 Poems For The Road*. Caroline works as Turkey Advisor for PEN Norway where she leads Turkey-based human-rights projects focussing on freedom of expression and the rule of law. She also runs their campaign #freethepoet for the imprisoned Kurdish poet Ilhan Sami Çomak. She lives in Bristol near her sons, John and Ali.

Louise Walsh

Louise Walsh is a Legal PA and lives in Cardiff. Her first novel, *Fighting Pretty*, drew on her knowledge of the amateur boxing world. Her second novel, *Black River*, was inspired by research into press intrusion at Aberfan following the 1966 disaster.

Louise was a participant on the Hay Festival Writers at Work programme from 2016 to 2018 and gained an MA in Creative Writing at Cardiff University in 2019. She is currently working on a police procedural set in south Wales.

Hazell Ward
Hazell Ward completed her MA in 2019, and is now working for a PhD by Practice in Creative Writing at Manchester Metropolitan University, looking at what readers and writers owe each other. As part of her thesis she is writing a crime novel. This also allows her to read lots and lots of detective novels, and call it 'work'. Hazell is also a freelance writer and teacher. She lives at the very edge of north Wales – almost, but not quite, in England. When not writing, she can be found walking through nearby woods or around (not up – she has a bad back) the many hills near her home. Having previously undertaken treks in Peru, Uganda and Nepal, she sometimes plans her next trip in her head while she walks, but mostly she is busy thinking about the characters in her latest story – and how much her back hurts!

She was shortlisted in the Margery Allingham Short Story competition in 2021.

ABOUT HONNO

Honno Welsh Women's Press was set up in 1986 by a group of women who felt strongly that women in Wales needed wider opportunities to see their writing in print and to become involved in the publishing process. Our aim is to develop the writing talents of women in Wales, give them new and exciting opportunities to see their work published and often to give them their first 'break' as a writer. Honno is registered as a community co-operative. Any profit that Honno makes is invested in the publishing programme. Women from Wales and around the world have expressed their support for Honno. Each supporter has a vote at the Annual General Meeting.

Honno, D41, Hugh Owen Building, Aberystwyth
University, Aberystwyth, SY23 3DY

Honno Friends
We are very grateful for the support
of all our Honno Friends.